D0088893

A STATION
ON THE PATH
TO SOMEWHERE
BETTER

Benjamin Wood

A STATION
ON THE PATH
TO SOMEWHERE
BETTER

Europa
editions

Europa Editions
1 Penn Plaza, Suite 6282
New York, N.Y. 10019
www.europaeditions.com
info@europaeditions.com

Library of Congress Cataloging in Publication Data is available
ISBN 978-1-60945-682-5

Wood, Benjamin
A Station on the Path to Somewhere Better

Book design by Emanuele Ragnisco
www.mekkanografici.com

Orginal jacket design by Jack Smith.
Silhouette figure by Stephen Arnold at Unsplash;
Forest picture by Pixabay

Prepress by Grafica Punto Print – Rome

Printed in USA

CONTENTS

for Nick

A STATION
ON THE PATH
TO SOMEWHERE
BETTER

SIDE ONE

TWO WEATHERS

U ntil that dismal week in August, when every plan he made was an attempt to cancel out another and every word he spoke was a diversion or a lie, I believed my father was a good man, somebody whose blood was fit to share. It's easy to say now that I was wrong about him, just as it's easy to dismiss his prior accomplishments in light of what occurred. But I was twelve years old that summer—as callow a boy as you could find, raised in a quiet street, pillowed by it— and I could tell a grown man's imperfections from his fatal flaws. Maybe this naivety of mine was wilful. Maybe I'd already fathomed the extent of his deficiencies, seen it in a glitter-smear of lipstick on his cheek one night when he came home, and decided to ignore it. The truth is, everything I know about his life is altered with each explanation of it, gets magnified to such a scale that I glimpse meanings in the grain that are not there. This isn't my attempt to rationalise him, only to account for what he made me. I can give you honesty, if little else.

That wretched week still slants the parts of me that should be upright, turns thoughts that should be clear and bright to murk. I'm not the Daniel Hardesty I was back then (by law, in fact: I changed my name when I was twenty) and yet I've been unable to erase the residue of him. How is it possible that a few short days of misery can corrupt a lifetime? How is it that we let ourselves be so defined by other people's sins? All I know is, from the moment I was old enough to recognise his absence, my father had the most peculiar hold on me.

He always had two ways of being—'two weathers,' my mother used to say of him—and he could switch between them without warning, without reason. There was gentle Francis Hardesty who stood too close to me in pictures, who hooked his arm around my shoulder everywhere we went, clung to me as though afraid that I'd forget the colour of his eyes if they weren't near. And there was the distant other, who vanished into upstairs rooms without me, who leaned in doorways with young women, pretending that he couldn't hear me as they giggled at his whispers; the Fran Hardesty who planted me on barstools to play fruit machines with pocket change while he attended to his own affairs, who let me have only the outermost of his attention, his perfunctory concern.

I loved him, and it shames me that I loved him, though everything he claimed to feel for me was just an affectation or a gesture of persuasion. I accept that this is not enough to vindicate my part in things. Still, when I think about that August week and what transpired, I know it is the fault line under every forward step I try to make. His mistakes are my inheritance. The rotten blood he gave me is the blood I will pass on.

* * *

I can't pretend to have been blessed with a prodigious memory for details, but I remember more than I care to, and there's one period of my childhood I don't need to recollect because it's documented for me. Here, for instance, are the items that were in my father's glovebox, catalogued the day his car was found by the police:

One half-eaten pack of Fox's Glacier mints, the wrapper torn back in a coil. Wooden golf tees of assorted colour, all unused. Three black Grundig cassette tapes bearing his careful handwriting in green biro: *Blue Bell Knoll*, *Treasure*, *Louder than Bombs*. A pair of nail scissors, bent. A 275ml tub of

Swarfega. one rumpled envelope containing a receipt from Bryant's Coachworks for 'repairs to rear side door,' dated 19th July 1993. A Volvo 240 owner's manual in a faux-leather case. A box of Anadin in which every capsule had been thumbed out of the blister-pack. Thirty-four pence in change: a twenty, a ten, and two coppers. What else? The red wax belt from a Babybel cheese, gone hard. A broken pen from the Hotel metropole, Leeds. An empty cigarillo tin.

These objects were not introduced as evidence, but their images still pad out his case file like expired coupons in a drawer. They are all inconsequential now, and yet by virtue of their placement in his glovebox at a certain point in time they've come to bear significance. So much of the fine print of our lives goes disregarded until one unlawful action makes it all portentous, worthy of examining for clues, and I can't help but scrutinise my past in the same way. As though the truth rests somewhere in these incidentals. As though what happened was a gradual accretion of small, ordinary things that no one thought to notice.

* * *

Our village had a life before my father, too, of course. Little Missenden was the kind of place that people still referred to as a parish. It was a pleasant rest stop in the Chiltern hills, known best for its Saxon church and manor houses: sites of niche historical interest that drew occasional visitors from London and beyond. Flannel-shirted men would often stop by to paint watercolours, and I would stand behind their easels while they sketched, numbing them with questions. They never seemed to capture the same landscape that I saw. They drew trees with bold distinctive shapes, birds of no velocity, cottages with characterful faces, country lanes mottled with shade. The Little Missenden I knew was harder to convey, a picture of entangled spaces. It was a rutted loop of track on which I rode my bike, the crawl space I'd spent years working underneath our garden hedge, the coin spout in the public phone box where my figurines camped out on recon missions, the flagpole on the belfry of the church that I could see from every upstairs window of our house, the perfect sleighing camber of the fields I prayed for snow to cover every Christmas. Things like these are how you separate a home from its location. If I had the courage to return to them today, I know I'd find them changed—and changed is just another word for gone.

* * *

The first change happened on a quiet Thursday morning, 17th August 1995, when I saw his old blue Volvo coming down our road like some dark clot inside a vein. I had woken early to look out for him, kneeling on the hardwood bench that spanned our guestroom window. For so long, the empty lane outside our house was just a dewy trail of bitumen, a parade ground for the crows, and I felt deflated every time I heard an engine revving in the distance that didn't materialise on our driveway.

My mother had spent weeks preparing me for disappointment: she wanted me to understand that Francis Hardesty, despite his many pledges and assurances, might not appear at all. 'Your father does whatever suits him,' she'd warned me. 'If he lets you down, it won't be personal. You'll just have slipped his mind completely.' I never liked it when she spoke of him this way. The more she levelled at my father in his absence, the easier it was to close my ears. He became less faulty in our separations. I believed that he would prove her wrong someday, demonstrate his true efficiency.

That morning, she was waiting to receive him in the hallway. Perhaps she had been standing there for hours. When the

bell rang, she was staring at the gilded clock over the door.
'Seven thirty on the dot,' she said to me, as I came downstairs.
'It can't actually be him. We mustn't be awake yet.' But we
both saw the looming smudge of his body through the door
glass, the pale disc of his face above the fabric of his shirt, the
blackness of his hair. I had never listened so intently to the
sound of our own doorbell before; it seemed to ring inside my
head longer than usual—now and then, I come across another
with the same artificial chime and its quaint music rattles
through me.

My father stood a moment on the front step, looking in. I
wish I could describe him for you in a way that makes him
seem a likely candidate for prison: tattooed fingers, skinhead,
biker's leather, someone who could overpower me with a simple shift of his blank eyes. But the fact is, Francis Hardesty was
not striking in his build. He was five foot nine and lean—
skinny isn't the right word for him, because there was still a
paunchiness about his middle. He dressed in polyester shirts
and crew-neck sweaters, always plain or faintly patterned, and
stonewashed jeans or navy cords that grew patchy where he
kept his keys and wallet. What gave him such an influence on
people was the texture of his voice—it had a radio announcer's
fullness, soft where other men's were sharp; deep and slightly
murmuring. And he was handsome, too; handsome in an inad-
vertent way. His nose, for instance, had a bridge as hefty as a
knuckle and yet the arches of his nostrils were slim and deft to
counterbalance it. His eyes had a colour that I've not encountered since: a honeyed shade of brown with inner spokes of
orange. He liked to stay clean-shaven, but if he let the stubble
grow for longer than a day, it lent his face a different quality,
kinder, less harassed. Somehow, his one eccentricity—a prefer-
ence he had for cigarillos—gave him an air of poise, of single-
mindedness, when it could've made him look pretentious. He
was a loyal smoker of the Café Crème variety, except he

thought that name was better suited to a pudding, so he called them Wintermans instead, as in, 'one more Wintermans for me, then I'm calling it a night.' The rims of his index and middle fingers were permanently yellowed by them; his clothes, his hair, his skin reeked of their musk.

He was squinting at my mother on the threshold. 'Kath,' he said, giving a timid wave. 'Good to see you. Is he ready?' She had barred one arm across the doorway out of instinct, and he leaned to stare beyond it. 'I hope you're ready in there, sunshine. Get your things. We need to beat the traffic.'

I was more than ready: bathed and dressed and full of cornflakes, my holdall packed the night before. I'd barely slept. But I was too elated by the sight of him to speak. It was so rare for him to live up to a promise that it left me partly disbelieving he was there at all. Also, blood was welling in my mouth and I didn't want to open it. In my excitement, I had jumped down from the ledge and nicked my tongue with my hind teeth.

'What's the matter—lost your voice?' he called to me. 'Grab your things. Let's go.'

My mother handed him my bag. He sagged to the left, pretending it was too much load for him to bear. 'How much has he packed in here?'

'It's mostly books, I think,' she said. 'I tried to make him scale back, but he's stubborn.'

'This must be the whole of the *Encyclopaedia Britannica*.'

'Give it a few hours, he'll need something to read.'

'What's that supposed to mean?'

'Nothing, Fran. Nothing.'

I tugged my mother's sleeve, showed her my tongue.

'Ooh, that looks sore,' she said. 'What happened?' She studied the wound under the light. 'Okay. Get yourself a piece of kitchen towel and wrap an ice cube in it. Hold it on there for ten minutes.'

I did as she advised—my mother had no medical expertise

or training, but she always knew the best methods for treating minor injuries, and seemed able to draw answers from a vast resource of knowledge. At the time, I found it vaguely mystical, though, of course, it was maternal instinct and sound logic.

When I came out from the kitchen, Francis Hardesty was gone and so was my holdall. I found him on the driveway with my mother, who was still in her silk dressing gown and slippers. He was bungeeing a clutch of short thin planks to the roof rack of the Volvo, and she was talking to his sweaty back while he got on with it. 'There,' he said, turning to her. 'That better now? Do I pass the inspection?'

She stepped away. 'I don't get why you didn't put them up there in the first place.'

'I don't get why I can't just store them in the garage.'

'You don't live here, Fran, that's why, and it's about time you got used to it. No more dirty boots in my kitchen, no more dumping off-cuts in my garage. No more taking liberties, full stop.' At this point, she saw me coming down the path with the wrapped-up ice cube pressed against my mouth. 'Everything's loaded now. Just making extra space.'

'We're clear for take-off,' my father said. He came and patted my head. 'Take a seat and buckle up. I just need to go in and use the toilet, if it's all right with your mother.'

'Use the one downstairs,' she told him, and he went off inside.

I got into the passenger seat. The car was warm and fragrant with chemicals, the plastic of the armrest singed, as though the bare flame of a lighter had been held against it briefly. My mother knocked on the window, so I wound it down for her. 'Listen,' she said, stooping to my eye line. 'Listen for a sec.'

I don't know how long this moment lasted—I didn't watch the dashboard clock while it was happening—but it often feels as if it took place over one slow stretch of time between two blinks.

'Look, you've heard all this before, but try not to get too

disappointed if it doesn't go exactly as you hope it will, okay? I mean, if you don't get to meet the actors like he said—if Maxine whatshername isn't there to meet you, or if you don't get to see them filming—just don't be too upset, all right? You'll still have fun, whatever happens. Your dad can be quite funny when he wants to be, and the important thing is that you spend some proper time together. I know that's important to you. So just enjoy yourself. Be good. Okay?'

I smiled, hummed in agreement.

She leaned in and took the wet kitchen paper from my hand. 'Let me see that tongue.' I pushed it out. 'Well, there's a proper lump, but it'll heal. Drink plenty of cold water. And phone me from the service stations, just so I know where you are. It's three and a bit hours to Leeds, if he keeps to the limit.' She was squeezing the paper in her fist. 'Hold on while I go and see what's taking him so long. I love you, son.'

'I love you too,' I said.

She stooped lower, pointing at her cheekbone, and I reached up to kiss her there. The skin felt slightly oiled. I caught the candy-lemon scent of 'Sunflowers,' her perfume.

I put my seatbelt on and waited. All the books and card games I'd selected for the trip, my figurines, my camera, were stowed inside my holdall in the boot. I had nothing to occupy myself except a fresh anxiety for what was taking place in the house. Imagined arguments were much worse than those I witnessed; in the peace and quiet when my parents were alone somewhere, beyond surveillance, my hands would glisten with cold sweat and I'd get a queasy feeling in my gut.

Before too long, my father came outside again, holding a blue coolbox. He was prolonging a dispute that must've started somewhere between the downstairs toilet and the front door. 'No, come on, I'm *on your side* about this, Kath,' he was saying. 'Of course it isn't fair. But I don't see why you're blaming me—you gave me two days' notice. Two days!'

'It would've made a difference, you being there. They like to see *both* parents at these things.'

'Well, I don't know what to tell you. If there aren't places, there aren't places. The man was hardly going to change the rules just 'cause of me. If I was that persuasive, we'd be on the kitchen floor right now, believe me.'

My mother crossed her arms and gave him an expression she usually reserved for cleaning dog muck from our footpath. 'My god, you're such a juvenile.' Above their heads, the sky was dimming. A gloom slow-skated on the bonnet of the Volvo, passing right to left.

'Or maybe you just take yourself a bit too seriously,' Fran Hardesty went on. 'And anyway, I'm not convinced it's right for him. Those places only mess kids up, from what I've seen.'

'You're unbelievable,' my mother said. 'Have you not been listening to a word I've said?'

'It's your old man behind this, obviously.'

'Fran. Stop. You're making it worse.'

'You always wanted him to go to Chesham Park.'

'Yeah, well, I wanted a lot of things . . .'

I needed a distraction from their squabbling, and my father's glovebox always had such great potential for discovery: perhaps he'd brought a present for me and had stored it in there for safe keeping? Maybe there would be a photograph of something adult cut out of a magazine, or a dangerous object like a penknife I could hide and use in secret? But I found nothing interesting (see previous). The giant road atlas of Britain was slotted in the gap beside the handbrake, so I drew it out and flipped to a page at random. I tried to lose myself inside the grid, in all the road numbers and junctions, all the places I had never been: Buckden, Little Paxton, Offord Cluny, Offord D'Arcy, Yelling—a town they must've named after my parents.

I'd only studied two pages by the time I heard my father

stamping down the path, calling: 'Come and say goodbye, then, if you're going to. We need to hit the road.' The coolbox was buffeting his thigh. He was hot-faced and shining. I thought at first that he was talking to me, so I unclipped my seatbelt. But then my mother appeared behind him, coming round the passenger side. She opened the door and moved to kiss my temple. 'Why haven't you got that belt on?' she said to me, and then towards the headrest: 'Fran—what the heck? He hasn't got his seatbelt on. What's wrong with you?'

My father said: 'Give me a break. We haven't even left the bloody driveway.' He was making room in the back footwell for the coolbox.

'Just make sure you drive safely. Take it slow. And please don't swear.'

'It's all the other idiots on the road I'd worry about.'

'Be extra vigilant.'

'Oh, sure,' my father said, under his breath. 'That's bound to help.'

She gripped my cheeks and shook me gently by the jaw.

'Make sure you behave,' she told me. 'Make sure *he* behaves. Don't let him feed you chocolate bars and Coke. And keep all your receipts.' If there was one thing that displeased me about my mother, it was this: the way she used me to refract insults in his direction, as though it would disguise her meaning. 'I'll miss you so much, darling. Phone me every time you stop. Whenever you've a chance.'

I promised—again—that I would.

The driver's door came open with a clunk and my father dropped into the seat. He gripped the wheel and straightened his arms, rolling his head until his neck gave a click. 'Right, come on.' He put the key in the ignition. 'I should probably get fuel at some point.'

As we backed out of the drive, I noticed that the front door of our house was hanging open. I knew that my mother would stand there, waving till our car was out of sight. But I didn't realise that this would be the final time that I would see the house I had grown up in as it truly was, a beautiful assembly of red-brown bricks and casement windows, a home so neatly curtained off by trees that you could only see its face when you were playing in the garden. I didn't know that we were making it a relic.

My father put the car in forward gear and we arced slowly past the house. He struck the horn twice with his fist. It was a friendly noise, intended for my mother, and it was loud enough to shoo the pigeons from the garage roof—they startled her. As we drove off, she was smiling at herself, a limp hand spread across her heart. It was the last I ever saw of her.

I suppose that every liar has to possess some credibility. My father understood this well and built half of his life upon the premise. He told mistruths in varying degrees: as letting agents put a shine on wretched houses with their bluster, as car salesmen adjust the mileage on a rust heap, as doctors conceal negligence by tampering with patients' notes. The lies that reeled me in towards the end were predicated on my faith in him, which makes them the hardest lies to stomach.

After his relations with my mother began to sour, he tried to use my weaknesses to gain favour with her. I was a studious boy with narrow interests and a tendency to turn the things I cared about into obsessions. For example, I was ten years old the day my mother—trying to introduce some sunlight to my 'librarian' complexion—took me to a jumble sale at St. John the Baptist church. On a trestle table there, displayed beside a set of romance novels and a letter opener, I saw what I assumed to be a broken pair of scissors, made of tarnished brass, all handles and no blades; but, inspecting them, I realised that they were spectacles, a strange old kind whose lenses moved around a central rivet, and I bought them with the small change that my mother let me have. They were, it turned out, French scissor-spectacles from 1901, not especially valuable in modern terms, given their condition, but far from worthless. And it should tell you something about how easily I give up on a fixation that they formed the basis of a spectacle collection that today contains over three hundred pieces, some of them (the early slit-bridge bow specs and the Adams-style lorgnettes) museum-worthy.

I'm not sure how my father learned about them—perhaps my mother let it slip about the jumble sale during a routine argument over the telephone, or maybe, in a teary lull after she passed me the receiver, I told him about the specs because I had nothing left to say. My parents weren't quite separated at this time, but their marriage was about to die as surely as a family dog that no longer gets up from the carpet, and my father was calling home every other night to fend off the inevitable. He was staying with a friend in Dublin and helping to construct the set for *Brand*, an Ibsen adaptation. I remember that he rang me to discuss my birthday gift. 'Listen, Dan, I've been a little short of time. But I went out to a few antique shops here with Lydia, trying to get my hands on some of those old specs you like.' His voice was breathy, tired. I didn't know who Lydia was or why he expected me to recognise her name. 'Well, we didn't have much luck with those, but we *did* find something— a fancy sort of magnifying glass. It's proper silver and the lens is in good order, so the lady said. How about I go back there and buy it for you? I mean, it probably won't arrive exactly on your birthday if I get it in the post tomorrow, but, anyway— how's that sound?'

I think this brief exchange gladdened my mother for a while, to know he'd been attuned to something I was interested in. After this, their phone conversations sounded cheerier, ran on longer, and she started to refer to him in kinder tones. Until his final days, he'd go on swearing that the gift got lost in transit; he even produced a letter of apology from a Dublin post office branch to persuade us of the fact. With my father, there were no straightforward apologies, no admissions of guilt, just this—an aftermath of make-believe excuses that grew more and more pathetic.

I expect he thought it quite unusual for a young boy to

obsess about antique spectacles, and I appreciate that it was difficult for a man like him—somebody who grew up baling hay and tending sheep with his own father—to rationalise it. But it's clear that my attentiveness to artefacts derived from him. In fact, I only seized upon those spectacles because I saw them as an opportunity to bring us closer.

Months before that jumble sale, he'd surprised me at the school gates, whistling to me from the kerbside where he'd parked the car—I'd walked right past him. 'Danno! Oi!' He was dressed in paint-streaked overalls, puffing on a cigarillo. The car's suspension rocked as he stood upright from the bonnet. 'You needn't look at me like that. It's fine. I've cleared the whole thing with your mother.' A lie, as it transpired.

It was the first time I had seen him in six weeks, since she'd filled a dozen bin liners with his clothes and dumped them on our driveway. I can only guess which of his infidelities had triggered the eviction. He was sleeping with a red-haired woman at the driving range around this time; I know because he often took me there to watch him swing and miss. He'd leave me in our cubicle with a bucket of golf balls and a baby five iron, whacking at the astroturf, while the redhead serviced him in the staff toilet. Her name is not important, though every man at the golf centre appeared to know it ('That Nadine is gagging for it. I'd love to peel those little shorts off'). I didn't witness anything explicit, you'll be pleased to hear—it's more that I observed it in my father's twitchiness when he resumed his golfing, in the pinched fabric of his shirt, in the flush of Nadine's cheeks when we returned our empty buckets to the pro shop.

'Come on, jump in,' he told me. 'I want to show you something.' He drove me from the school gates to High Wycombe that afternoon—about six miles west—and parked by the Swan Theatre. We went in through the loading doors in a back alley, and he marched me through the dark guts of the building, up onto the stage. 'There wasn't much of a budget,' he told me. 'It's all coming down on Tuesday week, so I thought I'd better bring you now.' He gestured at the set: a dingy bar with green-rinsed walls festooned in paper chains, two French doors backlit with a cityscape. It was for *The Iceman Cometh*. 'So, what d'you reckon? Will it do?' I don't know what level of response he was expecting from a ten-year-old, but I gave him an enthusiastic nod. He let me run around in circles on the stage awhile, observing from the wings, but I could've been anywhere in the world right then, circuiting the rubble of a landfill site with the same degree of interest, and he must've realised it. 'Okay, stop mucking about,' he said. 'Let's take you back. I thought you'd like to see what I've been up to lately, that's all. Never mind.' I was beckoned off the stage. He was always keen to show me things he thought made him extraordinary. 'Your mother seems to think I've had my feet up this whole time, living the good life in hotels. Well, take a look. You can see what I've been doing, can't you? Now when she asks you, you can tell her where my head's been.'

My attention shifted, then, to all the painted flats and groundrows that made up the set. There was a queasy angularity to the scenery—I admired the trick it played on my eyes from far away, how all the shapes lost depth as I got near. 'What's it all made of?' I asked.

'Well—' He paused, inhaled. 'Mostly wood and fibreglass. A bloke drew me a picture and I built it how I thought was best.'

I went to get a closer view of what was on the table, centre stage: wonky candelabras, clouded wine glasses, lustreless old cutlery. I lifted up a teaspoon. 'Did you make *this*?'

'No. That's real. The props department sourced it. Probably from a junk shop.'

'What's a props department?'

'Why d'you want to know?'

'I like to know things.'

He huffed, scratched at his temple. 'Well, all right,' he carried on, 'that spoon you're holding is what they call a prop. A prop's an object that the actors use during a play. The props department are the men—or women, in our case—who find the objects and make sure they're put where the actors need them to be in every scene. Sometimes, if the script asks for a certain object to be used but the real thing is too expensive—like that chandelier up there, or, I don't know, a fancy Chinese vase, let's say—the props department has to make it out of something cheaper. It'll look the same, except it won't cost much.'

'Can't people tell it's different?'

'Not from where they're sitting, no. Not if the prop maker's any good.'

I examined the teaspoon in my fingers. 'Can you make props too, Dad?'

'I can—I mean, I have before—but I prefer to build the sets, and furniture, occasionally. You know, structural things.'

'Why?'

'I don't know, son. I just do.'

I put the spoon back on the table. 'When can we make props together?'

'One day, when you're older.'

'I want to be your props department.'

'That'd be nice,' he said. 'Unfortunately, you need to be at least yay high to get the gig.' He levelled a hand against his chin. 'Why don't you start one at school? That's how most people get into it.'

'It's nearly end of term.'

'Doesn't matter. Any prop man worth his salt has to collect things between productions, store them up in case they're useful later—that way, he's prepared for anything; Shakespeare, pantomimes, you name it. If you want to start with something from that table, I won't tell on you.'

For a moment, I considered it. 'No, it's for the actors.'
'They won't miss one little spoon.'
'But I'll get in trouble.'
'Only if you're caught.'
I frowned at this. The mere suggestion made me shiver. He was leading me downhill. 'Your decision, son,' he told me, checking his watch. 'Don't take all day, though.'

I never admitted it to him—because it took a fortnight for my mother's rage over this episode to subside, and for us to be allowed to speak again—but when I saw the antique spectacles at the jumble sale a few months later, I thought they were the prop on which I'd base our future, his and mine.

The next school play was announced in September, and I went to volunteer my services with the teacher after registration, bringing her the specs and the stolen spoon to underline my credentials. I believe she laughed at me: not cruelly, just unthinkingly. 'Oh no, you keep hold of those, my love. They're much too nice,' she said. 'We've got boxes full of things already, don't you worry.' I felt some burning part of me extinguish. It didn't matter how robust that spark of goodness was I sheltered for my father, it always seemed to get snuffed out. I wonder if he sensed this, too. I wonder if, towards the end, he deemed it kinder on us both to forsake goodness altogether.

A pearly remnant of the moon was still hanging in the sky as we left Little Missenden. The low carriage of the Volvo meant that I could feel each lump and corrugation in the beaten track of Taylors Lane, passing the nurtured gardens of the manor house I never thought I'd miss, all the post-and-wire fences in the meadows. My father didn't say a word until we reached the junction. He stopped the car and let the indicator go on ticking left-left-left. A single lorry thudded by us. 'Right then, Danno,' he said, twisting. 'Think you're up to navigating?' He hooked his arm to fetch the road atlas before I could reply. Its flat weight dropped into my lap. 'I've already marked the route. All you need to do is keep your finger on the roads, follow the lines as we go. A clever lad like you can do it with his eyes closed.'

The *Ordnance Survey Road Atlas of Great Britain* is now an heirloom of the past. If it hadn't been so integral to my father's plans that week, I would probably reflect on it with the same dreamy sentiment I confer on the antiques in my collection. Instead, I picture it exactly as it was: an ungainly book of cold, stiff pages, warped by damp. It was not the simplest document for a child to read: a bizarre logic fused together sections of the country—on page thirty-seven was the fractured coast of south-east England, on page thirty-eight the witch's brow of northern Wales—so the first effect of leafing through it was bewilderment. My father's edition was a year out of date, but he said this didn't matter. 'I shouldn't think they've moved anything. Not without asking my permission, anyway.'

Looking through it earlier, I hadn't seen the highlighted tracks that he'd made on the middle pages, or noticed the home square (E3) that he'd coloured in for me on page twenty-two. Little Missenden was inked yellow, and branching away from it were all the roads and places that he wanted me to guide us through.

Cars were flashing past in both directions now. He waited for a minute, then became impatient, seizing a gap in the onrushing traffic. As we straightened up, he let the wheel spin through his fists. He said: 'Christ, you'd have thought somebody would've let us out there, wouldn't you? They could see I was turning.' He glared at the rear-view mirror. 'This idiot behind us, look. Where's he got to go that's so important? Joker!' I didn't know how to respond. He let me focus on the map. 'Anyway, who cares? We're on our way now. Bang on schedule.' His arms levelled. He leaned back. 'So, come on then, navigator: what's this road we're on?'

I had my index finger on the number already, expecting he would ask. 'The A314.'

'Ah,' he said, as though he hadn't driven it a thousand times. 'The trusty old A314. And where does this one take us?'

'Aylesbury,' I said. 'Dad, are you going to do this all the way?'

'I might check in every so often, yeah.' He sniffed. 'Just to make sure you're pulling your weight. I mean, we can't have you leading us off course. We might end up in the sea.'

He was trying to lighten my mood. But we had spent so little time together in the past two years I found it hard to interpret all the tiny fluctuations of his personality. I didn't know how much of it—the fatherly patter, the fleeting rage at other motorists, the bonhomie—was artifice, and how much of it was Francis Hardesty. I suspect he didn't know either. And I couldn't let myself relax too quickly in his company, because it felt disloyal to my mother somehow, to allow so easy a transition from estrangement to familiarity. 'Hey, see over there,' he said, pointing to my side of the windscreen. 'What's it got, a mouse?'

Above the dry beige grassland in the distance, a red kite was hovering. 'A vole,' I said. 'That's what they're meant to like.'

'Where'd you learn that?'

'Someone came to talk to us at school.'

'What, from the RSPB?'

I nodded.

'That sounds nice. Wish I'd seen that.'

'It was just an assembly.'

'Well, maybe they might come again and I can go next time.'

'Yeah, maybe. I don't think parents are allowed, though.'

The bird got more defined as we drove up to it. From half a mile away, it was simply a dark figure pinned against the sky, but all the subtle movements of its wings could be discerned from closer up, each elevating twitch. My father braked so I could see it properly. 'Majestic,' he said.

Its russet wings were spread out in a T, patched white. The deadweight of a creature dangled from its talons. 'I think it's a rabbit,' I said.

'What's it waiting for?'

'Huh?'

'Why doesn't it fly off and eat the thing?'

It disappeared from view, above the roof and into history. 'I think it was looking for more.'

'Must've been a female,' my father said. 'Maybe it's got chicks to feed, or whatever baby kites are called.' We were suddenly accelerating again. 'Kitelets. Kitelings.' The world became a smudge beside his head. 'Kitty-kites.'

I snickered at him. 'How many miles is it to Leeds?'

He eased off the pedal. 'You bored of me already?'

'No, I just want to know how many miles it is.'

'Well, you're the navigator, you tell me.'

'But you've done this journey loads before. It's easier if you say.'

'You've got the map there, haven't you? Work it out. Each square on that grid's about two inches high and wide. And there's roughly three miles to an inch. So, if you count them all—'

'Doesn't matter,' I said. 'It's about three hours away. Mum already told me.'

'And you're just going to take her word for it, are you? What a cop out.'

'I'll just wait for a sign to tell me, then.'

'Cop out.'

I shrugged at him.

'I thought you were a lad who liked to know things.'

'Why can't you just tell me?'

'Because,' he said, 'life's not always as straightforward as you want it to be. And the things that you remember when you're older aren't the things that just get handed to you, they're the things you had to work at. Like this car, for instance. You want to know how I got this car?'

He was going to tell me, of course, whether I cared to hear it or not.

'I got this car from an old lady whose house I decorated. A fantastic job I did on that place for her, believe me—something out of *Ideal Home* it looked like, after I was done with it—but I'll tell you what else, it was some of the hardest decorating work I ever did. Not just painting every room, three coats emulsion, two coats gloss, but she had wallpaper in that house from before the war that'd been glued on with something industrial. Like earwax it was, underneath. I had to strip and scrape and sand the place from floor to ceiling before I could put on a lick of primer. Still, by the end of it all, that old woman was so pleased she wanted me to take her husband's car—he'd died not long before, and she was going to sell it, but she said, *You know what, Fran? I've seen how hard you work, and that little van you've got just seems to make a lot of smoke, so I want you have Edward's car.* She said she wanted it to go to someone decent, someone who'd appreciate it. Now, see that number there?' He jabbed his finger on the Perspex screen that covered the milometer. 'Over a hundred thousand on the clock, right? Well, it had nine hundred on it when she gave it to me. Every mile I drive in this car makes me feel proud, and I've never regretted a single ache and pain I got from painting that woman's house. You understand what I'm telling you?'

'Yeah,' I said. 'I get it.'

'Good lad.'

If I'd known then that the Volvo we were sitting in was bought on hire purchase from a dealership in Chesham two years after I was born and was still registered under my mother's name, I would never have been pacified by his story of hard work and reward. As it was, I took his lies to heart.

He pulled into the first garage that advertised a decent price for diesel. The needle on the fuel gauge had reached empty in the middle of his fable, and we must've passed five other petrol stations before he settled on the one we ended up in: a ramshackle establishment you used to see a lot of in those days, which looked as though a motley co-op of retired locals ran it for a hobby. The forecourt was a dust-track and the pump handles were corroded. All of the carnations they left out for sale stood parched in margarine tubs.

While he filled up the tank and went in to pay, I waited in the car with the atlas open on my knees, tracing the bright-yellow route he'd charted for us. Map reading is a skill that other boys my age picked up at Scouts, but I happened to learn it in the context of my father's underhandedness. I tallied the grids, converted all the inches, got the answer I was searching for: it was 190 miles to Leeds, give or take. But I noticed something else, too. The route he had plotted was not the most direct. It took us on a snaking course of A-roads.

He ambled across the forecourt, studying the receipt. 'Not as cheap as I thought,' he said, getting in beside me. 'They haven't changed their sign for weeks, the lazy gits.' He stuffed the receipt into his pocket. 'Want a mint?'

A pack of Fox's glaciers was held under my nose. 'No, thanks.'

'I got us a Drifter each for later.' He leaned across me, flipped open the glovebox, tossed his haul of confectionery inside.

'How come we aren't going on the motorway?' I asked.

He slid a mint around in his teeth, turned on the engine. 'Roadworks,' he said. 'Once you hit Leicester, there's a wall of traffic. Best to skirt around it.'

'Oh.' I took him at his word. It seemed to me that fathers were supposed to have an intuition for such matters, just as mothers were supposed to have a native sense for flower arrangement. There was such nonchalance to his dishonesties, such a measure of conviction, that they left me feeling impudent for raising questions. 'Anyway, it's about the same in miles. I counted.'

'Does that mean you approve?' He rolled us away from the garage, back onto the road. 'Because a navigator and his captain have to stand together. I'm not having any insubordination.'

I stayed quiet.

'Know that word? Insubordinate?'

'No.'

He bit down on his mint, chewed it for a moment. 'Well, it's what happens when people get ideas above their station, start thinking they know better than you do. When a boat sinks in the middle of the ocean, it's normally because of that.' And he turned to me, eyes wide. 'But we're not going to sink, are we?'

I pressed my finger hard against the atlas, held it there. 'No way.'

* * *

There wasn't much that bound us, so I cleaved to any small thing that we held in common. Reading, for example. He said his favourite novel was *The Comedians*, but the books he renewed most at the library were historical doorstops like *Torquemada* and *The Name of the Rose*, which would take him months to slog through; I loaned mostly science fiction or boys' adventure novels where smart-talking youths rode motorbikes and hunted bounty.

We often watched old films together on TV, turgid Westerns with orchestral soundtracks (he liked to lie back on the sofa with a can of beer and give a running commentary: 'Whoever cast Bogart in this role needs hanging too, Sheriff'). On certain Saturdays when my mother had to work, he'd take me to whatever matinee was showing at the multiplex—we'd see films that were too grown-up for me, like *Brewster's Millions* and *Eight Men Out*. Afterwards, he'd say, 'Well, it wasn't art, but I'm not asking for my money back, are you?' He twice took me to play snooker at a gloomy club in Amersham, and I recall that he was impressed by my knack for potting balls, although he grew impatient with the minutes I spent measuring the angle of each shot—a third outing was not proposed.

We went to the golf centre a great deal, of course, and in between encounters with Nadine, he did show me how to grip a club correctly and the right way to plant my feet. There was also the fact that his favourite chocolate bar was a Drifter and so was mine: he had the sweetest tooth of anyone I knew. We enjoyed spaghetti Bolognese and cold toast with raspberry jam, we hated cauliflower and raw tomato. He kept a blonde Fender Telecaster locked in a black case inside his wardrobe and would bring it out every so often just to hold it in his arms, strumming it inexpertly with one thumb—it was the aesthetic of the instrument he admired most, not its potential sound, and I felt the same. What else? Our hair colour—tar black, identical—and I'm sad to say that I inherited my features from his end of the gene pool, which makes it difficult to stand before the shaving mirror these days, or sit in the barber's chair, or hold my head up as I walk into a lift.

The rest of our likenesses were so insubstantial they don't bear repeating. I'm not sure we ever saw the world with the same eyes. And yet, when I was twelve, I'd broadcast his achievements to anyone who'd listen. If babysitters asked me, 'What about your dad? Does he come over much?' my chest would swell with pride. I wouldn't think about the shortage of our time together, the places he no longer took me, the films we didn't watch, the meals we never ate at the same table. Because I knew that he was doing something more important with his life than taking care of me. 'He's away a lot. He works on a TV show,' I would say. 'Oh yeah,' they'd answer, 'which one?' And I'd watch their faces soften as I spoke its name— *The Artifex*—as if the words explained his absence and absolved it.

* * *

I've never had the mettle to review the scratchy VHS recordings of the programme I once made as a boy, though I've held on to them—for the same reason, I suppose, that people keep the urn after the ashes have been scattered. If I were to watch those episodes again, I would lose the final memory of their goodness, and I can't stand to close the gap between the poor expectant kid who made the tapes and the man who now possesses them. Had it not been for my father, it's unlikely I would ever have tuned in to *The Artifex* at all, and yet when I first saw the show it gave me a sensation that few stories ever have—a voluminous excitement slow-flooding my body, a recognition that I'd seen these characters and scenes before, that I was born with the show in me like some fossil waiting in a rock.

You'll have your own fixations, I am sure, and you'll recognise how difficult it is to move beyond them, even when they end or you outgrow them. *The Artifex* was mine, and I evangelised about it—at school, to my Sunday maths tutor, to my mother's friends, to any set of ears that entered my vicinity—believing that I had a more profound connection to the show than anyone, a deeper insight into its material, because my father was involved in its making. I will admit that it gave me a feeling of specialness. It was rare that I could make it through a day without re-watching it. This is still a problem I am working on, for different reasons.

It was much easier to avoid the show before the internet, of course, which only gets more complicated to navigate. Technology keeps generating new ways to disseminate the episodes. The web is a scrapyard of pixelated clips on YouTube, Vimeo, Dailymotion, Vuze, to name only a few—they appear whenever I'm compelled to type *The Artifex* into a search bar, which is much too often, and I have to summon the reserve not to click play. Many of the VHS originals remain in circulation, despite all my hard work to intercept them on eBay, Craigslist, Gumtree, and the other two-bit platforms people use to flog unwanted wares around the globe—I have at least a hundred copies boxed inside my storage locker because I can't quite bring myself to make a bonfire out of them. Facebook, Twitter, and Wordpress are the hardest to evade: nostalgia pages and devotional accounts are always rising up like cupboard ants and I'm forced to let them carry on existing. There's a stubborn mastermind out there who keeps restoring all the links I cull from Wikipedia pages, such as this one:

The Artifex Appears

From Wikipedia, the free encyclopedia

For the television adaptation, see The Artifex (TV Series)

The Artifex Appears is a science fiction/fantasy novel by children's author Agnes Mosur. Believed to have been written in the early part of her career (c. 1954), it remained unpublished until after Mosur's death from pancreatic cancer in 1986. The full typewritten manuscript was discovered with a hoard of uncompleted works at Mosur's home in Primrose Hill by editor Clarence Denholm. It was first published by Asphodel Press within the posthumous collection *In Otherland: New, Unseen and Unfinished Stories,* but was repackaged as a single edition in October 1993 to tie in with a successful adaptation of the story for children's television starring Maxine Laidlaw and Mike Egan.

Television series

Main article: *The Artifex (TV Series)*

Upon the book's release in 1987, ITV Children's Drama bought the adaptation rights for British television in a co-production with New Original. Screenwriter Joel Kasper (*Pantheon Nine*) was enlisted to write the first series of six episodes. 'I was asked to retain the darker aspects of the source material and ramp up the spookiness,' said Kasper in an interview with *Radio Times*. 'It's an old-fashioned story but I think most kids today will get a kick out of it—they don't like things sugar-coated.' Filming began in January 1993 on a sound stage at <u>Yorkshire Television studios</u> in Leeds; exteriors were recorded at various locations in Lancashire, London and South Wales. The programme debuted on Wednesday 13 October 1993 at 5:00 P.M.

—which is the date and time my father made me write down on a piece of paper and stick to our refrigerator door, in case my mother and I forgot to watch. The first five minutes of that episode were all it took.

* * *

It opens on a quiet shot of misty autumn woodland. A title card goes up: Devon, 1955. An overlapping sound of frantic footsteps on soft ground, a leafy rustle. Cut to the mud-spattered legs of children bounding through the trees. Close up on the face of the smallest child, a boy trailing far behind the pack. He is a wheezing curlytop in shorts and jacket. One of his shoes is missing. He calls out to the others, begging them to stop and wait, but they keep running. 'Last one there's a rotten egg!' they shout back, or something similar. They get further and further away. The boy has no choice but to stumble on. His panting worsens and his face flushes red. It's an asthma attack. A bad one. He falls onto the mulch, clutching his chest. The other children are too distant to notice. An eerie piano theme begins. The camera cranes upwards, showing the helpless boy left on the forest floor, until the screen whites out. A moment passes. The whiteness gradually dissolves into the quavering tips of pine trees. A woman's voice says: 'Drink up, little one. You'll be all right.' We see a pale hand lifting the boy's head up, a cup being pushed to his lips. As he gulps, a greenish liquid spills down his chin. 'Breathe now, breathe,' she tells him. 'A bit of ranyan tea, that's all you needed.' The boy's lungs fill with air again. He opens his eyes and sees his rescuer.

She does not seem human. Her eyes have strange pale irises. Her hair is ragged and wiry. She has a toothless mouth and scars across her brow. Her skin is pockmarked, stippled with blisters. The boy is startled by the oddness of her, but he's too weak to get up. 'Who . . . ?' he manages to say.

She seems surprised. 'You can see me?'

He starts to wheeze.

'No, no, no, don't be afraid, boy. Give those lungs a rest. Can you hear me, too?'

He nods at her, still fearful.

'I had a feeling you were different.' She has a strange accent: European with an American tinge. As she gets up, we see how tall she is: at least seven feet. She's dressed in a beige boiler suit, as a prisoner might wear, and she's barefoot. 'My name is Cryck,' she says. 'What's yours?'

'Albert,' he murmurs.

'Well, I think I'd better take you to my camp until you get your strength back. Then we'll find your friends and get you home. What do you say?'

The boy is exhausted. His eyes close again, dreamily.

'That'll be the ranyan kicking in,' she says. 'You'll feel better in an hour or two, I promise.' She bends and scoops him from the ground with ease. He lies cradled in her arms. 'It's just a mile to my compartment. Hold on tight. It's going to be bumpy.' She carries him into the mist between the trees.

The piano theme gets louder. Credits roll. Funny, how the order of the cast has stayed with me all this time: Mike Egan, Joy

Greaves, Kimberly Pope, Malik Asan, Eve Quilter, Gavin Wynn-Norton—and Maxine Laidlaw as Cryck. Based on the book by Agnes Mosur. Produced by Declan Palmer, Carole Reeves, Bruce Haswell. Directed by Alfred O'Leary. The title goes up, dead centre of the screen, where it glimmers like moonlight on water: The Artifex.

T he only thing worth eating at this dump is pancakes,' my father said. 'But order what you want.' We had made it as far as Lincolnshire unscathed. The town of Colsterworth, according to the map. He leaned back against the vinyl of the booth and drew out his tin of Wintermans, slotting one between his lips and mumbling, 'See an ashtray anywhere?' He beckoned the waitress over. 'You know there's a reason they put these places on the sides of A-roads, don't you? Same reason they put bookies next to pubs. Temptation for the desperate.' The flame of his cheap plastic lighter was minuscule, but he always seemed to make it work. 'The Little Chef,' he said, heaving the smoke out of his nose. 'I mean, what does that say to you? Inferior cooking, that's what. Tiny portions. One day I'll take you to a proper diner in America. You'd never find a place called little *anything* over there. They'd call it jumbo's, or Fat Dan's.'

I sat with the laminated menu, deciding between breakfast or dessert. The restaurant was almost empty. There was just a pane of glass between us and the car park, where the Volvo rested in the tepid sunshine. A cheerful bossa nova played on the house system, but it couldn't mute the din of tyres on the dual carriageway, which seemed no further from us than the kitchen.

The waitress arrived with a notepad. 'You ready to order?'

'First things first,' my father said, 'I need an ashtray.'

'It should be on the table.'

'Should be,' he said. 'Isn't.'

'Okay, I'll bring you one.' She fished inside her apron for a biro. 'What're you having?'

'He's still choosing, but I'll have raisin pancakes and a coffee. And can you tell me something?' He rubbed the sleep out of his eye and she waited while he scrutinised the goo upon his finger. 'Does your payphone work?'

'Last I checked,' she said.

'Does it take tens or twenties—you know, *minimum*?'

'Tens, I think.'

'Terrific.' He reached and took the menu from my hands. 'So, what's it to be then, Danno?'

'I can't decide.'

My father glanced up at the waitress. 'He'll have pancakes with syrup and vanilla ice cream. And a Coke. No, scrap the Coke—get him a glass of milk. And I'll have a bit of ice cream for my pancakes, too. Why not?'

She scribbled it down and left.

'I wanted scrambled eggs and beans,' I said. 'Or sausage and fried eggs.'

'Hard luck. If a man wants eggs, he shouldn't mess about.' He canted his head to get a view into the foyer—a cold entrance-way with a magazine stand and a podium that housed the cash register. 'Why don't you go and use the loo? It's a miracle you've held it in this long. Are you still sleeping with a bin bag underneath the sheet?'

'That was years ago, Dad.'

'Really? Not what I heard.'

I turned away from him.

'You'd better go before we leave. I'm not having any mishaps in the car.'

'Fine.'

He regarded the car park for a long moment. I can't say where his thoughts went. 'Think she's forgotten about that ash-tray. Can you grab one from another table?'

I slid out of our booth and checked the one behind us. There was a glass dish on the counter, full of dog-ends. I emptied it onto a plate of leftovers and brought it to my father. 'Good lad,' he said, weighing the heft of it, smiling at the franchise logo printed on the base. 'There's the little man himself. What's he looking so cheery about, eh? His bank balance, most likely. I might just have to keep this as a souvenir.' He set it down and dumped a scab of ash upon it. 'Unless we both get food poisoning.'

'If you hate this place so much,' I said, 'why did we stop?'

He snorted out more smoke, eyeing the window. 'When you get older, Dan, you're going to learn that there are two kinds of women: ones you love enough to marry, and ones who happen to be standing there when you're in the mood for something sweet. It's the same with restaurants.' A car was parking in the bay next to the Volvo, foregoing all the other empty spaces. He grinned at me. 'Plus, I knew they'd have a payphone.'

'Oh yeah, we need to call mum.'

'Right,' he said, dragging. 'Well, don't feel bad. You were busy with the map.'

'Should I do it now?'

'Nah, it can wait until you've eaten. Just don't tell her what I'm feeding you.'

The waitress arrived with our drinks. As she set the coffee cup down before my father, she noticed the ashtray and apologised to him. 'Head's like a sieve today,' she said—a phrase I'd never heard before, and which I now associate with her bony, tattooed hand upon his saucer. Her thumb was missing a fake nail.

'Not to worry,' my father said. 'I've got to say, it's a pretty good ashtray—nice and wide, not too shallow. I was thinking I might steal it. Don't suppose that sort of thing would be encouraged in such a high-class establishment as this, though.'

She laughed a little uncertainly, then said: 'You'd be surprised.'

'I bet I would, Kelly,' came his response. He must've clocked her name badge. 'I'll bet you've got at least five of these beauties at home.'

She pursed her lips. 'That'd be telling.' My glass of milk was still waiting on her tray, and she finally acknowledged it, spilling a drop as she lowered it down. 'Whoops.' She dabbed the paper mat with a tea towel. 'So where are you lads on your way to, then—anywhere special?'

My father was watching her through slatted eyelids. 'That depends on your point of view,' he said. 'I'm taking him to see the place I work.'

'And where's that?'

'It's up in Leeds. The TV studios.'

'Oh.' She looked at me. 'Exciting.'

I couldn't sit there waiting for him to tell her, as though it were nothing. 'He works on *The Artifex*.'

'Not everyone finds that as fascinating as you, Danno,' my father said. He stabbed out his Wintermans and peered up at her. 'It's a kid's show. Not like *Rainbow* or *Blue Peter*. A proper drama series.'

'Yeah, I've heard of it—haven't seen it, but I've heard of it.'

'You got kids? They probably watch it. Or they've read the book.'

'No. I think my nieces like it, though.'

'It's quite sophisticated for a kid's show. A little bit scary. But they keep letting us make more, so I suppose they must enjoy it. This one likes it, anyway.' He bobbed his head at me.

'It's amazing,' I said. 'Everyone says so.'

There was a ding from the kitchen.

'That'll be your pancakes,' said the waitress. 'I should fetch them.'

'You do that. We can entertain ourselves.' He plucked a pack of sugar from the stand and shook it. As she walked towards the kitchen pass, he held his gaze on her. 'What d'you think of her?' he said. 'Seems like a decent person.'

I drank my milk. Its coldness helped my tongue. 'I don't like her nails.'

'What's wrong with them?'

'They're all glued on.'

'That doesn't matter. You can't tell anything about a woman from her nails, believe me.'

'She's a waitress.'

'So what? Nothing wrong with that. Your mother was a waitress when I met her.' He stirred his coffee. 'A job's a job. I don't want you getting that superior attitude.'

'Mum wasn't a waitress.'

'She did catering. Same thing. Just because your grandpa didn't pay her for it doesn't mean it didn't happen.'

I couldn't understand why he wanted me to appreciate the lady. She was serving us breakfast at a roadside restaurant on the verges of a town we'd never return to—her life story was none of my concern. But I can see now that he was trying to bestow some of his better values unto me, or at least make me aware that he possessed them. 'Seriously,' he went on, 'you shouldn't just dismiss people because of what they do. Sometimes, what you see is what you get, and that's okay: not everyone has a dream to go chasing after. But most of the time—and I'll bet you that waitress is a classic case—there's plenty more to them than first appears. Like with me. When I was decorating, I wasn't just a decorator, was I?'

I shook my head.

'Right then, here we are.' Kelly appeared with our food. 'Who had the raisin pancakes?' She put them down in front of me. As she deposited the last dish before my father, he touched her hand. 'Is that a snowflake or a web?'

She blinked at him, took a slight step back. 'Oh that. I sort of regret it.'

'What's to regret?'

'You know, I was young and stupid. A boy dared me. Sad, really.'

'Not at all. I like it.'

She squinted at her hand. 'Well, either way, I'm stuck with it for good.' Folding the empty tray under her armpit, she set her eyes on me. 'Would you like another glass of milk, love?'

I shook my head.

'You can bring me some more coffee,' my father said.

She backed away, nodding. 'No problem.' And she smiled at him in the way I had seen other women smile at him before—that fleeting constriction of the mouth, a flinch to gauge his reaction. He flinched straight back at her. Then he turned to me and picked up our conversation: 'See, on the show, we just assume that Cryck is a weird creature to begin with, don't we? And then we find out she's a lot more complicated. Point is, no one writes her off.' He stripped the napkin jacket from his cutlery and started cutting up his pancakes. 'I mean, how d'you know that waitress doesn't have some secret of her own? Look at that tattoo she's got—could be a whatsit . . . an indograf. You never know.' A slick of ice cream dripped off his fork. 'Hey, these aren't bad. Eat up.'

I had a few bites, but it hurt to chew.

'I'm not saying she's from another planet or anything,' he said, 'but you can't just take one look at her false nails and think you've got her sussed.' He noticed, then, that I had barely touched my pancakes. 'Your tongue still giving you gyp, or what?'

'Yeah.'

'Just eat the ice cream.'

'It's making me feel a bit sick.'

'All that milk, probably.' He wiped his mouth. 'Okay, leave it, then.'

'Can I go to the toilet now?'

'Thought you'd never ask. Go on, hurry up.' As I slid out
the booth and headed off, he called: 'Make sure you get it all
out!'

I've always viewed men's toilets as sites of casual depravity—that pervading uric stench and dour strip-lighting, the
silent strangers who come and go from the urinals without
washing their hands—but I think the Little Chef's facilities
were likely where this attitude became ingrained. I couldn't get
the piss out of me quick enough. Standing at the hand dryer, I
noticed a beaded trail of syrup on the front of my sweatshirt. I
tried to smear it in, but that just made it worse. So I splashed
the stain with water and spent a while blasting it dry.

My father wasn't at our table when I came back out. He'd
abandoned his breakfast, left his tin of Wintermans on his place
mat, the knife and fork across his plate. I could see his saucer
but no coffee cup. 'He's over there, love,' came a voice from
behind me. It was Kelly, the waitress. She was taking an order
at a neighbouring table. There was something new about her: a
chalkiness about her face, as though she'd dusted it with different make-up. If she really was a delegate from another planet, I
supposed a dismal restaurant on the shoulder of an A-road was
a clever place to hide. 'Over there,' she said, pointing.

Fran Hardesty was inclined between the magazine stand
and the Coke machine in the lobby. He had the shiny brown
receiver of the payphone clasped against his ear. A coffee cup
was in his other hand and he was taking gulps from it as he
talked. I assumed that he was speaking to my mother. 'That's
totally ridiculous, that can't be right,' he was saying as I
approached, 'two weeks is what he told me. Have they even
asked her yet? Have they even bothered? . . . Come on, QC,
you *know* I didn't. You were with me the whole day. Don't
fucking start all that again. I've had it with all that . . .'

This was the first time I heard those initials—QC.

'No, the problem is—will you just listen? . . . How was I

supposed to *know* that, mate? She's gone way too far with all this. I'm telling you, it's out and out humiliation that she's after, and there's no way I'm—' As soon as he noticed me, he lowered his voice; his tone became conciliatory. 'Look, I've got to go, okay. My lad's showed up. But I'm gonna ring you back . . . An hour. You'd better be around . . . All right, good. But, look—you need to help me out here, it isn't right, all this. I'm trying to stay calm here, but . . . Okay. Later.' He hung up, necked his coffee, left the cup beside the cash register.

'Who's QC?' I asked.

'A mate of mine. Don't worry.' He ghosted by me. 'We should probably get moving.'

'Is everything okay?'

'I told you: don't worry.'

'You sounded upset, though.'

'Nah. QC can be difficult sometimes. It's fine.'

'Well, can I borrow 10p?'

'What for?'

'I need to call Mum.'

He surveyed the restaurant. 'You know what? I just tried her. No answer.'

'Oh.' The clock in the lobby said 9:48. She usually left for work around eight, but I knew that she'd booked the whole morning off as a contingency. 'Maybe she was in the bath. We'd better try again.'

My father pondered this for what seemed like an age. He reached into his pocket, spread out the change he had across his palm, and picked out a couple of tens. 'All right, if you need the brownie points that much, let's try her.' His bounding strides towards the phone were strangely rushed. He dialled the number and waited. 'Getting an engaged tone now,' he said. 'Listen.' The receiver was pressed to my ear as validation.

'One more time,' I said, before he'd got the phone back on its hook. 'Please. I promised her.'

'We can't hang around here all day, you know.' He shrugged and dialled again to placate me. When my mother answered, he dropped two coins in the slot and passed me the phone. 'Be quick,' he mouthed, and went back to our table.

My mother was glad to know I was safe. I could hear the relief wrinkling her voice. 'And where are you now?' she said, after I told her about my role as navigator. 'What are your co-ordinates?'

'Just a service station,' I said. 'Lincolnshire.'

'Not a McDonald's, I hope.'

'No. We just had the sandwiches you made.'

'I bet you picked out all the cucumber.'

'No, I ate it,' I said. 'Honest.'

'Sure, I believe you.'

'I was thinking—'

'About what?' she said.

'I wish you could've come with us.'

'Well, this is your father's thing.'

'Yeah, I know, but . . .'

Her hand rustled the mouthpiece. 'Look, as soon as you meet Maxine whatshername you won't even remember me. Next to Maxine whatshername, I'm dog food.'

'Laidlaw.'

'That's what I said, isn't it?'

She made this joke so often that I found it tiresome—I didn't understand that this was her intention, to irritate a smile out of me. 'I think my money's going to run out soon, Mum.'

'Okay. Just phone me next time you stop. Is your dad behaving?'

'Yeah. He's being nice. We're having fun.' On the far side of the restaurant, he was passing a small plateful of cash to our waitress. As she accepted it, she almost bowed: a dip of her knees and a swash of her hair. He touched her bare forearm as he went by her, whispered in her ear. Something was cupped against the inside of his wrist, a little souvenir half-tucked into his shirt sleeve. 'He thinks that I still wet the bed. Who told him that?'

'Not me,' my mother said, 'but it doesn't surprise me. Ask him what size shoes you wear. Ask him if he knows your collar size.'

'What is my collar size?'

'Thirteen and a half,' she said, 'last time I checked. You're going to have to catch him up, I suppose.'

'Yeah.'

'Be patient with him,' she said. 'I know it's not easy.' And then I lost her to the blips.

You need to be aware the show was not just entertainment but communion with my father. It was as though, when I switched on at five P.M. each Wednesday, our minds were connected by a cathode ray tube. I'd kneel before the television without moving—twenty-five minutes of intense concentration. I'd shut out the clatter of my mother in the kitchen and the waning music of the birds, forget the dust that dimmed the screen, ignore the niggling thoughts of homework. When the last scene faded to black, I'd wobble closer to the set so I could watch the end credits, pins and needles in my legs, hoping that I'd see his name scroll up with all the others. But it never did. 'I'm just a carpenter on set, Danno. You really think they're going to write my name in fancy letters? It doesn't work like that in television.' Strange, the things we celebrate. He wasn't credited for any of his work until his crimes made national news. And now you only have to type *The Artifex* into a search bar and it flushes out a hundred archived newspaper reports bearing my father's name, downplaying his connection to the programme. Like this one from the *Telegraph*: 'Hardesty, 36, was engaged as a freelance carpenter on the ITV co-production, a spokesman for the show confirmed. It is understood that Hardesty, who previously had worked as a painter-decorator and stage carpenter in regional theatre, had little to no contact with the programme's cast or senior production staff.'

How my father came to be involved in the show's making is

a story in itself. Given his mendacity, it's not easy to assemble a picture of his working life from the scant puzzle pieces I am left with: half-remembered conversations with him and my mother, letters he once sent to her and those she sent to him, small details he shared with others (friends and acquaintances, my grandparents), scraps of paperwork found with his possessions, contracts and invoices for jobs, outstanding bills, home videos, my mother's teenage diary.

What I know for sure is that he grew up in the Lake District, on a sheep farm at Wasdale Head, and was expected to raise Herdwicks with his father until he got old enough to inherit the land and its livestock. But he used to say the shepherd's calling was 'bred out' of him; he realised he wasn't built for it when he was very young. 'Men are born into that life,' he once wrote to my mother. 'If you don't feel it in the marrow of your bones your [sic] better off away from it.'

Strangely for a boy in his community, he enjoyed school (his Maths, English, and Science grades were good) and preferred the indoor life. 'The fells are great if you like the stink of sheep-shit and a lot of rain. I'd rather chase a pretty girl in the pub than a load of dumb animals in the mud. Who in his right mind wouldn't?' He left school with decent qualifications, was the first Hardesty to go to university. He wanted to be a town planner, and was accepted into an Architectural Design programme at Wolverhampton Polytechnic. one of his leftover drawings from that time is quite spectacular—a sprawling bird's eye view of an imagined city, sketched on tracing paper—and indicates his wasted talent. In the summers, afraid of going home, he worked picking tomatoes, shared caravans with foreign students. He seemed to like this period of his life: 'They're all training to be doctors. Bulgarians mostly,' he wrote to my grandma. 'They come over every year and get up to their elbows in tomato sap and bee stings. The wages are great if you pick fast enough. We're paid by the weight of each basket. The foreigners work so hard they can earn a year's tuition back home in a single season. You spend all summer with them, get to know them a bit, and then they're gone. I think it's kind of a shame.'

He dropped out of university at the age of nineteen, for reasons that elude me—his transcript shows all lower-second grades, and I expect he viewed this as a failure of some kind, an indictment of his potential. If you ever watched my father hanging wallpaper, you'd understand the great meticulousness he brought to his work—he tried to be the best at what he did, but people seemed to favour quickness over quality, and I suspect this wore him down after a while. If skill goes unrecognised for long enough, it suffocates. He laboured on building sites around the midlands for modest wages until he turned twenty-one.

At this point, an older man he'd been working with—a joiner called Eric Flagg—started his own company in Maidenhead, refurbishing and partitioning offices. My father took a job with him, learning the joiner's trade, renting a box room in a house-share. He got close to Eric and his wife, a dental receptionist who ran the local amateur dramatic society. One weekend, they conscripted him to help out with the set construction for an Ayckbourn farce they were staging at the community centre—the set designer had injured his wrist and Eric couldn't manage building all the flats and furniture on his own. I'm not entirely sure if this was my father's first encounter with the theatre (he rarely spoke about productions he'd worked on, or seen, or been inspired by), but this episode with Eric must've catalysed his interest somehow. I can only guess that the collaboration was an unexpected thrill for him, that taking the designer's plans and giving them shape, solidity, afforded him some satisfaction. Maybe he believed his talent and meticulousness would be valued in the theatre, if nowhere else.

He taught himself the rudiments of set design by reading

library books and absorbed the methods of stage carpentry from Eric. He experimented with the properties of materials (different timbers, fibreglass, polystyrene, cement, epoxy resin) in the makeshift workshop in Eric's garage. Through trial and error, he learned ways to build things cheaply, found techniques to convert the roughest sketches into modest scenery that could be rigged and flown. He made sets for plays at nearby grammar schools and comprehensives, working from the drawings of enthusiastic art teachers, impressing them with his ability. They passed his name and number on to arts centres with am dram groups, who passed it on to community and rep theatres, who passed it on to minor touring companies. He picked up a lot of small commissions: 'He was ten times cheaper than anyone else, that's why,' Eric told me, 'and probably ten times better. I always said he should negotiate himself a proper fee, but he didn't do the things he liked for money, your dad. He'd slave his balls off on a site for sixty quid a day, then he'd go off and build you a set for a pint and a packet of crisps. I always found him to be decent about that kind of stuff.' For about a year, Eric let him use his garage, stash materials there, borrow his tools. 'It became his little grotto. When he wasn't on the job with me, he was in my garage with the radio on, using my bandsaw. He was round more often than my brother. We couldn't get rid of him.' His experience accumulated into something befitting a CV. 'He never seemed to think he could make a living from it, though,' is Eric's recollection. 'I mean, we all said he was good enough to be a master carpenter at the National—I used to say I'd sack him if he didn't quit and make a go of it—but he didn't have much belief in himself, not about that sort of thing, anyway. And when he met Kathleen, well, let's just say I got my garage back after that.'

To hear Eric Flagg speak of my father is like reading a stranger's obituary. In his view, Fran Hardesty was luckless, thwarted, misunderstood. 'He lost a bit of purpose, I suppose is how I'd put it—anything he might've wanted for himself, Kath stepped in and replaced it. He was totally besotted with her, and she never understood that side of him—you know, that need to make something from nothing. She just wanted him to earn and pay the bills. He couldn't earn it fast enough for her. That's how it always seemed to me.' But this was not the father whom I saw at close quarters. If he was 'besotted' with my mother, he didn't reveal it in the day to day manoeuvres of our household. And for someone who reputedly aspired to a different life, he spent a long time avoiding the pursuit of it. He can at least be credited for not abandoning his responsibilities from the outset—stronger men than him have run out on their families, but he tried to endure.

He stopped working for Eric after I was born. 'Contracts in my game were either feast or famine, and he needed something steadier, so that was that. I wasn't going to argue with him. I'd hear from him every now and again, but then we lost touch. It was easier for him, I think, to just stop phoning or coming round the house.' He took a position as a maintenance worker for the Royal Borough Council of Maidenhead and Windsor, where he was assigned duties such as pipe repair, levelling pavements, relaying tarmac, renovating public toilets, and redecorating council buildings. During these years, he gave up on stage carpentry altogether. Whatever reputation he'd established in the theatre scene dissolved.

As far as I can tell, this was the point at which his slow drift towards trouble started. He was suspended from his council job for what they termed unsatisfactory conduct: 'remonstrating with a supervisor in a busy public concourse.' He was taken on by a large decorating company who had contracts with the NHS across the country. The hours were regular and he didn't mind the work: he paint-rollered corridors in drab hospital tones, grouted tiles in nursing homes, wallpapered dentists' waiting rooms, rendered the ceilings in GP clinics.

But he was let go from this job, too, after an altercation with his boss about a damaged company van.

It was decided, at my mother's urging, that he should start a decorating business of his own. She placed a notice for him in the local classifieds:

HARDESTY & HARDESTY

DOMESTIC AND COMMERCIAL PAINTING SERVICES INTERIORS & EXTERIORS, QUALITY PAPERHANGING, FRIENDLY & RELIABLE, FREE QUOTATIONS

The extra Hardesty was his idea—as a cultured liar he understood that it gave people the impression of a family enterprise, trustworthy and established, so when he rolled up on his own to give an estimate he could pretend his brother or his father were occupied elsewhere: 'We've a load of work on at the moment. They're finishing a job over in [affluent local town of his choosing].' This tactic—plus the skill of guessing other companies' quotes and undercutting them by just enough to appear reasonable—worked more often than not.

He earned a good profit from the first few house-painting jobs he took on, and his calendar soon filled up with others. He put an ad in the job centre, seeking an apprentice, and hired a gangly teen called Wes for measly pay. (Wes became enough of a fixture for me to know him as a gangly adult, the quiet passenger in my father's Volvo with a dog-howl laugh and a pink crust of psoriasis on his cheeks.) It was at some point in the early years of his business when my father got an unexpected call from a vicar in Bradenham—the church needed a set for a nativity play and could he do them a Christian kindness? He'd been recommended to the vicar by a member of his congregation—my grandmother, as it turned out (she didn't see the harm: wasn't her son-in-law supposed to have some talent, after all?). It was what my father liked to call 'a beggar's favour,' but he agreed to do it, and I guess it reawakened him to the pleasures of the work.

After this, he got in touch with some of his old contacts in the theatre. He enquired about stage carpentry work and found himself presented with more opportunities than he'd expected. This must've been one of the only moments in his life when he hit a wellspring of good fortune—he was told that the amount of skilled labour had dwindled at regional level; a dozen master carpenters in the West End had retired and most of the good craftsmen had found permanent positions. And so he was engaged as a freelancer to help build sets for shows in Stowe and Windsor, Castleford and Canterbury, Hastings, Northampton, Bolton, Aberystwyth, Wrexham, Maidstone, Newcastle, Poole, High Wycombe, and various other pinholes on the map—pick a region of the British isles, he'd probably served a theatre there.

Between decorating jobs, he drove to workshops up and down the country, taking his instructions from whichever master carpenter had hired him, sleeping in the car when it was necessary, or in the beds of women he encountered (I hate to think how many). He was called further afield—to Dublin, Jersey, the Isle of Wight—by other carpenters who vouched for him whenever work arose, staying on their couches and earning little more than his expenses back. His heart was in the fabric of so many productions in this six-year stretch (from 1986 to 1992), even if his work left not one smudge upon the national memory: from the highbrow plays (Chekhov, Pinter, Shakespeare, Beckett, Ibsen, Brecht, and so on) to silly pantomimes with tenuous celebrities (snooker players, Winter Olympians, television chefs).

These experiences could well have prompted him to chase something more permanent in a London theatre, to apply for master carpenter positions that would've been more lucrative and gratifying—not to mention stable. But, as he once wrote to my mother, 'At that level it becomes a job like any other. I love that I can come and go from it, pick and choose the work. I love the variety. Being in charge is too much hassle. Ask me to make something and I'll make it. No point adding on a load of stress.' He seemed content to fill out the dead spaces between carpentry assignments with decorating jobs. This became the settled mode of his career. He spent a lot of time in other people's houses and little time in his own home—I can only infer that this was how he wanted it, and maybe this was the contented state he should've stayed in.

When I think about the last few years he lived with us, the symptoms of his presence are what I recall, not the feeling of his company: the dry throttle of his car returning to the driveway in the dark, the sudden brightening of our landing curtains, the tired percussion of his keys on the hallway table, the uneasy rumble of his conversations with my mother in the bathroom, his washed-out jeans and overalls spread out to dry on radiators at weekends, the tinkling of aluminium ladders being carried from the garage, long spring evenings punctuated by the grinding of a mitre saw. I've come to the conclusion that what he liked about his life as a stage carpenter was being appreciated for something he was good at—and who could blame him for wanting to maintain it?

But television was my father's ruination. It changed the way he saw himself. First, it gave him false humility, which is worse than having no humility at all: 'Yeah, people keep telling me it's such a special project to be part of, and I suppose they're right,' he'd say to us. 'You just have to look around and see the kind of talent they've got working on this show, it's frightening—and there's me in the middle of it. I keep saying, are you sure it's really *me* you want? I mean, that's *Dame* Maxine Laidlaw—surely I'm not good enough to be standing in a room with her.' Later, he behaved as though the platform of success he had ascended to was nothing special. 'You don't want to hear me droning on about this stuff again,' he'd say, then carry on regaling us with details.

The day he rang to inform my mother that he'd landed a position on the show, nobody was home to take the call—it was the Christmas holidays, so it's likely that she'd taken me to see my grandparents or into town with her on errands. At this juncture of his life, he had no fixed address: the last we'd heard, he was a lodger in a guesthouse outside Gillingham. I wish someone had thought to keep the answerphone cassette that bore his message: I would like to hear it back again just once, so I could check his words against the transcript in my memory. Because I can't tell how much I've misremembered the weight of his voice that day, the joyful yet mocking tone, the insinuation of *I told you so* that ran through it.

Still, the facts are clear enough: a carpenter he'd met while he was working at the octagon in Bolton had been made the chargehand on a new TV show and was assembling a crew. My father had been hired and was delighted. The job began in three days' time, and it required him to be in Leeds for several months for pre-production and filming. There was a camp bed in the workshop with his name on it, a communal kitchen and a shower room: it'd do him for a while. He planned to head north in a few days. He'd be in touch as soon as he'd got settled. It was a massive opportunity for him, he said. A massive opportunity.

I've often wondered what my mother might have told him if she'd been at home to answer. Would she have divested him of the idea that she still cared about his opportunities? Would she have been able to persuade him not to go?

The box was in my holdall, right where I had packed it. 'You found it yet or what?' my father called to me from the driver's seat. 'Chop chop.' We were still in the car park. The Volvo was a dull reflection in the tinted windows of the Little Chef. An apathetic brightness steeped the sky. The engine wasn't running, but I could smell the burned-on fumes of the exhaust pipe. I was under the spread wing of the boot door, both knees on the bumper, but my bag was slightly beyond reach. 'I can't get to it.'

He didn't turn his head, just watched me in the rear-view. 'You need to climb right in.'

I did as he suggested, trampling his possessions: a long-handled toolbox, the bin liners that contained his entire wardrobe, a bouquet of golf clubs, a bucket crammed with wallpaper brushes and old Stanley knives, bottles of turpentine and varnish. Thrown against the upright of the back left seat, upon a set of dustsheets, was my holdall. I dragged it close, unzipped it. 'Get a move on, Dan, or I'm driving off with you still in there.' The box was jammed in tight among the other things I'd packed, but I managed to free it.

'Coming!' I called, and my father started the car. I had to jump to close the boot.

'Seatbelt,' he said, as I got in beside him. He pressed the clutch and joggled the gearstick. 'So, how come I've not heard about this before now?' he asked, reversing. 'They only just brought it out on tape. Mum ordered it for me.'

'How long is the loan on it?'

'A few weeks, I think.'

'Ah,' he said, 'so we don't have to listen right away. We can put some music on for a bit. I've got The Smiths with me—you'll like them.'

My shoulders sagged. 'But I've never heard this one before.'

'I've never heard it before either, and I work on the bloody show. You're a proper fanatic, eh?'

'Yeah. So what?'

He was laughing at me. 'How many times would you say you've watched it?'

'Shut up, Dad.'

'Ha ha. Go on. I want to know.'

I hesitated. 'Which episode?'

'The whole series, start to finish. How many times?'

'I don't know.'

'Ten?'

I shrugged.

'Twenty?'

'Something like that.'

'Wow,' he said. 'And now you want to listen to the book on tape—I mean, doesn't the same old story get boring after a while?'

'The book's quite different from the show.'

He pretended that he knew this. 'Not *that* much.'

'And the tapes are read by Maxine Laidlaw, so they're different as well.'

'Okay, I get it.' He eyeballed me. 'You're smitten.'

'I just like to know as much as I can. What's wrong with that?'

'Nothing,' he said. 'But sometimes knowing too much can spoil things, don't you think? It's like when you hear a song and the lyrics make you feel *wow, this band*, this band really *knows* what it's like to have your heart ripped out, and then you hear them interviewed about it—turns out the song is really all about them being off their heads on LSD.'

'What's LSD?'

'It's something you shouldn't . . . Never mind,' he said. 'All right, you win—we'll put the first tape on, if it means that much to you. But just the first one, okay, or I'll get queasy.' He waited for a clearing in the traffic and rolled us back onto the carriageway. 'I don't see the point of talking books myself. Same person whining on at you for ages. I'd rather use my own imagination, make up my own voices.' He glanced down at the box again. 'How many tapes are in there, anyway?'

'Four,' I said.

'Bloody hell. That must be hours' worth!'

'You swore again, Dad.'

'Oh, come off it, that's not swearing.'

'Yes it is. And so is damn and piss and git.'

'What?' He laughed. 'Who told you that? That's ridiculous!'

'Mum says that piss is rude. And damn is only *half* swearing, but it's still bad.'

The 'Oh' of recognition he made was long and exaggerated. 'Well, your mother's got her good side, but she's wrong most of the time. Have you seen her record collection? Two of the worst words in the English language for you there: Simply Red.'

I let him go on chuckling at himself, until a lorry tried to move into the lane in front of us without indicating. 'Look at this moron!' My father hit the horn. As we accelerated past, he stooped to glare up at the driver in the cabin. 'Dickhead,' he muttered.

'Can I put the tape on now?' I said.

He gave a little exhalation, just to register his annoyance. 'Yeah, go on. But no shirking on the map reading. I still need those directions.'

The cover illustration on the box was quite unusual: a pencil crayon drawing of a rangy silhouette emerging from a forest. in plain red lettering across the top, it said:

Now a major ITV series

The four cassettes were housed in moulded plastic, packed so snugly that the first tape squeaked as I lifted it out. I clunked it into the mouth of the stereo and waited. It was the inaugural airing; I'd been saving it especially for our trip and I felt a sudden apprehension that it might not be as good as I was hoping for, that this might reflect poorly on me. 'You'd better crank it up a bit,' my father said. 'Speaker's blown on my side.'

White noise filled the car. And then there came a throaty voice, familiar but different, more present in my ears than it appeared on television. Her otherworld accent was much less pronounced—barely discernible, in fact—and her articulation of the words more ponderous, theatrical. '*The Artifex Appears*,' she said. Long pause. '*By Agnes Mosur.*' Long pause. '*Read by Maxine Laidlaw.*'

'Crikey,' said my father. 'She doesn't speak this slow in real life.'

'I can't believe you know her.'

'Oh, sure.' He let a small moment of hush settle. 'She's very friendly, Maxine, actually. Quick with a joke. You'll see.'

'*Chapter One*,' said Maxine Laidlaw.

'I mean, I wouldn't say we're best mates or anything—'

'*The Compartment.*'

'It's more of a nod-politely-at-each-other-in-the-canteen state of affairs.'

'*On a cold bright day in late October, the Artifex appeared—*'

'But, yeah, she knows who I am.'

'Shush,' I said. 'You're talking over it.'

'Oh, well—pardon *me*. Here, wind it back.'

* * *

The final carefree moments of my life unfolded on a section of the A1 between the villages of Colsterworth and Sprotbrough, as nondescript as any other length of highway in Great Britain. It's an ordinary stretch of asphalt that joins the heel of Lincolnshire with the base of Yorkshire, so devoid of character that to drive along it is to undergo an anaesthetic at seventy miles per hour. But when I think about that slice of road I find its uninspiring details have stuck with me. I suspect this has a lot to do with yearning. If I could reset the clocks to any point in time, it would be the hour we spent en route to Sprotbrough, listening to Maxine Laidlaw read *The Artifex Appears* in her slow, lurching voice. I know what I'd do differently. I would tell my father that I loved him more than any television programme. I would make it clear that my respect for him wasn't contingent on his level of success or what other people thought of him. I would tell him that I admired him more for taking me on this trip to Leeds than for anything he planned to show me when we got there. I would tell him that he had nothing to prove to me, even if it wasn't true.

Instead, I stared out of the windscreen, listening to that book on tape. Images got processed, filed away. Interminable grass verges. Median strips and corrugated girders. Newly planted saplings on the banks like headstones. Daisies, buttercups, and bracken. Patched-up tarmacadam. Overpasses hewn from bunker-grade concrete. The ridged grey backs of road signs on the right, the bright green squares of road signs on the left. Ragwort on the central reservation. Wheat fields, corn fields, onion fields, cabbage fields, potato fields. Telegraph poles and bellying wires. A million and one traffic cones. The ghostly jetsam of collisions gone before us: shattered brake-light plastic, broken hubcaps, tyre tracks that streaked off-road. Suddenly, a lone tree in a meadow. Clouds like mountain ranges. Slip lanes. Hay fields scored by tractor wheels. Pylons getting more and more enormous, linchpins of the earth.

Today, I live an entire ocean away from the A1, and yet I stalk it daily. Its nothingness pervades my thoughts in lonely moments as I ride the subway into work. I wish that I could drive a car without hearing the voice of Maxine Laidlaw. I wish that I could be in anybody's passenger seat without my fingers twitching on the door handle. But I'm part-marooned on roads like these and always will be.

* * *

[. . .] On a cold bright day in late October, the Artifex appeared to save his life. He was racing through the back-woods of his family's estate with his two sisters. For once, he was ahead of them, and it meant so much to be out in the lead that he ignored the burning in his chest when it began. But soon the pain got worse. They overtook him in a flash. He watched them bounding on, mud splashing up in chunks. His lungs were shutting down. He kneeled in the mush of leaves and dirt to rest, hoping it would pass. His sisters did not hear him wheezing. Not once did they look back. He knew their minds were on the finishing post: that ancient sycamore deep in the woods. One of them would get to notch a victory upon its trunk again, but it would not be him. It would never be him. Albert Bloor, eleven years old, was gasping in the dirt, alone. His eyes started to close. The world was drifting out of sight, further and further away. But then, with an intake of breath, she appeared.

He did not know from where. One moment he was staring at the tips of evergreens tilting above him, the next she was lifting his head and pressing a cup to his lips. 'Drink up, little one. You'll be all right,' she said. He slurped warm tea until the tightness in his chest relaxed. When he looked at her for the first time, it made him shake. How ugly and unusual she was: her catkin hair in the half-light, her toothless mouth, the scars across her brow, her chapped and blistered skin—and those white eyes, as pale as clock faces. But he was not afraid—not for a second. He trusted in her kindness from the start.

It was she who helped him find the air again. It was she who scooped him up and carried him through the pines and brambles. It was she who steered him past the snatching tree limbs without slipping. It was she who hauled him up the muddy hummock to her camp. At the top of that hill, she scraped a patch of mulch with her bare hands, exposed a rusty cover in the ground. She threw it aside. 'Hold on around my neck now,' she said, and twisted him across her shoulders. 'We're going down to my compartment.' He was lowered, rung by rung, into the dark.

She put him on a bed of hay and burlap, turned a handle overhead: a rush of soil came flooding in and brought a shaft of light. There was a metal crate for cooking on, holes punched in the sides for ventilation. She prepared a salve to soothe his chest. Three parts kardlach, two parts grish, one part mesckital. He would come to know this recipe by heart one day. The only asthma medicine that ever worked for him.

She mixed powders in her flask and added cold water, shook it. Testing a drip of the slack gum with her finger, she nodded— 'Perfect!'—then tipped it on his clavicle. 'We'll let that do its work,' she said. 'You rest.' From a flask, she poured out steaming tea. 'Another dose of ranyan to relax that chest and you'll be fine in a few hours.' She steeped a clod of leaves that looked like mistletoe in the hot liquid. 'It's a bitter flavour, but it makes you feel brand new, I promise.' So he gulped it down.

'Thank you,' he muttered, feeling his eyelids closing again. 'Thank you for saving me.'

She told him not to mention it. 'You sleep,' she said. 'Get your strength back.'

***

My father hit the pause button. 'I need a break. This is making me carsick.' He wound down the window on his side. A dirge of air pressed at my eardrums. I opened my window to get rid of it. 'What do you think of it so far? Nowhere near as spooky as the show. The piano music and the mist: you don't get that from a book, do you? And what about that good bit when she chucks her axe into the tree-trunk and it sticks? That's one of my favourite parts.'

'Maybe it's coming,' I said.

'I thought it happened at the start.'

'Yeah, but maybe they just added that part in for TV.'

'To make it more intense, you mean?'

'I don't know.'

'You could be right. It's better that way.' He smacked his stomach. '*Urgh.* Too much coffee, burning up my innards. Can you get me that Drifter out?'

I did as I was asked. He unwrapped it with his teeth and took a bite. 'I remember building the compartment for that scene, though—day one of the job, that was. They were going to use the barrel from an old cement lorry, but it cost too much. So we had to build it on a frame with sheets of ply. It was like a big half-section of a pipe, in the end, like something they ride skateboards on. We raced toy cars on it for a bit, until the scene painters got to work. That was a pretty good laugh while it lasted.'

'Really?' I said.

'Yeah, we were just messing about to kill some time.'

'No—did you really build Cryck's compartment?'

Pride registered on his face: a smiling nod. 'Of course. I've told you that before.'

I never tired of hearing it. Just as I never lost the impulse to run to the kitchen telephone after each new episode was broadcast to give my verdict, even if I could not reach him, even when the messages I left with housemates weren't returned, even when we had no contact number for him at all. Because, on those rare evenings when the phone did ring, and I was upstairs dreaming, my mother would come to nudge me awake and say, 'Your father wants a word,' and I'd go drowsy-eyed downstairs and hear his voice rousing me: 'Evening, Danno. Didn't mean to drag you out of bed. I couldn't sleep.' There'd be a sound on the line like water. 'So come on, then, don't keep me in suspense: what did you make of the last few episodes? I'm not so keen on those delegate characters, personally. I think they're a mistake. Way too much screen time for them. I'm more interested in what Cryck is building with that thing they found last week.' His words would smudge together. While he spoke at me, I would endorse his opinions with yeses and mm-hms, and then he'd trail off and tell me how late it was and wish me goodnight. I craved these private moments with him, and their infrequency and imperfection only made them more addictive.

We had moved into the fumy wake of an aggregates truck with a bumper sticker that said HOW'S MY DRIVING? and offered a number to dial. 'Think anyone ever rings that?' my father said. 'I always picture some old lady sitting in a porta-cabin somewhere, manning a hotline.'

'What else did you make?' I asked. 'On the show.'

'Almost everything.' He chewed on his Drifter, edged us into the middle lane. 'When we get there, I'll show you. The only set I didn't really work on was the Bloors' conservatory.'

'What about the conducer?'

'As if I'd let them build that thing without me! There's a hundred different pieces went into the shell alone, and I must've cut eighty of them by hand. It was like building a house. Then about a million tiny holes for the lights had to be drilled in.'

'What's it made of?'

'Wood and polystyrene, mostly. Horsehair and plaster. Chicken wire. A few struts from a marquee. It looks like it'd weigh as much as Nelson's column, that thing, but you could lift the whole lot on your own without much effort. They had to load it up with sandbags for the shoot in case it blew away.' He scrolled his window up again. There was an easing of his shoulders. 'Shut that window on your side,' he said. 'I'm all right now,' and pushed play on the stereo.

* * *

[. . .] When Albert awoke, it was pitch dark and raining. He heard the patter on the ground above. The candlelight was skittish and she loomed beyond it. 'How are those lungs feeling now, eh?'

'Much better,' he said.

She came to mop his brow with a cool rag. 'Time to get you home then, I suppose.'

'What should I call you?'

'Cryck,' she said.

'I'm Albert.'

'You must be from the big house, are you?'

'Yes, miss,' he said.

She winced. 'I told you my name, boy. Use it. I'm not one for formalities.'

'Sorry.' He sat up and stretched. 'I don't know how to repay you.'

'No need for that,' she told him. 'I'm glad to've sorted you out. You've got a better colour now.'

'What sort of name is Cryck?' he asked. 'Are you foreign?'

'In a manner of speaking.' Her giant nostrils flared. 'We've

got one thing in common, you and I. We're both a way from where we ought to be.'

'How long have you been hiding here?'

'Oh, I'm only passing through. Not hiding.'

'Passing through to where?'

'Aoxi,' she said. 'You have a lot of questions for a little one, if you don't mind me saying.'

'Is that where you come from? Aoxi?'

'Your pronunciation isn't right, but yes.' She moved in closer then and took him by the chin, turning his head left to right. 'You've really got me wondering now, Albert,' she said, softly. 'How is it you can see me? Are you a different species?'

'No.'

She inhaled so deeply that her skin cracked. 'You must have Aoxi in your blood. An ordinary child wouldn't feel a breeze if I were near. But you—not only do you see me, you aren't even revolted. And it leads me to believe that you're the only person on this rotten planet who can help me.'

The dirty red phone box where he placed the call was on the junction of Main Street and Boat Lane, set off in a lay-by near the boundary wall of a church cemetery. I would imagine it's still standing there today. Perhaps his thumbprints linger on the door glass. Perhaps some vestige of his spittle clogs the perforations of the mouthpiece. Sometimes, I'm plunged into anxiety that everything my father touched during our trip needs to be revisited and cleansed with bleach, in case his madness is contagious. That phone box in Sprotbrough would be the place I'd start, because it's where the first clear signs of his disturbance were presented.

We had taken a detour to get there. As we were coasting down the A1 in the thrall of Maxine Laidlaw's soft narration, my father said, 'Shit, is that the time already?' It was 11:02. At the sight of the next slip road, we veered off course. The track he'd plotted on the map for us continued on to Doncaster and Pontefract, all the way to Leeds, but we branched off into some drowsy South Yorkshire town: an ordinary suburban strip divided by two lanes of traffic and flanked by car dealerships. He pulled into a bus stop, turned off the stereo. 'Give me that a sec, will you?' he said, and took the atlas, spreading it upon the wheel.

'What are you looking for?' I said.

'It's fine. I've got it.' He tossed the atlas onto my lap. We drove on, crossed a viaduct over a canal, the water still and mirrored, anglers on the banks with landing nets. Then we emerged into the village, confronted by a church tower with a belfry not unlike the one I knew from home. The grounds of the church were similarly sculpted, a grey stone path skirting a lawn beset with tombstones, a phone box by the entry gates. 'This'll do nicely,' my father said. 'Let's stretch our legs for a minute.'

He parked right up on the kerb. There was a small parade of shops across the street, fringed by trees. 'What d'you reckon the odds are they'll have Wintermans in that newsagents?' he asked, stepping out. 'A little country town like this, plenty of old men about—I think my chances are good.' He walked around the bonnet, a passing cloud before the sun. 'You coming, or what?'

I climbed out. As we headed for the graveyard, he put his arm round me. After half a circuit of the grounds, we paused at a memorial skinned with moss. I can't remember what was carved into the stone, but it might as well have been: HERE LIE HARDESTY & HARDESTY. 'Listen, you stay here. Have a run around the church or something. I need to make a phone call.'

'Can't I just get back in the car?' I said.

He mussed my hair. 'You're a real outdoorsman, aren't you?'

'I don't want us to be late.'

'We won't be, son. In fact, that's why I need the phone.'

'You said everything was organised.'

'It is. This whole thing's been arranged for months. Look, I just—' He stepped forward, took me sharply by the elbow. 'Let's get you back in the car.'

'Can I play my tape?'

'Not until we're moving again,' he said. 'You'll drain the battery.' He steered me by the shoulders, back towards the road. 'Don't you have anything else in that bag of yours?'

'Figurines,' I said.

'That all?'

'Top Trumps.'

'That's a game for two.'

'Not always . . . I've got my camera, I suppose.'

'Any film in it?'

'No.'

'Well, that's useless then. I'll get you some from the shop. You'll want it for later.'

'What time do we have to be there?'

'It depends,' he said. 'I was told one o'clock, but I need to double-check that with my boss. The filming schedule changes all the time. And nothing pisses people off—I mean, *cheeses* people off—on a TV set more than someone interfering with the schedule. That's why I need the phone. Might take me a while to reach who I need to, though.' He was such a comfortable liar. 'You'd better get those Top Trumps out.'

I sat in the car with the windows open, sun splintering behind the visors, shuffling my deck of World's Best Aeroplanes. My father went into the phone box and shut the door. I dealt the passenger planes into two stacks, face down—one for me, one for him. Picking up his stack, I tried to plant myself inside his mind, guessing which of the planes' attributes he'd value, his tactical approach, before flipping over my cards in the other pile. I lost twenty in a row this way on his behalf.

He was still in the phone box, smoking and talking. His body seemed to sway. His voice was only just perceptible, more a thud than a whisper. I lost the next ten cards, too, depleting my father's pile. His voice got louder, more persistent. The temperature rose in the car. I took off my sweatshirt. What if I adjusted my strategy? Instead of playing *as* him, I'd play *for* him, use my own judgement. He won the next card, and the next, and the next, and I felt consoled by this, in better balance. He won the next card, too: nothing beat a Concorde. And then—*pop pop pop* from outside, three brisk punches to the phone box glass. When I turned my head, I saw there was a webbing in the door pane, a sudden opacity where my father's face should have been visible. I got out of the car and went to him.

'And that's precisely what I'm fucking telling you! That's exactly what I'm—' He was startled, angry, when I tugged back the door. A spume of smoke poured out at me. 'Jesus Christ, hang on a minute will you, mate, just give me sec.' He slid his palm over the mouthpiece, a cigarillo viced between his fingers. On his other hand, the knuckles were blood-raw. 'What the hell, Dan—get back to the car and wait for me, yeah? I'm trying to sort things out for us here. This is *serious*. Get it?'

I was stung, muted. I must've looked frightened.

'Look, I didn't mean to snap,' he said. 'I didn't mean it to come out like that.'

'It's okay.'

'No, it isn't. It wasn't right. Thing is—' His eyes were round and dewy, pleading. 'I've *really* got to settle things with QC before we get to Leeds. He's got it in his head that we were coming tomorrow morning instead of today, the moron. I'm trying to straighten things out.'

I recognised the doomy mood that settled in me then. The worst side effect of faith is the anxiety of disappointment nearing, the crack exposed in the foundations. I did everything I could to deny it. 'Are you hurt? You smashed the window.'

'Oh, *that*. That was nothing—that was just your dad being an idiot. I'm fine. It was a stupid thing to do.' He laughed sheepishly, raised his left hand, tensed and relaxed it. 'I've got tough bones, me—all that full-fat milk I drink. Now, go on—' His gaze shifted to the church. 'Be a good lad and wait in the car. You can put your tape on if you like. Don't worry about the battery. I'll get a jump-start if we have to. And, anyway, this won't take long.'

'All right,' I said, and began to back-pedal.

'Good man.'

'Are we still going to Leeds?' I said.

'Of course we are, son. If I've got to carry you there on my back, we are going to Leeds and I'm showing you that conducer.'

'And Cryck's compartment.'

'Yep. First on the list.' He tapped his temple.

I smiled at him, placating myself, and turned back for the car.

'Danno, *here*—' As I twisted round, I saw a black shape like a beetle flying towards me. It struck me on the chest and hit the floor with a rattle. 'You'll need those to play the tape. Don't turn it all the way. I'll be done in a minute.' I picked up the keys and headed for the Volvo. 'QC, you still there?' my father said behind me. 'Don't tell me you've hung up . . . No, he's all right. A bit stroppy, but it's understandable . . .'

The upholstery was hot under my legs when I got in, the air fusty and dry. I reached to put the key in the ignition and turned it carefully, one notch. Warm breath heaved from the fans. I turned the stereo on, and waited to hear Maxine Laidlaw. Meanwhile, my father was rocking on his feet inside the phone box, head down, raging. 'No fucking way. No *way* am I doing that.' His voice came through the broken pane. 'Do you think I'm going to let them do this to me? Because of what, QC? She wasn't even in the fucking room!'

* * *

[. . .] *Cryck had an explanation for everything. When he asked her to describe Aoxi, she told him it was seven million light years from Earth and forty times its size. Almost three quarters of its surface was covered in water and the land was spread across it in many distinct continents called ilphics. Every scrap of vegetation on the planet had a use, from medicine to fuel to food to fabric to building material. The terrain was rocky in the southlands, where the climate was drier, but in the northern ilphics—where she lived—there was only marshland. In the winter, there were ice winds, blizzards, hailstones like bottlecaps; in the spring, a downy flock from the imbok trees blanketed the land; it was harvested by large machines and used as tinder. There were no countries or entitlements to land. No birthrights. Aoxins had no patriotic duty to each other. They were free to move and live wherever they wished. There was one common currency between them: the handshake, and its value never changed. It was a sprawling planet and its spoils were so rich that everyone had what they needed. There were big variations in languages between the ilphics, each more complex and ancient than any on Earth.*

Cryck said she had taught herself to speak English in half a day, by reading the collected works of Ralph Waldo Emerson and Harriet Beecher Stowe, the Pears' Cyclopaedia and the Webster's Dictionary: four 'thin' volumes she discovered in the first house she took shelter in upon arriving. 'A remarkably simple language, but not without beauty.' When he asked her to talk in Aoxin, it came out of her lips so fast, punctuated by so many ticks and frills—his mouth was not elastic enough to utter one word of it. When he asked her to write something down on paper, she made a page of nicks and glyphs in pencil, recited it out loud, first in Aoxin, then in English: 'There once was a woman named Cryck, who was stuck on a useless moon planet by accident. She was a very long way from her husband, whom she loved, and her work, which she loved more . . .' He asked if that was true—did she really love her work more than she loved her husband? 'An Aoxin husband loves his job more than his wife, too, I assure you,' she said. 'My husband, Sem, is an engineer. Chemical engineer would be the closest categorisation. We are opposites in almost everything.'

When he asked about her job on Aoxi, her white eyes twitched. 'There's no term for what I do in English. The closest

I have seen is "artifex"—an artist, a craftsman, but also a thinker. I invent things, mostly.' I was the inventor of a very important technology for my people. It allows us to send materials from moon to moon and down to Aoxi in milliseconds. Except, when we tested it—'

The machine's malfunction was the reason she was here, stranded. 'We used to send the worst of our criminals to Earth. Murderers and thieves. If you know where to look, you'll find their old compartments everywhere—we're in one of them right now.' She banged the ceiling; soil rained down on her . . .

'I don't understand how little shops like that survive,' my father said. His bloodied fist was resting on the mouldy window rubber. A blue carrier bag swung from his other hand. 'No Wintermans, no film, but d'you reckon they had fishing tackle? You bet your arse they did. And here—I got you a Lilt. Pause that, would you?'

I stopped the tape, took the icy can and wedged it in the slot beside my seat. 'Thanks.'

'Thought you'd be gasping for that. Not thirsty?'

'I don't really like Lilt.'

'What? Since when?'

'Since that time I tried it once.'

'I'll drink it, then.'

His attitude was quite serene now. He reached down to open the glovebox, the lid kissing my knees. Drawing out his tub of Swarfega, he lathered his raw knuckles with a dollop of the gritty paste and rubbed. His sloppy fingers delved into the carrier bag and brought out a bottle of water. He twisted the cap off with his teeth and poured the contents over his hands. Then he went to the boot and ferreted around in a bin bag of his clothes, took out a T-shirt and padded his knuckles dry. 'There's been a slight change of plan, son,' he called to me. I heard the ripping of cloth. When I twisted to face him, he was winding a ribbon of the T-shirt fabric round his palm. 'Seems like they aren't quite ready for us in Leeds yet. Like I said, the schedule changes all the time up there.'

'Yeah.' I tried to hide my deflation. 'When *will* they be ready?'

'I dunno. At this stage—' A roll of masking tape was gripped between his teeth now. He coiled it round his makeshift bandage, bit off the end, tossed it aside. 'At this stage, it's a bit unclear. But QC's going to come and meet us. He's the one with all the up-to-date information.'

'Meet us *here*?'

My father pursed his lips and studied his surroundings as though deciding whether or not to set up camp in the church grounds. 'No, I don't think this place has much to recommend it. Can't even buy a simple roll of film.' He shut the boot. 'I mean, the face on the woman in there! I said, *It doesn't matter what type, love, as a long as it's thirty-five mil.* You'd think I'd asked for lobster thermidor.'

All his riffing was diversionary, of course—I'd come to understand this well enough by then. But an artificial state of calm was always preferable to rage, in my experience, and I didn't want to unsettle it. So I didn't tell him that my camera was a Kodak Pocket Instamatic that took 110 film cartridges, not ordinary 35mm. Nor did I tell him that it had been a birthday present from my mother and had come in a plastic presentation box with an attachable flash unit and a leatherette carrypouch—the same birthday that his imaginary parcel had fallen victim to the irish postal service.

'What did you say?' he asked, getting in beside me, but I swore I hadn't spoken a word. 'Have you been messing about with this seat?'

'No. Why would I?'

'It feels a bit off to me.' He adjusted it, then turned the key in the ignition. The car made a desperate grating sound. He pressed his forehead to the wheel and sighed. 'You turned the blowers off, right? Please tell me you turned the blowers off.'

'I—'

'Ah, Daniel, for crying out loud . . .' With a long huff, he tried again.

The engine fired.

He revved, elated. 'Thank Christ for that!' He revved again in celebration. 'A bit of luck for once.'

'Dad,' I said, over the din.

He turned us onto Main Street. The blood had already seeped through his crude bandage: four red crescents in a row beneath the masking tape. 'Yeah?'

I fetched the atlas from the dashboard. 'Where are we going?'

The trip my mother had agreed to was supposed to last two days. It had taken us a long while to convince her of its merits. As per every plan my father ever sold me, it came veneered like a brochure, all the problems absent or glossed over, all the brightest features emphasised and amplified. We would make an early start on Thursday, reach the studio by the afternoon, in time to catch a good few hours of filming; he'd show me around the set while everything was being packed up, introduce me to the cast in their dressing rooms. 'It'll depend on who's got scenes to shoot that day, but it's a sure bet Maxine will be there,' he'd said. 'I don't know about Mike— kids can only work so many hours. But probably Eve and Malik. Definitely Joy.' The nonchalance with which he'd referred to the actors by their first names was exhilarating. We would stay overnight at a hotel, have what he called 'a proper cooked breakfast,' and be on the road home to Buckinghamshire by Friday noon. My mother was sceptical about the prospect from the beginning. For weeks, she endured my needling at mealtimes ('I'll think about it'), on car rides into town ('I said *I'll think about it*'), when she paused at my door each night to ward against the bedbugs ('That's enough now, Daniel, it isn't helping'). Why couldn't she see that he was trying to be good, that *The Artifex* was the only thing I'd ever truly shared with him and she was spoiling it? She held out for a month before relenting. Perhaps she thought that if I spent some time alone with Francis Hardesty that summer, a single dose of him would be enough.

She had certain conditions, which she relayed to him over

the phone: 'The hotel has to be at least three stars. No dingy pubs or campsites. I want to recognise the name.'

He consented.

'You're to have him back here no later than six o'clock on the Friday. I don't want any excuses about weekend traffic or slow punctures or accidentally oversleeping—you'll organise a wake-up call, or I'll do it for you.'

He consented.

'It's direct to Leeds, there and back, none of your little detours. You can stop at the motorway services, but I know you, Fran—don't be arranging any pit-stops to check in with your mates along the way—and you understand *exactly* what I mean by *mates* here, don't you? Not to put too fine a point on it while our twelve-year-old is listening . . . Laugh all you want, Fran, I've known you far too long.'

He consented. If she had asked for him to sign an affidavit to attest to these conditions, I'm sure my father would've enacted the charade of autographing it.

* * *

By a quarter past seven that Thursday night, my father had abandoned me to the darkness of an upstairs function room in a pub on the outskirts of Wakefield. He'd set me up at a sticky round table with a lukewarm glass of Coke, facing a small wooden stage lit by a single tasselled floor lamp, and told me he'd be back before the music started. But at least twenty minutes had elapsed without a trace of him, and since then a beer-bellied man had walked up to the front and introduced himself as the stand-in host of the White Oak Folk Club. 'Simon's off in Tenerife till Tuesday, so you're all stuck with me tonight,' he said. 'And more to the point, I'm stuck with you lot.' After asking the crowd for a D and getting back a volley of shrill hums and twanged guitar strings, he began tuning the dainty mandolin that was harnessed to his neck like a bell on a heifer. I was tired and twitchy, sitting there alone, picturing my father's movements outside in the car park. 'Nice to see a young face in the crowd—first time for everything,' said the host, sighting me. 'If you'd like to play us a tune, lad, just let me know, all right? Always good to hear from the younger generation. You'll not finish that pint on your own, mind.'

My heart jounced inside my chest. People were gawping at me. 'It's my dad's,' I said. 'He'll be back in a minute.'

'Then you'd better neck it before he shows up, eh?' The host grinned and turned away. 'This one's an old favourite of mine that you're all sick to death of.' There was a tone of camaraderie in the crowd's laughter. The room was barely half full. A clutch of locals with wet eyes and cardigans were constellated on the cushioned bench seats; most of them seemed to have instruments of their own within arm's reach: acoustic guitars, accordions, a banjo, a fiddle, and what appeared to be a portable loom. 'Anyway, it's my version of "Shenandoah" and it goes something like this . . .'

Everybody hushed. He strummed a few tinny chords on the mandolin—a surprisingly sweet and tuneful sound for a man so large—and then out came a voice so faint and timid that I had to stop swallowing my Coke to hear it. '*Oh Shenandoah, I long to hear you far away, you rollin' river. Oh Shenandoah, I long to see you far away, you rollin' river. Away, away across the wide Missouri . . .*'

For a moment, I lost all sense of where I was. His voice was mediocre but the melody was so transporting.

After the song finished and the applause trailed off, the back door of the room opened and a burr of conversation from the pub rushed in. An old man walked past me with a lute and took a seat in the gloom. Other latecomers filtered in, carrying their ales and G&Ts. My father was among them. He took the chair beside me, picked up his pint of lager and continued draining it as though he hadn't been away. He was freshly marinated in smoke and very pink around the face and neck. I couldn't tell if he was exhausted or upset. Leaning in, sniffing, he said: 'Hope I didn't miss any sea shanties.'

'Can we go yet?' I said.

'Not quite.'

The host snapped his head in our direction.

'We'll talk after,' my father said.

I slumped into my chair.

'This next tune is a new arrangement I've been working on,' the host announced, 'so if I mess it up, you all know where the door is.'

My father scanned the space to our left. He was trying to catch the eye of the young woman we'd met earlier—Karen, the gaunt blonde with the braided fringe and the kindly demeanour. She was at the next table, lamplight on her cheekbones, guitar on her knee. He raised his chin to acknowledge her, and she gave a slow lift of her fingers.

'When are you on?' my father asked, a mite too loudly.

She mouthed *Shshh* at him, nodding at the stage. He mimed the zipping of his lips.

The host lifted the head of his mandolin, poised. 'It's "Make Me a Pallet on Your Floor",' he said, 'as you've never heard it butchered before.'

My father leaned back with his arms crossed to appraise the sound, pint rested in the hinge of his elbow. His flushed complexion settled to its normal pallor. '*Make it soft, make it low, so your woman don't know,*' the host sang, '*make me a pallet on your floor . . .*' I was surprised to see Fran Hardesty so pacified by such a sweet and simple tune.

* * *

We'd driven north, the land rising into dales ahead of us,

rows of terraced houses cleaving to the undulations of the land like studs pressed to a belt, grey smoke ascending from the power station chimneys. Leaving Sprotbrough, he'd insisted on ejecting my audio book and replacing it with a tape of his own. 'I need to think,' he'd said, his bloodied knuckles dancing on the steering column. 'A bit of *Treasure*, that's what we want.' My father didn't claim to have an eclectic taste in music, but he had a refined ear. He'd become a devotee of Cocteau Twins at some point in his twenties, and tried routinely to impress their qualities on others: to me, their music was no different to roadwork noises. There'd been nothing to do except submit to it—those strange, reverberating drums and synths, the clanging bells, staccato breathing, brash guitars, a woman singing with the voice of a girl chorister, mumbling nonsense words that might as well have been Aoxin. I'd comforted myself with the thought that at least we were getting closer to Leeds with every passing mile, though our deviation from the plan gave me a hollow feeling.

QC's instructions were to wait for him at the White Oak pub in Rothwell—my father couldn't pin him down to an exact time of arrival. 'He's a busy man, you know,' he said, 'and he's doing me a favour coming out here. We'll have to be patient.' The pub was still shut when we got there, and so we sat in the empty car park eating the salmon sandwiches from my mother's coolbox.

We'd parked in the cool of the pub's shadow, eyeing the road and the cabbage fields beyond. Cars beat steadily across our sightline and Francis Hardesty regarded each vehicle that passed as though studying the comportment of racehorses in a paddock. The dashboard clock edged towards one thirty. 'He drives a Beamer, a three series, I think. Can't remember if it's black or silver now. Actually, it might even be blue. I've only been in it the once.' He drew the Lilt out from the gap beside my seat and offered it again. 'Last chance,' he said, and cracked the ring pull.

Every minute that crept by felt like a step away from him. We should have been in Leeds already.

'See, this is the thing about QC: he goes round acting like he's straight off a hard-knock estate, when I know for a fact that he went to a posh school like your mother wants to send you to. And, okay, he claims he was expelled and all that, but still. His parents are barristers. That's why we call him QC. Barnaby's his real name, but you didn't hear that from me.' My father was chuckling at the thought. If he liked QC at all, it wasn't evident from the sneering tone in which he spoke about him. 'Not sure how he got into carpentry work, but I'll bet you he had plenty of help from mummy and daddy along the way, if you know what I mean. Brand new tools and his own little workshop, just to help him get started. Apprenticeship at the Old Vic. Connections at the Beeb. No problem.'

I didn't know how to respond to this. But if I had the opportunity to answer him again, I'd tell him his philosophy was backwards: why should parents with the means to help their child ever withhold it? Wasn't that just selfishness?

And still the cars went by.

'I've been wanting to ask you,' he said, 'about your grandpa—how's he doing lately? He bearing up or what?'

My grandfather had chain-smoked his way to the age of sixty-four and developed cancer in his lung. The last time I had visited his house—a six-bedroom mansion in Bradenham with a rolling lawn the gardeners had to cut with a ride-on mower—he'd been unable to raise himself from the banquette in the conservatory to kiss my mother hello. We hadn't even sat at the piano, as we always did, so he could play me tunes from the book he called 'Chopin for Dummies'. He had an oxygen tank and a translucent tube hooked to his nostrils. When I explained this, my father said: 'Oh, that doesn't sound too good . . . Who's he got running the show while he's laid up, then—your mum?'

'I don't think so.'

'Well, she must be doing all she can to wriggle out of it.' He lifted his brow at me. 'No one's going to make her give a toss about the catering business. The old man needs to sell that company while he's still got his wits about him.' He belched quietly into his fist. 'Excuse me.' A chain of traffic hauled itself beyond our view. 'What's this school like, anyway? The one they're so keen on you going to.'

'I was only there for a few hours,' I said.

'D'you *want* to go there, or what?'

My experience of Berkhamsted School was limited to a brisk walk along the path between the chapel and the cricket pavilion, down a long corridor where the names of ex-Head Boys were painted gold on tall oak panels, into a teaching room that looked down onto a copse of evergreens, to a desk where I had written the two-hour entrance examination. I had spoken to nobody except a wiry teacher in a gown who'd told me I could leave as soon as I was finished. There was one troubling aspect of it I couldn't forget: the sense I had, ambling away, that I was a much less exceptional person than I'd been led to believe.

'I don't know—Mum wants me to,' I replied. 'They only put me on the reserve list anyway. My maths mark was bad.'

'Seventy-six per cent is what I heard. If that's bad, I don't know what's good.'

'It's bad at Berkhamsted.'

'Well, there are plenty more important things in life than school, believe me.'

'Like what?'

He began to pick the gungy bread out of his teeth. 'Like doing what you're good at. Finding a way to do what you're good at without all the other garbage getting in the way.'

'What garbage?'

'All the stuff you can't escape when you get older—bills and rent and debts. The ties that bind.'

'Oh.'

'You've got to know what you're good at when you're young and go for it—don't waste your time worrying about how you'll cope, just *cope*. That's what I've learned.'

'How do you know when you're good at something?' I didn't think I had any particular gifts. I was skilled at playing Top Trumps, but I didn't see it as a valuable asset, long-term.

'That's the tricky part,' he said. 'If I'd started doing this ten, fifteen years earlier, I'd have been a lot better off.'

'Building sets and stuff, you mean?'

'Yeah. I never *knew* that I was good at it, that's the problem—people told me that I was, but I thought they were just saying it because that's what mates do. You don't really know until you're *in it*, and suddenly it all comes naturally, and the time just goes *phoof* when you're doing it. I wish I'd worked it out sooner, that's all.'

'But then you'd never have met mum,' I said.

'True.'

'And you'd never have had *me*.'

'No . . . I suppose not.'

His eyes were glassy now, gone to the distance.

We sat in the quiet for a while more, projecting the arrival of QC onto every movement in our sightline. My father took his cigarillo tin out of his shirt pocket and flicked it open: empty, as it was the last time he'd checked, an hour ago. He tucked it away again. An old Beetle slowed, indicated left, and pulled into the car park, piquing our interest for as long as it took to make a U-turn right in front of us and rejoin the road, disappearing in the opposite direction. 'Oh for god's sake, mate, where the hell are you?' My father threw his head back, juddering the seat rest. 'It's almost two.'

'How come we even need QC?' I asked.

'Because he's the man in the know, that's why. He can make things happen.'

'Yeah, but don't you know things, too? You both work on the show.'

'It's not as simple as that, son.'

'Why not?'

'Nothing ever is. There's always someone's arse you've got to kiss to keep the peace. QC's ten years younger than me so he's much better at all that. I can't play the game that way. It's meant to be one big collaboration in TV, but there's still a hierarchy—you know that word? A ranking system.'

'Like the army,' I said.

'Yeah, almost.' He wobbled the sun visor in exasperation. 'See, QC and me—we're just privates taking orders from the generals. Sometimes the orders you get handed aren't ever going to work in practice, and it's obvious, but you've got to go along with them to please the generals. Everyone's so afraid of upsetting everyone else that the job takes six times as long as it should. There's a lot of that, in TV, I've found out. Pleasing the generals. And the lieutenants and the sergeants, and anyone else who looks down their nose at you, which is more or less *everyone*.' He upturned the Lilt can over his mouth till it was empty. 'Watch this,' he said, cradling the base of it in his right hand; then, in a flurry, he pitched it at the open glovebox. It rebounded into the footwell and splattered my shoes. 'Bad shot—did I spray you?'

'A bit. It's fine, though.' I wiped them on the carpet.

'Anyway, I'm not afraid of telling the generals how it is sometimes. Never have been. It puts noses out of joint occasionally, but they all know I do good work and they respect me for it. Downside is, the other privates start thinking you've gone over their heads when you do that. They get the idea that you're not one of them, and then you start to get problems. Squabbling and resentment. You get left out of certain conversations. Which is why I need QC. He's an ally. He gets it. D'you see what I'm telling you?'

'Yeah, I think so.' But there was nothing he had said that made our situation any more transparent. Extracting the truth from my father was like trying to wring the taste of dinner from a dishrag.

It was past two o'clock when a man in a white vest and Bermuda shorts emerged from the pub's entrance. He went inside again and then returned with a blackboard sign on a stand, displaying a list of beers on tap. 'Reckon they've got a pool table?' my father said.

'I don't know how to play.'

'Rubbish—I taught you that time in Amersham.'

'That was snooker.'

'Same difference. Pool's just snooker for idiots.' He pulled the handle, nudged the door open with his knee. 'Come on, there's no point sitting here all day. Whenever QC decides to show up, he'll find us.'

'Is there a phone in there to call Mum, d'you think?'

'I can ask.' (Later, he'd deliver the bad news: 'There *is* a phone but it's behind the bar. And the landlord says it's staff use only. I tried to reason with him, but he wouldn't have it. Tight old git.')

Inside, the White Oak was dim and decorous. There was no pool table, just a lot of equine paraphernalia, a wall-mounted jukebox, and a fruit machine. I needed the toilet but couldn't bear to go alone, and didn't want to ask my father to accompany me, as though I were an infant. He left me at a table by the entrance while he went to order at the bar. Staring out at the car park, I tried to overlap the image of a silver BMW arriving ceremoniously on the tarmac, QC stepping out to save the day like Joe Durango, the brash youth from my favourite boy's adventure novel, short and denim-clad, hair greased to a shine. But no one came. We were the only patrons in the pub for quite some time. All I could hear was my father chatting to the landlord and the subdued carnival refrain of the fruit machine.

The longer we waited for QC, the less likely it seemed that he was coming for us—I know my father sensed it too, but he carried on his show of positivity. 'You bring those Top Trumps with you?' he said. We played a round together, his enthusiasm for the game unprecedented and suspicious. After I took his last card—a Hawker Siddeley Trident—he threw his hands up in surrender. 'Okay, that's it, I can't stand any more punishment! You're too good!' But this was just his way of tempting me into a few more rounds, diverting me from the delay. As we went on boasting the statistics from our cards, the pub slowly filled up around us, the minutes amassed, the bright day washed to grey, and thoughts of *The Artifex* and all my father's promises somehow escaped me.

When I couldn't ignore my bladder any longer, he took me to the gents' and we stood at adjacent urinals; he, whistling the theme from *Grandstand* and pissing noisily; me, eking out a weedy stream, trying not to stare at the detritus in the drain, the pubic hair and viscid yellow stains. He'd already rinsed and dried his hands by the time I was done, and was ogling his reflection in the mirror. 'Look at that,' he said, pointing out a rash of paint-specks on the surface. Leaning close, he scraped the dried spots of emulsion with his thumbnail till they came away. 'How can you leave a job like that? It's criminal.' He held the door for me, ruffled my head as I went out.

There was no trace of QC or his car outside, so we went to check the deeper reaches of the pub, nudging aside old men in muddy wellingtons with tabloid newspapers spread across the bar, and a sunburned farmer who was leaning on the counter at an angle just sufficient to obstruct the aisle; I stepped over his enormous hobnail boots. On our way past, my father asked the landlord: 'Any sign of that fella I told you about?'

'Nah, pal, sorry,' came the reply. 'Heard there was a bad collision on the six-three-nine, though. Perhaps your mate's got caught in the congestion.'

'You could be right, there,' my father said. 'Cheers.' And we carried on into the next section, walled with dark wood. There was a fireplace without flames. A giant set of bellows. An old mantel clock that needed winding. I didn't know the time and was afraid to ask.

'Do you think he's really coming, Dad?' I said.

My father halted. 'What?'

'QC.'

'I know who you meant.' He was peering downwards, but not at me—at the vacant space between us. 'What's put that daft idea in your head? Of course he's coming! You heard them out there, didn't you? There's been a crash on the road from Leeds. He'll be stuck in a tailback or something like that. He's a mate, he'll be here.' And he crossed his arms. 'I'm a bit surprised at you, son. I thought you had more trust in people.'

'QC isn't perfect,' he went on, 'but he's the sort who puts himself out. You're going to see that for yourself when he shows up. And, by the way—just in future—don't do that, okay? Don't be like your mother. Don't go questioning the people who are trying to help you. I'm doing my best for us here, okay? Give me some credit.'

I yielded.

'Sit there,' he said, gesturing towards the corner table.

'Where are you going?'

'To find something to smoke. Maybe there's a machine or something.' He nodded at the window. 'Keep lookout.' And he went off to scout for Wintermans.

In the relative quiet, I gazed at the mantel clock and thought about my mother. She would've been at work by then, with her wristwatch laid out on her desktop and the number of the Leeds metropole scribbled on a slip of paper, ready to dial if the hour hand reached six and she was still to hear from us. She would've been contemplating the prospect of speaking to the hotel manager and being told: 'No, madam, it seems they're yet to check in.' Worse, the truth: 'Sorry, madam, that booking was cancelled several days ago—did you want to make a new reservation with us?'

I was alone and deflated, and every time I heard the clunk of a car door outside, my heart rabbited. Still there was no BMW in the car park.

' . . . so he pulls up another screen on his computer and types it in . . .'

The room dulled at the edges of my vision. Two young women were carrying half pints of beer to the table opposite.

' . . . and he's eyeballing me the whole time, like, *you're taking the piss, you, aren't you, love?* Surprise, surprise, there's nothing available. So he turns his screen right round for me to look. Ha ha! As if I thought there *would* be. And he goes to me, *There aren't any vacancies for backing singers. You might need to lower your expectations a bit. Cleaning work, call centre jobs, things that don't require any experience.* It was so embarrassing. Total waste of time.'

'You'll never get a job if you're that picky,' the blonder of them said.

'Good!' said the other. 'I don't bloody want one, do I? That's the whole point. Weren't you listening?' Her dye-job was seven shades subtler than her friend's. She was hippyishly pretty: a fine-boned face, two meals away from scraggy; pale skin; a waifish set of eyebrows. There was a braid in her fringe, a neat little ropeline across her forehead.

'So, you're just gonna sign on for the rest of your life, are you? Good plan.'

'No, I told you,' the braided woman said. 'Gary's lending me enough to make a demo, then we'll see what happens. I've got it all worked out.'

Her friend coughed out a laugh. 'Shit. You're really pinning all your hopes on the music, eh? I don't think that's actually a plan.'

After so long in the car, the tune of someone else's conversation was a welcome sound.

'What's *your* plan, Vee? At least I've got some ambition.'

'Don't need one, do I? I've got qualifications.'

'Right, yeah, with that BTEC they'll be making you Prime Minister.'

'Shut up. It's a start.' Vee raised her glass. 'Anyway—*cheers*. It's nice to be out.'

'Yeah, cheers.' As they clinked, the braided woman took notice of me. I must've seemed especially glum or lonesome, because she said: 'You all right over there, kiddo?'

I smiled at her.

'Is anyone with you? You look a bit lost.'

'Leave him, Karen—he's fine,' said Vee.

'It's okay. I'm with my dad. He's gone to—' I realised the truth would cast him in a poor light. 'He's gone out to the car, I think.'

'Ah,' said Karen. She canted her head. 'Are you on your holidays? You don't sound like you're from round here.'

'We're supposed to be going to Leeds,' I said.

'Supposed to be?'

I shrugged.

She took a sip of beer.

Vee said, 'Where's Gary getting the money from for all that, anyway? I thought he was skint.'

'He got that payout, didn't he—from work.'

'Yeah, but I thought he'd spent all that by now. I would've.'

'I know you would've.' Karen's attention was still on me. 'Leeds,' she said, 'why Leeds? You got family there?' She had a gentle manner, a sympathetic tone.

'Have you ever watched *The Artifex*?' I said.

'Er, *yeah*,' she answered, bug-eyed. 'It's ace.'

Vee glared at her. 'What's that?'

'*The Artifex*. It's on the telly.'

'A kids' show?'

'Yeah, but it's weird. Loads of people watch it. Gary watches it.'

'When's it on?'

'Can't remember.'

'Five o'clock on a Wednesday,' I said.

'What side?'

'ITV.'

'Loads of adverts, then.'

'Yeah. But it's not on at the moment, anyway. They're still making the next series.'

Karen beamed at me. 'The lad knows his stuff.'

I shrugged again.

'Who's home at five o'clock on a Wednesday?' Vee said. 'I'm still at the shop at five o'clock on a Wednesday. My shift don't finish till seven. You're such a layabout.'

'I can't help it if I work from home.'

'Yeah, right. *Work.*' Vee stared at me now. 'She reckons she's a musician. But all she does is sit on her arse and listen to the Bee Gees. I don't think it's the same thing.'

'No *way* do I like the Bee Gees.' Karen elbowed her. 'Button it.'

'Watch my drink. You're gonna knock it over.'

Karen settled down. She seemed to be pondering my situation intensely; her lashes were convulsing. 'I still don't see what *The Artifex* has got to do with Leeds, though.'

'That's where it's filmed. Well, most of it,' I said.

'No way! I never knew that.'

'Can't be that good then, can it?' Vee said.

I let a moment skid by. 'You know, my dad's actually on . . .' I trailed off.

'Yeah?'

'My dad's on the crew.'

'No way.'

'Yeah. He's taking me to see the studio.'

'That's amazing,' Karen said. 'He sounds like a right cool dad. Mine's a window cleaner. He's never even let me up his ladder.' I didn't say anything, and she probably mistook this silence for an affirmation. 'Well,' she went on, 'you're not far away now. What is it, Vee, ten minutes?'

'To Leeds? More like fifteen.'

'You must be dead excited.' Karen rubbed her palms. 'I'm excited *for* you. Jealous, to be honest.'

'It's taking forever, though. To get there.'

'Good things usually do,' she said.

'I suppose.'

Vee coughed. 'So where are you recording this demo, then? I thought that place you found was too dear.' And Karen turned to answer her, letting me continue my surveillance of the car park.

They were still discussing the ins and outs of it when my father returned, empty-handed. The bandage was gone from his scabbed knuckles and the swelling had worsened, yellowed. He sat down next to me. 'I just went round everyone in the pub, and no one smokes. Can you believe my rotten luck today, or what?' He directed this to me, but he was facing the women. 'A boozer full of farmers, not a pipe or a rollie between 'em. What kind of a town is this, eh?'

'The crap kind,' Karen said to him.

'*We* smoke,' Vee added, a bit too keenly. 'You need one?'

'Yeah,' my father answered, 'but I'm fussy about the type.'

She wet her lips. 'What's your type?'

He prodded my knee with his own. 'Tell her.'

'Wintermans,' I said.

Vee snorted. 'And what're they when they're at home?'

'They're like those little cigar thingies,' Karen said. 'My granddad smokes them. Crème Brûlée, or something.'

'Café Crème,' said my father.

Vee snorted again. 'You what?'

'I can give you Silk Cut,' Karen said. 'Otherwise you'll need to walk about three miles to the shops.'

'You know, I think I'm desperate enough to take you up on that. Thanks.' My father stretched his arm over my seatback, sighing.

Karen went fishing in her handbag. She brought out a pack still in its cellophane, tore it off. 'You can have the first one.'

'Is that meant to be lucky?'

'I don't know. I don't think so.'

'Shame.' With the slowest of movements, he leaned close enough to draw two cigarettes from the box. He enclosed one in his fist, tucked the other behind his ear, holding his gaze on Karen all the while. She watched him in return. 'Aren't you going to have one?' he asked.

'Maybe later,' she replied. And there it was—that testing smile, barely a crease.

He reciprocated.

'You've a good lad, there,' she said, motioning at me. 'He's been telling us about your trip.'

'Oh yeah?' My father's arm sunk round my shoulder. 'Things aren't quite going to plan at the moment, but it'll turn out fine in the end, won't it, son?'

Vee broke in before I could answer: 'He says you work in telly. You must know a load of famous people.'

'One or two.'

'Oh my god, have you met Noel Edmonds?'

'She has a thing for Noel Edmonds,' Karen said. 'Don't ask.'

'Crikey,' my father said. 'It's always the ones you least expect.'

Vee blushed. 'It's not that weird. Have you actually met him?'

'Yeah. Doesn't it show?' My father winked. 'Am I not bathed in his almighty glow?'

'Shut up. You don't have to take the mick.'

Karen was laughing now. 'I can't believe you work on *The Artifex*. I mean, I know it's for kids and everything, but it's still good telly.' She toyed with her braid, sipped her drink, fidgety all of a sudden.

'Thanks,' he said. 'The book's better, so they tell me.'

'Was it a book? I never knew that.'

'Yeah. We've just been listening in the car. I don't think it's quite as weird as the show is, personally.' Then he seized his opportunity: 'D'you girls want another drink? Least I can do for you keeping him company.' He tousled my hair again, fingernails roughing my scalp.

'I'm meant to be driving,' Vee said. 'But, go on, I'll have another half.'

'That'd be nice, yeah, thanks,' Karen said.

'Same again?'

She nodded.

He got up and made for the bar, then paused in the doorway. 'Sorry, I didn't get your names.' He was only looking at one of them.

'Mine's Karen,' she said.

'It's Vee.'

'I'm Fran. That's Daniel.' He took the cigarette from behind his ear. 'You don't happen to have a lighter in that bag of yours, do you, love? I'm going to take this outside. Prefer to do my smoking in the fresh air.'

'Yeah, I know what you mean.' Karen started rummaging, then a better thought came to her. 'Y'know, I think I'll come out with you. There's a bench in the back. It's not raining, is it?'

'Don't think so.'

'And what about *me*?' Vee said. Her jaw was hanging slack.

'Well, obviously I meant you, *too*.'

'Obviously,' my father said, and he muttered to me: 'You'll be all right here for a bit, won't you, Danno?'

I was expecting this. 'Can't I come with you?'

'I don't want you breathing all our fumes. Look what's happened to your grandpa. It's really bad for you.' To Karen and Vee, who didn't know him, this must have seemed like fatherly concern. 'Hey, tell you what—' He walked over, dug into his pocket for a handful of small change, and counted it off on the table. 'There's three quid. Let's see if you can make it fifty by the time we get back.'

'How?'

'I'll show you.' He wagged his head towards the door. Karen and Vee were gathering their things.

'But what if QC shows up?' I swept the coins into my hand all the same. 'I don't even know what he looks like.'

'Who's that?' Vee said to my father.

'Nobody. A mate of mine.'

'He single?'

'*Vee.* Honestly!' Karen slapped her arm. 'Ignore her.'

My father snickered. 'Yeah, he's single. But he couldn't hold a candle to Noel Edmonds.'

'Ha ha. Not many can, sweetheart,' said Vee. 'Not many can.'

I followed the three of them through the pub, into the room we'd left earlier; it was busy now, rumbling with chatter. My father dragged a stool to the fruit machine and lifted me onto it. 'You girls head out,' he said, over his shoulder, 'I'll catch you up.' And they did.

When they were out of earshot, he gripped my collarbone. 'Right, son, put your money in.' The machine's lights intensified as I dropped a coin into its guts; it made newer, brighter noises. But I couldn't summon any interest in the game. 'If someone comes and says you're not allowed to play on it, you run and fetch me, okay? I'll be back in five.'

'But, Dad—'

'I know, I know. QC. Don't worry.' He checked the doorway,

trying to extend his neck enough to take in the entire car park. 'If you see anyone wearing bright red trainers and a hooded top, that's him. Tell him you're my lad, and there won't be a problem. You show him where to find me.'

'When are we going to be leaving?' I said.

'Soon, I promise. As soon as he gets here, we'll be on our way again.' And he backed away, firing the gun of his hand in my direction. 'Win me that jackpot, yeah?'

I sat there playing the fruit machine until my eyes became imprinted with the after-images of cherries and my pocketful of change was almost spent. The coin tray never rattled for me once. With every failed nudge and hold, I willed the arrival of a stranger in red trainers and a hooded top. I prayed that QC, whoever he was, could deliver us to Leeds in time for me to call my mother from the Hotel Metropole—for my father's sake, as much as mine. It was clear that if we didn't make it to the metropole that night, we'd never be allowed to see each other again. The last skein of our connecting tissue would be severed. Our lives would not recover. I could see it all coming. I was twelve years old, but I was better equipped to understand it than I was to appreciate the workings of a fruit machine.

I had three coins left.

At the bar, a line of people leaned and perched. A man whistled to the barmaid, brandishing a tenner. An elderly couple were eating stew and dumplings, chatting to the landlord about tomorrow's weather. I climbed up on an empty stool and waited to be noticed.

It was the barmaid who saw me. 'Can I help you, love?' she asked, putting down a set of dirty glasses. 'You shouldn't really be up here, you know.'

'My dad sent me to ask something.'

'Which one's your dad?' She scanned the room.

'He's in the back.'

'Well, what is it you need?'

I showed her the coins in my hand. 'I've got 60p. I was won-dering, if I gave you this, would it be all right to use your tele-phone?' Her expression gave me hope. 'Let me ask the boss,' she said. 'Hang on.' She went straight over to the landlord and posed the question. He came bounding down to meet me. 'Is it an emergency?' he said.

'No. I just—my mum's expecting me to ring her.'

The landlord crossed his arms. 'She's not in New Zealand or anywhere, is she?'

'No. Little Missenden.'

'Where's that?'

'Down south.'

'Right. Well, I can't let you through the bar, I'm afraid. Against the law. But you can come round the side and—'

'There he is: *Harry Houdini*,' my father said. 'I've been looking for you everywhere.' His hand settled on my shoulder, tightened. 'I thought I told you to stay out of people's way.' He lifted me down from the stool by my armpits. I kicked my heels into his shins, but he didn't let go. 'Sorry about this. I had reins for him once but he chewed through them.' The barmaid tit-tered. And he ushered me towards the corridor, pushing at my back. My legs weren't quite fast enough.

'They've got a phone,' I said, twisting.

'Shshh.'

'We can use it right now if we want to. He just said so.'

'Dan, hush, will you? People are staring.'

'We need to phone Mum.'

'Not right now,' he said, 'not right now. We'll call her from our room, later.'

An old woman came out of the toilet and sidled past, apolo-getically. Then the corridor was ours.

'Are we leaving?' I said.

'Not yet.'

'When is QC coming?'

'I don't know, but we need to sit tight until he does.'

'But how much longer?'

He sucked in a sharp breath. Then, as casually as a man fanning a bluebottle from his food, he slapped the side of my head. It was not a hard blow, but it jarred me. I thought of crying. My eyes brimmed but didn't spill. 'Listen to me, okay? You're acting spoiled,' he said. 'You know I can't get you on the set without QC. We've no choice but to wait. And if we ring your mother now, she's not going to understand about the change of plan. You know her: she'll panic. She'll make me bring you home, and then what, eh? The whole trip will be for nothing. I don't want to let you down like that again. No way am I giving her another thing to rub my nose in for the rest of my life. So this is happening. Believe me, it's happening.' He loosened his stance. 'We might not get to Leeds exactly when I thought we would, but I'll get you there—I swear on my life and the Holy Bible—and all this hanging about is going to seem like nothing in the long run.' As he drew me close, I could smell a different scent on him: a cheaper, more savoury smoke. I blotted my eyes on his shirt. 'Look, don't cry, all right? I shouldn't have clipped you round the ear like that, I know.'

I said nothing.

'But we've got to toughen you up a bit before you get to that new school. You don't want all those posh kids picking on you, do you? Sometimes you need to dish it out, sometimes you need to take it on the chin. That's how the world is. At the minute, we're taking more than our fair share on the chin, but all that's going to change. It has to.' He paused. 'You okay, or what?'

I nodded.

'There you go,' he said. 'I knew you had some Hardesty in you somewhere.'

He steered me back to the dark-wood room where we had

met the women earlier. They had reclaimed the same table but weren't sitting at it. Karen had an acoustic guitar strapped upside down against her back and was standing there while Vee assessed a pad of paper, saying, 'I don't know, Karen, I'm not one for poetry. They look all right to me.'

'Do you get what they're about, though?'

'Not really . . . Gary, I suppose.'

'Shut up.' Karen snatched the paper. 'As if I'd write *that* about Gary.'

'So it's not a love song, then.'

'No, you duffer. It's a protest song. Anti-war.'

'What war?'

'Not *the* war. Any war.'

'Oh.' Vee made a face at me. 'Well, that'll come in handy, soon as one breaks out.'

My father knocked the wood of Karen's guitar as he approached. She spun round. 'Hey. You're back.' Her smile was beautiful, I thought—it softened the bonier parts of her face, lent them pleats and ley lines.

'What time does it all get going, then?' he said.

'They'll start letting people up around sevenish. First act's normally on by half past.' She peered down at me. 'You going to come and hear me play, Dan?'

'She's got a gig,' Vee told me.

'Not really—it's just a folk club. Anyone can sign up. But it's regular and they let me play my own stuff.'

'All good experience,' my father said.

We sat with them while they finished their drinks. I helped Karen tune her guitar by holding an electronic box up to the sound-hole as she picked the strings with her thumbnail. She and Vee explained the tribulations of life in Rothwell to my father, and he offered a few drips of detail about his own life in return. He asked them veiled questions about what they thought they'd missed out on at school, if they felt they'd have had a better chance in life by going 'somewhere fancier.' They spoke as though their school lives were only recent memories. Karen was noncommittal: 'There's no point looking at things that way. You get what you're given and you try to make the best of it, don't you?'

Meanwhile, I watched the static mantel clock. I imagined us arriving in the plush, bright lobby of the Hotel Metropole. And I resolved that I would do exactly what my mother thought was best for me from that moment on.

Eventually, there was a trickle of foot traffic through the room. Karen gathered her guitar and said it was time to head up. My father went to get himself a lager and a Coke for me, which I didn't want or ask for. When he came back, he guided me upstairs, and grudgingly removed his wallet to pay the five pounds cover charge.

The room had a grimy light, an air of damp. We shuffled to the table closest to Karen and Vee. My father put our drinks down. We took our seats. There was a nervous quiet. I watched a man on the far side of the room skim resin up and down his fiddle bow. I ate the ice cubes in my Coke. *The important thing is that you spend some proper time together*, my mother had said on our driveway that morning. *So enjoy yourself.* I tried to fathom how much of the trip I had enjoyed so far, and realised I'd been most at ease during the moments I had spent away from him—in the world of Albert Bloor and Cryck, under the spell of Maxine Laidlaw.

Then there came a sudden weight beside me. Two bright red trainers pressed the carpet by my chair. 'They told me you'd be up here, Francis.'

He was nothing like I'd pictured him. A closely shaven head, concealing baldness. A bronze skin tone that can only be achieved with artificial lotion. A gold chain round his neck as thick as the brake cable on my bike.

'Why I've got to come and fish you out a bleedin' folk club

in the middle of Christ knows where, I'll never know. But here I am.'

'About time,' my father said. 'Where the hell've you been?'

'I'm not talking in here. Downstairs. Car park. Two minutes. Or you're on your own.' He made for the door.

'QC, hang about, I'm coming,' my father said, and hurried after him.

Our parents' lives before we're born are merely phantoms, as unthinkable as what becomes of them after they're gone. I don't recommend reading your teenaged mother's diary if you can help it. There are some details of a woman's life that are better lost to history. My mother wrote a lot about the early stage of her relations with Fran Hardesty—or rather, what she called her 'raging appetite' for him. At least thirty pages (passages dated 10th June to 14th July 1982) are devoted to transcription of prolonged sexual encounters at hotel rooms in the Buckinghamshire region. Trust me when I say that there are only so many times a son can read epithets for the male organ scrawled in his mother's handwriting before his uneasiness turns to nausea, shame, alarm. But, in another sense, it's helpful to understand the strength of their physical attraction, because it was the single aspect of their lives in which they were compatible, and it provides the only valid explanation for them ever forming a relationship.

I heard my mother justify it many times to friends who came to sit with her at our kitchen table in the aftermath of arguments, asking, while she wept aloud, 'What did you ever *see* in a bastard like him?' The way she accounted for it, the two of them were brought together by an unhappy coincidence. She was eighteen years old, due to start a degree in finance at the University of Exeter that autumn and was partway through a summer internship at Tyler Graves, a firm of accountants based in Beaconsfield. That she was undertaking low-grade secretarial work instead of travelling in Africa as she'd planned was the fault of my grandfather. He knew Malcolm Tyler from the golf club and the placement had been organised ad hoc, over a round of drinks without my mother's knowledge—she had no choice but to uphold the arrangement. I expect, by interfering in this way, my grandpa had the best intentions, but without this intervention in her life, who knows what she might have become, what better things she might've experienced?

One morning, she arrived at Tyler Graves to find the back section of the office had been screened off with particle board and plastic sheeting. A contractor had been brought in to expand the conferencing facilities: E. E. Flagg Construction Ltd. That afternoon, as she went to heat a can of soup for lunch, she found a man (my father) measuring the corridor. She describes the moment in her diary:

He was scribbling all these calculations on the wall in pencil. I had to ask him to step out the way & he just looked at me with his eyes scrunched up. He wasn't being rude just extremely confident. He said no you'll have to wait while I finish this last bit unless you're going to share that soup with me. I told him I preferred eating alone & he said suit yourself. So I stood there for something like a minute while he got on with his measuring & scribbling on the wall & it was like he knew I was watching him. He had the most amazing arms. Muscly but not from the gym. From proper hard work. & my god his hair was kind of amazing. Long & dark & tied back with elastic to keep it out his eyes. He didn't look over at me once & then finally he backed up to let me through taking this little tin of cigarettes out of his jeans & he goes all done is there a good place I can smoke without getting told off? His voice was sort of whispery but there was nothing quiet about him if that makes sense. It made you really listen to him even though what he was saying wasn't all that interesting. Nicest voice I've ever heard. & I felt like there was more going

*on inside his head than he let on. It's kind of hard to explain. I
said we aren't at school you know, everyone smokes, you don't
have to hide it & he laughed & said he liked to smoke in the
fresh air. I told him about the terrace on the roof & he said okay
nice one thanks & walked off straight away & I didn't see him
for the rest of the day. Don't know if he'll be coming back tomorrow but at least it's something good to think about.*

This has to be one of the few times in her life that she
referred to Francis Hardesty as something good. They were
married eight months later; I was born just four months after
that; and all their differences would eventually be exposed as
problems they could not surmount. But what this single entry
from June 1982 reveals is the strange effect my father had on
women. He seemed to magnetise them with the most routine
behaviour—a two-handed lean against a lintel, a slide of his
forefinger across his bottom lip, a casting of his eyes into the
distance. He didn't dazzle them with repartee, beguile them
with his humour—in fact, I often sensed antagonism in his
manner ('Hey, Nadine, you over-charged me—there were only
forty balls inside my bucket. We counted them, didn't we,
Danno? You can refund me next time. With interest'). His flir-
tatiousness was fairly subtle ('Cute handwriting—look at that.
You still dot your I's with little hearts. How old are you?'),
sometimes brazen ('Why don't you pick it up for me? Slow as
you can. I want the mental image of that rear end to stay with
me'). And I suppose for every woman who was immediately
attracted to him, there must've been a thousand more who
were immune to the sly quality he possessed or who rebuffed
it. But it was enough to make my intelligent, discerning, ambi-
tious, unimpressionable mother wilt the moment she met him.

So perhaps this odd facility he had for winning her affection
also worked on me. By which I mean that everything my father
said and did on our trip was part of the same process of seduc-
tion. That I was persuaded of his goodness by a similar hope

for intimacy. That he relied on this, used it to his own advantage, as he did with them.

* * *

I can't say what became of Karen after her encounter with my father, but I know she gave a statement to police before the inquest, accounting for his movements on the evening of 17th August, offering opinions on his 'state of mind.' Often, I'm drawn to wondering about the details she left out of her testimony. Was it shame or disgust that made her deny the extent of her contact with him? Did she worry their association would stain her reputation? I only hope she never gave up singing—or, if she did, I hope it wasn't due to him.

That night in the White Oak, she sang full-bloodedly, a pleasant wobble in her voice when she unravelled the high notes. And even if her skill on the instrument didn't match the level of her singing (each chord was hacked, clumsy, a little off tempo) I could see her talent might one day outgrow the boozy drabness of her local folk club.

Her set received only a mild ovation—from everyone except Vee and my father, who clapped his meaty hands above his head. When she sat down, her face was ruddy with embarrassment. The host took to the stage to introduce another act—that pensioner with his fiddle—and we endured his scratchy, two-tune repertoire of jigs until the interval was called. As the room emptied out, my father said to Karen, 'Blimey, I had a feeling you'd be good, but that was something special.'

She beamed at him. 'You really think so?'

'Yeah. Reminded me of Laura Nyro.'

She shook her head, eyeing Vee. 'Never heard of her.'

'Look her up. She was big a long time ago—your voice is similar. Better, though.' He stood up and stretched.

'Dad,' I said, reaching for his sleeve.

He ignored me. 'That sort of talent's going to take you a long way. Believe me. You can forget about signing on.'

'Aw, thanks, Fran.'

'*Dad*,' I said.

He lowered his chin. '*What?* Can't you see I'm talking, son?'

I couldn't stop thinking about QC and his red trainers, the urgency in his tone. I didn't understand why we were still waiting round. 'Did you speak to him?'

'Yeah, we've sorted something out.' He sounded unimpeachable.

'So, can we leave now?'

'I was about to ask the same,' Vee said, overhearing. 'There's only so much of this folky rubbish I can take.'

I stared up at my father.

His tongue stroked his bottom teeth. 'We'll be off first thing tomorrow.'

'*What?*' I said. 'But—no—you said—'

He raised his palm to stifle me. 'Don't bother, Daniel—I know what you're going to say, and I don't want to hear it. I practically had to give QC a kidney to get us on that set tomorrow. We'll be here overnight.'

'Here?'

'Yeah, I've got us a room.'

'But you said—as soon as he came—you *said*.' I was almost shouting.

'I know what I said, and I told you: we're *going*. Tomorrow.' He rolled his eyes at Karen, as though he was inured to such behaviour on my part. Then he slung me his sternest look. 'It's all organised. Eleven thirty at the studio gates. He's given me his word.'

'Eleven thirty?' I said.

'Eleven thirty on the dot.' He crossed his heart. 'We'll still have time for that cooked breakfast if we get a good night's rest.'

'Okay,' I said. It came out like a sigh. 'Tomorrow, then.'

'This mean you'll be stopping a bit longer?' Vee said, coming near to him. 'She always makes me sit through the second half out of politeness, but I might as well shoot off now, and meet you downstairs after.'

'You're just going to sit on your own down there?' Karen said. 'You're not even drinking.'

'Yeah, what's wrong with that? Seems to work for Daniel.' Vee was more perceptive than I'd thought. 'Maybe a nice lad'll buy me an orange juice.'

'Go home, if you're tired. I'll get a cab,' Karen said. 'I don't mind.'

We joined her table after the interval. She installed a modest distance between herself and my father on the bench seat to begin with. The second half was given up to the main act, an accordionist from Whitby. I was not accustomed to the sound of the accordion, though I found it nicely diverting for a while, to observe the huff and puff of it, the bellows swelling and shutting, the keys going *clack clack clack* under the drone. My father pretended to enjoy the spectacle for as long as Karen seemed attuned to his reception of it. Still, forty minutes of sombre Russian circus music would test anyone's resolve—I fell asleep against my father's shoulder. He must've lowered me down sidelong on the seat afterwards, because I awoke to the strip lights blinking white above me. I looked up to find him prodding my shoulder with two fingers, as if I were a vagrant who'd passed out in a bus shelter. Karen had her arm around his waist, and he had her guitar strapped over his right shoulder. 'Think it's time we put you to bed, sunshine,' he said. 'You did well to withstand that racket for so long. At least I had the beer to take the edge off.'

'Yeah, I reckon you did right to sleep through it,' Karen

said. Her words came out a little sloppily, her eyelids seemed more leaden. 'I thought he'd have to sing eventually—his mouth kept moving but nothing came out. Just more *twiddly-diddly-dee*. He went on for-bloody-ever.'

'I don't see why you couldn't have played a few more,' my father said. 'You should've been the headliner.'

'I *know*. Two songs are all I ever get. Tightarses.'

'All right, come on, I've got the room key here.' Digging into his jeans, he retrieved a single Chubb key on a wooden fob the size of a salt cellar. 'It's nothing fancy, but it'll do for tonight.'

The pub's lodgings were exactly of the type my mother had prohibited. Two single beds with floral coverings that matched the curtains. An en suite bathroom with mouldering green taps that looked to have been dredged from a canal. There was no telephone with which to report all this to her, so I had to abide it.

My father asked me which bed I favoured and I chose the one nearest the window; if I knelt at the headboard end, I could see the glow of lamp posts in the car park. It was from there I watched him traipse across the tarmac to collect my holdall and his suitcase from the Volvo. The return leg took him twice as long. When he got back, he sounded five short raps on the door and I went to unlatch it. He deposited our bags on the foot of his bed with a groan. Then, reaching underneath his shirt, he unhooked an object from his belt and disentangled the coil of plastic wire and metal that came with it. 'A little present from Karen,' he said. 'Just on loan, mind you. Here.'

It was a cheap orange walkman. 'Thanks.' I flipped it open. There was no tape in it.

'Oops—nearly forgot the most important bit.' He pulled a cassette from his back pocket. 'I wasn't sure where you'd got up to with it all, so I brought you the third one from the box.

Hope that's okay. You'd better check the batteries are working in that thing.'

I pushed play and felt the mechanism of the walkman move. He leaned to slot the tape in for me, setting the band of the earphones over my head. 'Just in case you can't get back to sleep,' he said, but these gestures of concern didn't convince me any more. I knew they were a ploy to soften his departure from the room. There was no point trying to stop him going downstairs to resume things with Karen in the bar. I would be left alone again, in another strange place, with a crummy bedside lamp casting a yellow light across the textures in the anaglypta; with the rising sadness of my thoughts, and the steady chink of glasses in the pub below, and the roil of voices spilling out at closing time, baiting my window; with the dread of further disappointments lying in wait for me tomorrow, and the feeling that my mother would be angry when I made it home, because of him.

* * *

[. . .] *He would come to cherish those days out salvaging with Cryck, examining the contours of the land for scars. Acres, they covered together, heads bent to the soil and grass, stopping every time he thought he saw a marker. Hand-drawn strokes of Aoxin were not easy to determine—so many of the figures in the dirt that he mistook for language were only scuffs from landed birds or prints from deer's hooves or smudges left by rabbits— but he soon got the hang of it, and Cryck was grateful for his help.*

The more complicated markings had no consistent size or shape. One day, he saw her stoop over a streak in the wet mud by a ditch and leap up in exhilaration: 'There, you see it. There!' She was pointing to a slight circular impression, no bigger than a sixpence. Another day, she paused next to a shallow square chipped from the tree roots at his feet. 'It's an indograf—these woods are full of them,' she said. 'This one says to be alert for weapons. Might be some rich pickings on this track.'

In all this time he spent walking the land with Cryck, they were not seen by anyone. He believed that his Aoxin blood made him invisible too. But there were occasions when, crossing an open field, he thought he saw a farmer stand up at the wheel of a tractor with a hand screening his eyes, as though spotting him, a trespasser.

He came to feel more Aoxin than human. He was never bored or tired of learning, never frightened, never melancholy. His heart and mind seemed bigger, fuller. These days with Cryck were the best of his life.

* * *

Karen and my father came back to the room long after midnight. They must've thought, because I had the headphones on and lay unmoving in the bed, that I'd be oblivious to the sweep of corridor lights across the floor, the flurry of their shadows on the carpet, their stage whispers to each other, 'Shshhh, keep it down, you'll wake him.'

'Sorry!'

But I heard and saw it all.

I watched their drunken shuffle to the bathroom with my lids half closed. I heard Karen's meagre protestations to 'Wait, wait, wait, hang on, he'll see us, stop,' while my father's hands worked loose the dainty zip along the hipline of her skirt and, with a single downward tug, reduced it to a dumb suede hoop around her feet.

The angle of the hallway mirror gave a view of them. It was something I was not supposed to see but felt impelled to watch, to understand. She tried to shut the door behind them with a trailing hand, but it bounced in the latch and hung ajar.

At first, their bodies moved inside the tiny bathroom like two lobsters in a tank. They held each other caringly. They kissed. But then the groping became heated, forceful. He pushed his thumb into her mouth and she bit down on it and grinned. I watched him kneel and press his nose into the mound between her legs, hitch off her knickers, haul her upwards by the thighs to sit her on the basin as though setting down a barrow, and then unbelt himself, lower his jeans, bring out the mystifying private flesh my mother wrote whole paragraphs about, a distended thing that I could barely reconcile with the colour diagrams in Biology or my own equipment.

He tried to mute her gasps of pleasure by covering her mouth, but nothing could be done about the thump of Karen's shoulders on the thin partition every time my father thrust at her. His forearm came towards her throat. His thumb pressed beneath her jaw. 'Oi, *don't*,' I heard her tell him. '*Don't.* That's too much. Stop.' And she slapped his arm away. 'Okay, okay,' he said. His breathing sounded pained.

Afterwards, they stayed there, clinched and statuesque. They panted and they sniggered. I saw Karen hop down from the basin, scavenge for her knickers on the lino, out of puff. 'How often have you, I mean, I don't—I don't even know what to say—I haven't ever—I mean, it's *never* been like *that*—with anyone,' she said, while my father put himself away and rinsed his hands and face under the squealing taps. 'Can I sleep here?' she asked him. 'It's late and I'm—well, *you know*.'

'Stay if you want,' he said, 'but you'll need to be gone before he wakes up—it'll only confuse him. He's angry with me as it is.'

'I'll walk to the cab rank, then.'

'Up to you.'

'Yeah . . . Yeah, that's probably best. I don't want him to think bad of me.'

'All right. Whatever you reckon.'

Karen found her skirt and said, 'Is there a number I can ring you at? It'd be good to see you again some time.' He reminded her that she was meant to have a boyfriend. 'I know, I know,' she said, 'but, if there's a number?' and, on the bedside table next to me, he wrote it down for her. I couldn't make out the digits, though I doubt they were correct.

'What about your walkman?' he asked. 'I could try to slip it off him.' But she told him I could keep it—something to remember her by—and he didn't even thank her. She collected her guitar and left.

My father stood shirtless at the foot of my bed for some time after, smoking a cigarette and flapping the fumes out the window. A cool draught bothered my neck. I knew that he was staring at me, but I didn't dare acknowledge him. The pretence of my sleep was sheltering. I counted every inhalation, exhalation, until he settled in the bed across from me, turned off the lamp. And for what seemed like hours, I listened to his agitation of the bedsheets as he struggled with his dreams.

SIDE TWO

HIS CONSTANCY

We came through silhouettes of overpasses, navigated roundabouts, flashed by pylons and sheer grassy banks, zipped past stuccoed houses, dipped under the legs of bridges, left behind the pasture and the meadowland to join the concrete city. We had the music turned up high, the speakers fizzing Cocteau Twins, a thick echoing noise in which my father hid from me. It took sixteen minutes to arrive in Leeds. I sat on my hands the whole way there. A flat nest of buildings in the distance became a one-way system lined with patchwork architecture: Sixties apartment blocks the colour of wet mud, brick warehouses, viaducts, angular office complexes, sandstone tenements, the mirrored glass of brand new high-rises, the colonnaded splendour of the town hall, the spires of law courts blushed with soot. I expected Leeds to be as sprawling and mysterious as London, but it was smaller, dimmer, less engulfing. The streets were emptier; the clouds hung lower overhead; the sunlight had a drear quality when thrown against the pavements, as though filtered through crepe paper.

I don't know if my father noticed these things, too, but he was quieter than usual as we crawled through the city centre. He turned the music down until it was a murmur and let me absorb the sights outside the window—it must've occurred to him that I was seeing them for the first time. All he said was, 'No one's in a hurry to get anywhere round here. Look at them all, just trundling along. Not a care in the world.' I couldn't tell if it was praise or condemnation.

In the quiet, the ticking of the indicator irked me, a countdown to something I couldn't quite interpret. I was so anxious about what lay ahead of us that morning I couldn't speak, and I kept tasting the half-cooked breakfast sausages we had eaten at the White Oak. We didn't pass the metropole, but coming through the main square we skirted by the Queens Hotel, whose entrance was adorned with plush red carpet and gold handrails. 'See that fancy place,' he said, as we drove past, 'next time we do this trip, I promise we'll stay there. No more dodgy Cumberlands for breakfast. No more stale toast and jam. The royal treatment. That's what we deserve, right?'

'Yeah,' I said, but my gut twinged at the prospect.

'Well, anyway.' He sighed, noting my reluctance. Every gear change was a maddened heave from this point on, until we reached the Kirkstall Road, where he took his scabby hand off the lever. 'Do us a favour and dig out the paracetamol,' he said. 'This thing's really starting to ache now.' He was waving at the glovebox. I fumbled around inside it, laid my eyes upon the yellow pack of Anadin. 'Any left?' he asked.

'A few,' I said.

'Get us out a couple, would you?'

I did as I was told, handed them over: a pair of white tablets on my palm like milk teeth I'd pulled out. He took both and dry-gulped them. 'So, then—how d'you feel? You ready to see some compartments, or what?'

'I suppose.'

'You don't sound very excited about it. All you've been banging on about is Leeds, Leeds, Leeds, and now we're here you aren't even fussed.'

'I am. It's just—I don't know. I'm tired.'

'Hmm.' My father thought he understood me well enough to second guess me. 'Look, I'll smooth things over with your mum later on, don't worry. She won't mind once I've explained it all to her. I'll be the one who gets it in the neck, not you.'

'It's not that,' I said, though she was fully on my mind.

'What's up with you, then? You've had a sour face on you all morning. This is meant to be a treat.'

I didn't have the words to express my disillusionment. I could only feel it in the fibre of my body. Something had expired in the night, vacated me. It didn't matter if the outcome was the same or better—we could spend the afternoon on set with Maxine Laidlaw in full costume, the director could invite me to guest star in an episode—it wouldn't change my disaffection with my father. I wanted the journey he had promised. I wanted him, for once, to prove his constancy. But he seemed to spend each new day of his life promoting compensation for the day before.

A little further on, the traffic thinned and we passed the smoking metal chimney of a factory; all the properties on both sides of the road began to look more corporate, bearing shiny monograms and logos. He gave a salute through the windscreen: 'There she blows,' he said, so cheerily it was conspicuous. 'Yorkshire Television.'

It looked like a suburban hospital. A collection of low brown buildings fronted by an unkempt lawn. Thin, dark windows set into the bricks at even intervals. A satellite dish on the outermost roof the size of an aeroplane wheel.

'Not very spectacular from here, is it? But wait until we get you through the door. All kinds of magic on the inside.'

'You're driving past it,' I said.

'Can't get in from this end. We need to loop around.'

He took us a few hundred yards along the carriageway and turned uphill, towards what seemed to be a council estate. There was a long procession of terraced houses with FOR SALE signs before the studios came into view again. The buildings looked broader from the rear, and more ordinary. In the vast

car park, fenced off with steel, a fleet of white lorries was waiting to be loaded. We hung a right at the junction. 'Hey, look at
that,' he said, spotting something in his periphery. 'Eleven
thirty on the button.' And just as we were closing on the
entrance gates, he braked and pulled up on the double yellow
lines. He motioned at the clock. 'Ye of little faith, Danno. Ye.
Of little. Faith.'

I checked the side mirror, hopefully.

QC was striding up to meet us: those bright red shoes were
unmistakable, his listing gait unusual. His arms hung crablike
by his torso, hardly moving when he walked. There was a
clumping sound behind me as he opened the door. He didn't
so much sit down in the seat as dump his whole weight into it.

'Are you feeling okay, Fran? You're actually on time for
once,' he said.

'Good morning to you too, mate.'

'Yeah yeah. I'm still not happy about this.'

'Ah, you know I'd do the same for you. Stop moaning.'

'If only that were true.' QC gripped my headrest, leaning in.
He offered up his other hand for me to shake. 'So, your dad
says you're a proper fan.' His fingernails were oddly pristine,
buffed. 'I'll have to quiz you a bit later. See how much of a
Fexhead you are.'

'He doesn't like being called that,' my father said.

'What?'

'I'm saying, don't call him that.'

'Oh, well, pardon me for breathing.' QC slumped back.

'I don't mind actually,' I said.

My father coughed at me. 'Oh, I see—like *that*, is it? One
rule for him and one for me.'

QC called from the back, 'Let's just get this over with, eh?
We're on a schedule here, in case you need reminding.'

We drove another hundred yards or so, up to the entrance
gates. There was a set of automated barriers with an intercom.

My father stopped the car, wound down his window. He pushed the button on the intercom and waited.

The barrier didn't lift, but after a moment a man in a white uniform came out of the gatehouse. 'Good news, it's Foz—we should be okay here, mate,' said QC from the back. 'He doesn't like me much, but I can handle him.'

'Just do what you need to.'

'Don't forget to smile,' said QC, patting my shoulder. The joss-stick sweetness of his aftershave was smothering.

The guard came round to the driver's side and peered in at my father. 'You got an access card there, pal?'

'He's the one you want to ask,' my father said, thumbing at the back seat.

QC strained to get his wallet from his jeans. He took out a small laminated card and stretched forward to present it.

'Oh, hey, never saw you there,' the guard said to him.

'No problem, Foz. How you getting on today?'

'Yeah. Can't complain.' The guard studied the ID cursorily. 'Barnaby,' he said, grinning. 'What kind of name is that?'

'Sixties, wasn't it? Blame my old man,' QC replied. 'My sister had it worse.'

'What'd they call her?'

'Ophelia.'

'Yeesh. Poor lamb.' The guard passed back the card to my father, laughing. 'These two coming in as guests, are they?'

'That's the plan,' my father said.

The guard gave him a submissive look, but the warmth drained from his eyes. 'You'll be on my list then,' he said.

QC slotted the card back into his wallet. 'Yeah, I put them on it yesterday.'

'Well, I should probably check it to be sure. You know how they are in this place.'

'Tell me about it, mate.'

The guard nodded towards me. 'What's the lad's name?'

I felt QC tapping the back of my seat, so I flashed the guard a smile.

My father blinked. 'Daniel,' he said.

'Daniel what?'

'Jarrett.'

I flinched.

My father barrelled on: 'It's two Rs, two Ts.'

'And you are?'

'Philip Jarrett. One L.'

'All right, I don't need a spelling lesson.'

'*Dad*,' I said. 'That's Grandpa—'

'Shshh, it's all right, son. We'll see your grandpa later.' He angled his head to the guard. 'He's a bit excited.'

The guard hitched up his trousers by the belt. 'I'll get my clipboard.'

'Can't you just let us through, Foz?' QC called. 'You know *me*. And we need to be on set by noon.'

'If it were down to me, I'd not get off my chair all day. But I've got a boss like everyone else. And he likes his paperwork in order.'

'Fair enough,' said my father.

'All right, do what you need,' said QC.

The guard ambled away. We watched him head into the gatehouse.

QC huffed. 'Bellend.'

'Likes a chat, doesn't he? *Jesus*,' my father said. 'How long's *he* been on the gate?'

'Since a bit after Sid left. He's all right to have a smoke with, I suppose, but the stick goes right back up his arse once break time's over.'

'Well, anyway—so far so good.'

I felt like I was stapled to my seat. 'Why did you lie to him?' I said.

No one answered.

'Why did you *lie*?' I said.

My father kept his eyes on the barrier. 'I'm not lying. Who's lying?'

'You just gave him Grandpa's name. And you said I was called Jarrett.'

'Well, you'll be a Jarrett one day, if your mother gets her way—I'd start getting used to it.' His nails worked the stubble on his cheek in tiny strokes. 'And I wasn't lying, just acting—there's a difference. It's like checking into a hotel under a—you know, whatever the word is. A fake name.' He landed his eyes on me, a resoluteness to his posture. 'Do you want to get on that set or don't you?'

'Yeah, but why can't we just be ourselves?'

'It's complicated, Dan. You're going to have to trust me.'

'You always say that, though.'

In the backseat, QC snickered.

'And, anyway,' I said, 'you work here—why can't you use your *own* card?'

'Because.'

'Because *what*, though?'

QC chimed in, amused: 'Oh, Fran, mate, this is ridiculous. Just tell him what the problem is, for crying out loud. Save yourself the hassle.'

My father toyed with the handbrake button. 'Thanks for all your help here, Uncle Barnaby. I appreciate it.'

'I think I'm helping you enough for one day.' QC sniffed. 'Actually, this is the last favour you'll be getting off me for a while, don't worry. We're even.'

My father's eyes were on the gatehouse now. 'What's taking him so long in there?'

'Fucked if I know,' QC said.

'Language.'

'Sorry.'

'You still haven't told me *why*.' I had to bend forward to get his attention. '*Dad*.'

'Why what?'

'The card,' said QC. 'For starters.' He must've smirked, because my father glared into the rear-view.

'You're enjoying this, aren't you?'

'Maybe. Yeah. Just a bit. Ha ha ha.'

When the explanation came, it wasn't what I hoped to hear. 'If you really want to know, my own card doesn't work right now,' my father said. 'That's why.'

'How come?'

'I—it just doesn't.'

'Why not?'

'Look, Dan, if I'm under arrest you need to tell me, 'cause all this *why not this* and *why not that* is doing my head in.' He shook away the loose strands of his fringe. 'Honestly, I didn't think there'd be an issue. It's like that time we couldn't rent a car on holiday. Remember we had to take the bus everywhere 'cause your mum's licence had expired? Portugal, I think it was.'

'No.'

'Well, maybe you were too little. But it's the same thing— my card's out of date, and I didn't realise till yesterday. There's a whole rigmarole about getting a new one. So QC's getting us in with his card—it's just easier that way. We'd have to postpone the visit otherwise.'

'But it's wrong,' I said. 'It's dishonest.'

I heard QC cackling again in the back.

'Don't be soft. I work here, remember?' my father said. 'We're not breaking and entering. Just bending the rules.'

Except that we were still on the wrong side of the barrier and the guard was taking a very long time to check his list of names. Part of me hoped he was on the phone to my mother. An acid pain was brewing in my stomach, thinking of how worried she was getting. The backs of my knees were sweating.

My father sat beside me peacefully, examining his knuckles,

hopscotching the fingers of his other hand over the scabs. His chest rose and fell beneath his seatbelt. He began to whistle *Grandstand*. 'Stop it,' QC said. 'Are you trying to piss me off?'

The wait felt interminable.

I said, 'Dad, I think we ought to just leave it.'

He glowered at me. 'What?'

'Let's just go home. If we can't get in, it's okay—honest, I don't mind.' Maybe if I'd withheld the next thing out of my mouth, he might've listened to me. He might've backed away from the barrier. 'Mum said it might turn out like this, so it's fine. Honest. I'm not even fussed.'

QC made a pained noise.

My father didn't react. His eyelids dropped and opened. There was hardly a movement in the car park. I could see the motion of his tongue behind his teeth. The engine shuddered underneath us. 'You know, I just had the weirdest *déjà vu*,' he said, eventually. 'Ever get one of those?'

'No, and I don't believe in 'em,' QC replied.

'Wasn't talking to you, fella.' His voice seemed to crackle. 'Maybe it's not a *déjà vu* exactly—more like an old familiar feeling coming back to me. I was thinking about this bloke Tom Pascoe, used to work with us on the farm.'

'You're not making much sense here, Fran, I hate to tell you.'

'Can you shut up, please? I'm talking to my son.' My father addressed me without facing me. 'Pascoe worked for us when I was little—this weird-looking Geordie who my dad took on. People said he maimed two lambs on someone else's grazing land, but I never really bought into that story, personally.'

'What's maimed?' I asked.

'Injured, *hurt*.'

'Oh.'

'There was no proof he'd done it, mind you, not a scrap of it, but he got pinned with the crime just because his face was an easy fit. He'd been in borstal as a kid—that's what they used to call prisons for lads your age—and people didn't really trust him once they'd heard about all that. Can't say I liked him that much. He was a narky sort of bloke, but he was a hard grafter on the farm, especially when it got to clipping time, so my dad thought the sun shone out of him.'

He made us wait for it, wetting his lips—and I can see now, because I'm convinced this was the only truthful story he told on the whole trip, that he was trying to resist the urge to reconstruct it.

'Thing is,' he went on, 'once these kinds of accusations start being thrown about, they make an awful stink. Folks had all made up their minds that Pascoe did the crime, so that was that. The stink was on him. And because he worked for us, the stink was on my dad as well. We lost a load of money that year. You've got to deal with a situation like that, don't you? Make a stand either way—you can't let it drag on. So my dad gave Pascoe the boot—I suppose he never had a choice. He let him have a few months' pay and found him a job at a dairy out in Devon or somewhere, I forget where exactly. But, I tell you what, I never saw my old man so upset about anything before. I mean, he didn't shed a tear when I left home, but when Tom Pascoe went, *wah*, he was in a mood for weeks.' My father grasped the steering wheel now, twisted to look at me.

I knew he wanted me to ask what happened to Pascoe, so I did.

'Probably topped himself,' said QC in the back.

'Not far off . . . Turned out, those lambs were hurt by someone else—two lads on another farm with a crossbow, shooting at things just for something to do. They'd bought it from a catalogue, would you believe. Well, they got caught doing it a second time. Pair of idiots. So, right away, my dad rang up his mate at the dairy to get Pascoe back to work for us, but, nope—too late. Way too late. Pascoe was in prison, wasn't he?

He'd got eight years for robbing a post office about a month after he'd left our farm and no one had told us a word. The old man couldn't get over it. He was so bloody relieved. The way he thought about it was: *Phew, close shave, eh? That Pascoe was rotten all along. Good riddance.* But that wasn't how I saw it then, and I still don't see it that way.'

Another car was waiting in the bay behind us now, motor running.

'Sounds like it *was* good riddance, to be fair,' QC said.

My father turned to him. 'Where's this list he's checking, mate—Alaska?'

I was still pondering his sermon. 'But, wait, I don't get it— Pascoe was bad. He didn't hurt the sheep, but he *stole* from a post office. That makes him bad.'

'Dan, come on, not you as well, son. I thought you had more sense.'

'It's obvious, though,' I said.

'Well, *I* wouldn't say so. It all depends how you look at it.' He squeezed the sore spots of his knuckles. 'You can say that he was rotten from the off, or you can say his circumstances made him that way, can't you? That's what I think. My old man let him down. Big time.'

The car behind us beeped. He ignored it. 'I don't know. maybe.'

It beeped again.

'What the bloody—?' He spun round. 'Are you hearing this?'

'Yeah. Head up, though,' said QC, nodding at the wind screen. 'Movement.'

The guard was coming now, and he had company—another guard in a navy-blue jumper with a walkie-talkie.

'Shit,' my father said. 'That other fella knows me.'

'Don't panic. Wait and see.'

They approached the car and stood at my father's window.

'Did you manage to sort it for us, then?' he asked them curtly. 'There's a bit of a queue forming now.'

The guard in the jumper spoke first. 'Sorry, I'm afraid we need identification for you and the boy.'

QC rolled down his window. 'What's the problem, Foz?'

The guard tapped his clipboard. 'Got the names right here, like you said. Just need to check some IDs before we can oblige.'

'Hey, come on, that can't be right. I work here,' QC said. 'I'm allowed to bring in any guests I want.'

'Not without ID you're not,' the other guard insisted. 'It's procedure.'

My father stared up at him. 'I don't have any. For either of us.'

'Then you'll have to back up. I'll give the car behind a nudge.'

'No, no, no, come on. This is crazy. I work here!' QC pleaded.

The guard in the white shirt planted his hands on the roof. 'We've been told not to let anyone through without ID, mate, sorry. Unless you have a driver's licence or a passport or something like that?'

'Dad, let's go,' I said. 'I want to go home.'

But he just scowled at the guards. '*Who* told you? *Who* told you not to let us in?'

'It's just procedure, that's all.'

'Yeah, right. He works here, we're his guests and we're on the list—I don't see the problem.'

The guards were unmoved. 'Look, if you're not going to shift your car, we'll have to wait for the police to sort this out.'

'The police! The police now! Oh my god, what *is* this?'

'You want to calm down, mate,' said QC.

'Dad, let's go. Let's just *leave*.'

'What business is it of the fucking *police*?'

'You should listen to your lad there,' said the guard in the jumper. 'He seems to have his head screwed on.'

'Yeah?'

'*Yeah.*'

'Yeah, Dad, come on, let's go.'

'This is all *her* doing, you know,' my father told QC. 'She won't stop till I'm humiliated. I told you, didn't I? Didn't I *tell you*? Once was bad enough. This is fucking uncalled for.'

'Fran. Calm down now. Seriously.' QC was buckling himself in. 'You're landing me in it here.'

'I can't believe this. I mean, is this beyond the pale, or what?'

The guard in the jumper stooped, a staunch expression on his face, meant for my father. 'Listen to me now, I work this gate quite a bit, and I know who's who, all right? That's all I'm saying to you, pal. You're not fooling anyone. I've a decent memory for faces. This isn't the way to get your access back, all right?'

'Yeah, yeah, dickhead, I get it, I get it.' My father jabbed his leg down on the clutch pedal and joggled the gearstick. 'You're humiliating me in front of my son. Thanks a lot for that. Well done.'

'You're humiliating yourself, pal. Don't let me see you here again or there'll be bother.'

'*Dad*,' I called.

'Just back up, Fran. Or you'll get me in the shit.'

'You're already in it, mate,' he said. 'Are you stupid?'

'What's that supposed to mean?'

'You know what it means.'

'Let's just go. Before you get me sacked.'

My father huffed. 'Yeah. Fuck it.' He revved the engine hard. The car behind us arced away, heeding our reverse lights. As he wheeled us backwards, he stuck two of his bruised left fingers up towards the guards. They didn't seem to mind. One spoke into his walkie-talkie, one smoothed down his sleeves. Our wheels spun and squealed.

QC went for the door but my father had the child lock on. 'You've lost it, mate. I'm getting out.' He rattled the handle.

My father took his foot off the accelerator. We rolled back with sheer momentum, and everything seemed to go quiet and still, as though we'd left the tow of gravity. Then he slotted into forward gear again. My belly lurched. The tyres shrieked beneath us. We were streaking down the road with all the clouds retreating from the windscreen and QC pinned against his seat. My father's fists were clenched tight on the wheel. I wanted to cry right then, but didn't, fearing it might worsen his behaviour, that he would see my tears as a disgrace, another provocation. As we neared the junction, our pace gathered. The lights flicked green to amber, but he dismissed them, taking the turn at such a speed that QC's body swayed behind us. His weighty hand thudded the window. 'Christ, Fran, what's got into you? Slow down, you arsehole. This ain't funny.' But my father wasn't listening.

I had seen a different kind of rage in him before, watching through the uprights of our bannister. He would prowl the limits of our hallway as my mother's insults rained on him. *Selfish*, *worthless*, *lazy*, *stupid*, *heartless*, *shameful*, *coward*. She'd exhume all of his past mistakes and indiscretions, spitting names of other women like obscenities, reminding him she'd never really loved him anyway, saying how he couldn't even do the simplest thing she asked, how all her friends detested him, and even his own son had lost respect for him. An hour or two of this and he would break.

He'd put his boot through the flank of the sideboard. He'd kick chunks from the door under the stairs. Pictures and ornaments would get hurled against the dado rail, swept from the walls, trodden. Later, with him safely gone, the shattered pieces would be folded into newspapers; my mother on her knees, a wreck. 'Get the hoover out, Daniel, please. Don't say anything. I know, okay? I *know*.' (Children of unhappy marriages become adept with vacuum cleaners. We grow accustomed to unpacking them in the small hours, using them in lieu of fixing things we can't. A well-vacuumed carpet is an equilibrium.)

He never hit my mother while he lived with us—at least, not to my knowledge—but our repainted doorframes looked like avocado skins, our furniture was patched and crooked, most of the family photographs had no glass in the frames. It seems alarming to me now that I once admired him for his restraint, as though not striking her required some extraordinary act of will.

I can't pretend to understand what all my parents' arguments were about, or who was to blame for starting them. Hindsight makes it easy to link every problem in their marriage to my father, but perhaps this is too simplistic a view to take—because, despite what happened in the end, and all his cruelty, can it really be that he was responsible for each defective moment in their life together?

I know what my memory has recorded. And I recall that when they fought, he'd stand there, doing nothing, while she punched and punched and punched, as though he were acquiescing to her right to beat him, taking all her puny blows the way a tree accepts the birds. I think this means he recognised the badness that lurked in him and wanted to suppress it. A better man would not have failed to, I suppose.

* * *

When he realised the cars ahead were stationary, he stamped down on the brakes. It seemed the entire chassis was sliding out from under us. The tyres made a ripping noise. The seatbelt bit my collarbone. I shut my eyes, expecting to be swallowed up in metal, showered with glass, but there was no impact at all. There was a pure, remarkable hush.

Glancing up, I found we'd stopped a yard from a van's rear bumper. A Labrador was panting at us gormlessly from the back window. There was a smell of cooked rubber. My father's face looked sunburned. He sounded starved of air. 'Come on, move it. Fucking move it!' He pushed at the horn with both fists. 'It's green, you idiots!'

'Stop beeping, for fuck's sake,' QC shouted from the back. 'Where exactly are they meant to go?'

'Anywhere. Out of my way. I don't care.' He blasted the

horn again. And in the lull of his frustration, he turned to me and saw that I was terrified and padding tears with my sleeves. 'Don't fucking cry—it's not my fault, okay? Don't fucking *cry* on me.'

'Never your fault, is it, Fran?' said QC. 'Jesus bloody Christ. Let me out. Right now.'

My father paid him no attention. He edged us forward as the queue of cars began to filter left. We were heading back down Kirkstall Road, in the opposite direction. 'You know, I'm putting two and two together here,' he said, 'and I don't like the answer that keeps coming back to me.' I gave a spluttering noise he didn't care for either: he glared at me with vague disgust, the type I thought he only harboured for strangers. 'Will you be quiet?' he said. 'You've got to toughen up, son. I tried the best I could for you, I really did. I tried *everything*. And, all right, I messed up. I know, I know. I couldn't get you in there like I promised. But I'm telling you right now, the entire fucking universe is up against me at the minute. I swear to god, it is. And I just can't compete with that. Nobody can.'

'It's all hot fucking air with you, isn't it?' said QC. 'Give the lad a break. He's frightened, mate. How stupid are you? You're acting like a loon.'

'Is that right? How many kids you got, Barn? You've no fucking idea.'

'Pull the fuck over.'

'No, I don't think so.'

'Pull over, Fran. I'm not playing any more.'

My father fixed his eyes on the road. We were keeping to the speed limit, trailing behind average people having what I hoped were pleasant interactions with the voices on their radios, but I could tell that he was itching to race past them. He kept changing lanes, creeping closer to the car in front, as though trying to couple with its tow bar. When we drove by Yorkshire Television again, he wouldn't look. I watched the buildings slip into the gloom behind my shoulder. 'I'd keep my mouth shut if I were you, mate,' he called back to QC, who was now leaning across the back seat, trying to figure out the child lock. 'Because, like I said, when you add two and two, I mean, it really looks like you just stitched me up back there. In fact, the more I think about it, the more I know you were behind it.'

QC didn't answer. He was pulling and pushing at the door lever in vain.

'You told them we were coming, didn't you? Not Foz—that bloke was clueless. I mean, you must've flagged my name up with the other fella somehow.'

'Stop acting paranoid,' said QC. 'You're making things worse.'

I was still trying to stop my jaw from yammering. My eyes felt leaden and stung. I wanted to hear sirens, to see the rescue lights of police cars nearing, but I knew they wouldn't come. Instead, the vapid corporate buildings we had passed less than an hour ago receded from my view again, and I was so removed from them, so disconnected from their normalness, that stomach acid rose into my mouth, left an astringent coating in my gullet. I've come to know the taste of it too well.

'Don't hear you denying it,' my father said. 'You told them we were coming, didn't you? You piece of shit.'

'Hey, you wanna mind what you say to me. I just did you a favour, remember?'

'Right. Some favour.'

'Don't go blaming me. You had a plan. It didn't work, mate. Simple.'

'Yeah, because you dobbed me in. You went and spoke to Palmer.'

'*Palmer.* Palmer! You're losing it, mate. Get a grip.'

'You still haven't denied it.'

'It wasn't me, it wasn't me, it wasn't me. All right? That what you need to hear?'

'Yeah. I don't fucking believe you, though.'

'Pull over.'

'No.'

'Pull over.'

'No.'

At this, QC sprang forward. He grabbed the upper section of my father's seatbelt, tugging on it like a boat rope. He hooked the other arm around my father's windpipe. 'Pull the fuck over. Now.' And though I heard myself calling weakly, 'Don't, QC! Let him go,' my body stayed planted in the seat. I wanted it to end. I wanted him to squeeze just hard enough to make my father faint, so we'd career into the central reservation, smash the barrier. With any luck, I'd wake up in the hospital and find my mother tending to my injuries.

But then I felt the car begin to slow. We turned down a side road and pulled into the disused car park of a bankrupt carpet showroom. The windows of the shop were whitewashed, swirled with gypsum. My father, for some reason, steered into a bay right by the entrance, bumping the nettles on the kerb. I could see our dumb reflections in the frontage. 'If you take your fucking arm off me, QC,' he said, half strangled, 'I'll let you out.'

'Don't do anything stupid.'

'Like what?'

'Like I don't know. Just don't try anything.'

'I honestly wouldn't know what to try.'

'Yeah, right.'

QC released his hold. My father got out and, for a moment, he just stood beside the car. I could only see his midriff, his pink hands on his hips.

'Hey, snap out of it,' said QC, knuckling the window. I expected he'd bolt as soon as the door opened, but he didn't. He stayed there, blinking at me, while my father held it back for him, chauffeur style. The local sunshine angled in, a feeble brightness. 'He used to be all right, your dad, you know. He used to be all right.' And he gave a sigh of great finality, twisting to get out. 'Watch yourself, Dan, eh?' I thought he was going to abandon me, too. It seemed hopeless to stop him. But no sooner had QC laid his trainers on the tarmac, he turned round. 'Hang on, I don't like how this feels. I want to know what you're planning to do, Fran.'

'I thought you wanted to get out,' my father said, flatly.

QC slid further along the seat. 'Yeah, but first I want to know where you're heading.'

'I don't know yet.'

'Well, in that case,' said QC, 'I don't think in all good conscious I can leave him with you.'

'Is that right?' Fran Hardesty was laughing. 'That's my son you're talking about. You're not his social worker.'

'Someone's got to look out for him, haven't they?'

'Are you saying I'm not?'

'I'm saying you're not thinking straight right now.'

'You're not *my* social worker, either.'

My father's shadow wavered in the shopfront glass. By a strange trick of the light, and the way the car door covered him, he almost seemed to levitate. A block of flats was visible beyond him, in the reflected distance. A new development trussed with scaffolding. I could've reached it, if I'd thought to run.

QC said: 'The fights you're fighting don't involve him, Fran.'

'Do I look like I'm fighting anyone?'

'Maybe not yet. But I know where you're going.'

'And where's that?'

'Chloe's.'

'Just get out the car. You're bothering me now.'

'Nah, I think I'll stay.'

'Okay then. Suit yourself. But *you* go where *we* go.'

'Fine.'

My father slammed the door. When he dropped back into the driver's seat, he gripped the rear-view mirror and repositioned it so it was trained on nothing but QC. 'By the way, genius,' he said, 'it's in all good *conscience*, not in all good conscious. And that child lock's still on back there.'

'Just drive,' QC told him. 'I'm sick of all your dramas.'

'Yeah, yeah.' My father didn't put his seatbelt on. 'Keep your hands where I can see 'em this time.'

As he fired the ignition, I asked: 'Who's Chloe?'

He seemed heartened by my question. 'Chloe's the reason we're sat here,' he said, reaching for the glovebox. 'And I'm tired of sitting, Dan, aren't you?'

S ome houses are more vulnerable than others. The place
that Chloe Cargill rented stood at the summit of a slop-
ing avenue. It was semi-detached, with a large bay window on the ground floor and a gable roof, and was adjoined to
what appeared to be its better turned-out twin—next door had
a coat of white emulsion, neat black drainpipes, privets freshly
clipped; Chloe's place had drab beige render, wonky guttering,
bad grass. And it had the disadvantage of being first on the
row. The south-facing part of it was open to a side road, which
divided it from a long bank of terraced properties. These were
mostly flats whose back windows were all barred and looked
out over wooden sheds and flagstone yards and garages. Trees
and wild hedges lined the path. There was one lamp post covering the juncture where this side road met the avenue proper,
but the hood of it was smashed and the bulb was missing. The
track itself was gravel-chipped, and the further you looked
along it, the more of it was swallowed up by weeds and mud;
it was hard to imagine that anyone used it as a short cut, given
that it led to nowhere any quicker, but dustbins were left out
there in an ordered fashion, so it must've been a through-route
for collection lorries. None of this took my attention at the
time, of course, but I've since studied pictures on the news
reports, and I'll say again: some houses are more vulnerable
than others. Most people see a family home on a quiet suburban street, they imagine what it might be like to live in it, where
they might position their own furniture inside, how differently

they'd dress the windows, plant the garden, paint the brick-work. But the days when I could see a house without gauging how its weaknesses might be exploited are long gone. Now every house has the potential to be Chloe's house again.

* * *

By the time we got there, all the summer promise had been lifted from the sky and a fine rain had accreted on the wind-screen. My father parked up right outside the gate, on the gravel of the side road. It was hard to tell if anyone was home—bamboo blinds were rolled down in the porch and the curtains were still drawn in the bay window. But my father took another view on this.

'How exactly are you going to play it?' QC asked him, in the calm after the engine noise. 'What if she's not there?'

'She's there,' my father said.

'How d'you know that?'

'The curtains are all shut. She only opens them if she goes out.' He yanked the door lever. 'And, anyway, you're staying in the car. You wanted to play families? Fine. You're the babysit-ter.' He got out before QC could muster a reply.

We watched him take a slow spin on the asphalt, his eyes scanning the house. He stood by the bonnet while he tucked his shirt-tail into his cords. 'What the fuck's he up to?' said QC to me, under his breath. I didn't like the look of it, either. There was a slant to my father's gait, a restlessness about him. He kept rub-bing the sores on his knuckles. I heard him say, 'Christ, I need a proper smoke,' and saw him spitting drily at the ground. After a moment, he came around my side of the car and opened the boot. QC kneeled up on the seat to get a view of him; I did the same. My father started rummaging around inside the bin liners.

'What are you looking for back there?' QC said.

'My jacket,' he answered. 'If that's all right.'

He continued pulling clothes from the bin liner, casting them aside. The boot began to clot with crumpled jeans and shirts and jumpers.

QC pressed him: 'What d'you need a jacket for? It's barely raining.'

My father carried on. There was a set of painting overalls at the bottom of the bag, and he considered them for half a second before dropping them on the pile. 'Shit, where is it?'

'There's two jackets right there,' said QC, pointing.

'That's not the one I need. I want the one *she* gave me.'

'Oh.' QC turned to glance up at the house, as though the walls were listening. 'Why?'

'She wanted it back.'

'But you're gonna wear it?'

'Yep.'

'Why?'

'To make a point.' My father ripped the next bin bag apart and let the contents fall into his hands. 'Found it.' He gathered up the jacket—a limp denim thing with a sheepskin collar— flashing it at us briefly, as though it were a matador's cape. And, with that, he shut the boot. As he went back around the car, he stopped by my window and pulled on the jacket. My holdall was at his feet.

'Hey, that's *my* bag,' I said, instinctively.

QC leaned forward to call to him: 'What's the bag for, Fran?'

My father reached and opened my door. 'Changed my mind,' he said. 'It's best if you come with me.'

'Let me out, then,' said QC.

'Not you. *Him.*' My father hooked his hand under my armpit and tugged upwards. 'Take off that seatbelt. Hurry up. I want Chloe to meet you.'

I unclipped it.

But QC took my elbow, and started pulling down as I tried to get out. 'Hang on, hang on, I don't think—' he said.

'Just sit tight,' my father told him. 'This won't take long, I promise. I'll drop you both home straight after.' And QC must've heard the evenness of his tone and trusted it, because he let me go.

My father stooped to collect my bag, then I felt his hand move to the centre of my back. Prodding at my spine, he guided me towards the gate. My legs obliged him. I undid the latch and went into the front garden. The porch step was crested with dandelions. 'Go on, press the bell,' he told me. So I pushed the button and it rang out a sharp buzz, almost industrial. For a time, it seemed that nobody was going to answer, and my father's patience was short. He strode forwards and held the button down. That's when I saw the bulk of something nestled in the rear pocket of his cords.

I could go on claiming that I had no inkling what this object in his pocket was before he brought it out and used it. But I knew—I had to know. Maybe I only saw the shape of it under the corduroy, but I understood where it had come from. He'd swiped it from a bucket in the boot.

* * *

Chloe took a while to unbolt the door. It was long past noon, and she gave off the shuffling, fragile quality of someone who'd only just awoken from a night of heavy drinking. Her dark hair was lustreless and limply knotted. She was wearing dungarees and a white vest, one strap hanging at her hip. Her feet were bare, and she had a beaded ankle bracelet, rainbow-coloured. The drizzly daylight seemed to affect her whole constitution—she withered in the face of it. Her response to seeing us on her porch step was a disbelieving sort of laughter: a breathy *Ho, ho, ho.* 'No way. No way on earth,' she said, a coarseness to her voice. 'You just don't listen, do you, Francis?'

But he was not deterred. He pulled me closer. My head fit in the hollow of his armpit. 'A polite hello would've been nice,' he said. 'I mean, seeing how we've travelled all this way to see you. Well, not *you* exactly, but you get my drift. We've definitely travelled a long way.'

She turned her eyes to me, brow tensing, but said nothing.

'You needn't look at him like that,' my father told her. 'He's not done anything wrong.'

At this point, she seemed to recognise that the exchange was veering in an unforeseen direction. I could tell she was perturbed, if not yet frightened. Her leaning arm moved to the deadbolt. She retreated a pace, saying: 'Look, just leave me alone, okay. I've said everything I want to say to you.'

'Well, no. I think you owe my son here an apology.'

'Who?'

He ruffled my hair. 'His name is Daniel, by the way. But you knew that already.'

She didn't acknowledge me.

'Look, if you don't go away, I'll have to—'

'What? Come on, it's Dan that wants to talk to you, not me,' my father said, getting nearer. 'He's confused about what's been happening. So much disruption and waiting around. See, we couldn't get on set today. Nor yesterday for that matter. You know, after all the promises I made him. So I was thinking you'd explain to him why that might be.'

The silence was cut only by the birds.

Chloe wiped her mouth and glanced back into the house. I noticed how thin she was compared to Karen and my mother, especially: the caps of her shoulders jutted from her vest like hard-boiled egg-tops, her breastbone was a dish. She was trying to think of something to say to me. Then I suppose it dawned on her—she must've decided that my presence was somehow benign, even protective. She must've thought I was indemnity. Looking down at me, at last, she said, 'I don't know what to tell you, Daniel. Your father made some very bad decisions.'

'Okay,' I said.

'No. *Not* okay,' he said, shunting me forwards. 'Not okay at all. Can we come in and talk to you?'

'Sorry,' she said, 'I'm not letting you in,' and she tried to shut the door on us. But my father had prepared for this: he threw my bag into the threshold, jamming the door, and before she could remove it, he said: 'At least let him use your toilet.'

'No, Dad, I'm all right,' I said.

'Shush. Chloe doesn't mind.'

She mused on it a moment, narrow-eyed. '*Then* what?' she said. 'Then you'll leave?'

'Yeah. Absolutely.'

Without peering down, she drew my bag in with her foot, into the hallway. 'You're not getting this back until you're out of here,' she said. 'I'll go up and chuck it out the window.'

'Don't get shirty. I wanted you to look him in the eye, that's all,' my father told her. 'You've done that now, so I feel better. I think I've made my point.' He stood there, scratching his stubble. 'Oh, and here. I brought you this, too. You said you wanted it.' Off came the denim jacket. He gave it the politest of throws, and she caught it, one-handed.

She said, 'I never lent it to you in the first place.'

'That's right, you didn't. I'm just not very good at letting go of things. You know how it is.' He waited. 'So, can we use your loo, or what?'

'*He* can.' She nodded at me. 'You're staying right there.'

'Off you go then, Danno.'

I didn't move.

'Don't get stage fright on me now,' he said.

I started walking.

'He's been really upset,' my father told her. 'Maybe you can tell. Look at his eyes. He's cried the whole way here.'

She had no reply.

If I hadn't drunk two cups of tea at breakfast, I might've been able to resist for longer, but Chloe started beckoning me towards her like a landed aircraft, so I did what I thought was best. She kept her eyes locked on my father as she hinged the door back. 'It's straight down the hallway, past the kitchen, to your left,' she said. 'Don't touch anything.'

There was not a single light on in the house, just a permeating brightness from the kitchen. Music was playing inside. Trumpets squealing to a syncopated dance beat—jazz, but not. The woodchip in the hall was painted over, dolphin blue. Whoever did the decorating in that house was not my father—every wall was patchy, badly finished. The kitchen sink was full of dishes; the window gave a view of plastic lawn chairs toppled in high grass. A giant pan was cooling on the stove. Imagine walking right in off the street, into a stranger's home—that was how it was, and that was how it felt.

In her downstairs toilet, she had hung an old dressing-room mirror; it was edged with bulbs that did not work. And there were pictures of her everywhere in crooked Perspex frames, in which she postured happily with other women—friends, I assumed—at weddings, in sunny foreign resorts, on snowy pistes. I studied them while my bladder emptied, looking for my father's face. He wasn't pictured. Maybe, I thought. Maybe things are fine now. Maybe he'll take me home.

I washed my hands and dried them on her damp orange towel. On the way out, it occurred to me that Chloe would have a telephone—I hadn't seen one in the hallway, but perhaps I'd missed it in the kitchen.

I found it mounted on the wall next to the fridge. It had one of those long wires, stretched so much the plastic coils were slack. I dialled my house and waited. The gentle dance loops were still pulsing in the living room, a saxophone filling the blanks. When I heard my mother's formal voice, the buoyancy went out of me: '*Hello, you've reached the answerphone of Kathleen Jarrett. If you leave your name and number, I'll get back to you. Here comes the beep. Thanks a lot!*'

How many times had I lain on the carpet of our lounge with the television on while she sat behind me, checking her messages? How many times had I listened to those clumsy little orations people left for her and giggled at them? But, when the time came to record a message of my own, I became so self-aware, so concerned about the right way to phrase it that I rambled like a child reporting back the plot of some new film he'd seen.

I told her not to worry, I was fine. I told her I was still in Leeds—did she know a friend of Dad's named Chloe? We were at her house. I didn't know where it was exactly, but we'd passed the cricket stadium to get there. I told her that we never made it on set, as promised. I told her about the pub in Rothwell. I told her that I didn't know exactly why we couldn't get on set, but it had something to do with Chloe. I played the whole thing down. I told her that I thought we might be coming home soon. I told her I would ring her when I had the chance, but didn't really know when that would be yet. I told her that I wanted to spend the rest of summer with her in Little Missenden. I told her that I wanted to see Grandpa. I told her that I missed her and I loved her, and hung up when I sensed that the machine was going to cut me off.

The next thing, I was standing in another person's kitchen. Speaking to the answerphone had transported me away. I'd been picturing my own house, the worn arm of the sofa where my mother perched to replay messages, and now I was alone again. The rhythms on the stereo had mellowed into snare-drum patter. I went out along the hallway. Chloe was not there. In fact, the door was hanging open where Chloe should've been: I could see all the way across the street. The house opposite had bedsheets for curtains, hung on plastic washing lines. 'Dad,' I called. 'Where are you?' And I checked the living room on my way past. But there was no sign of them, only a grey couch covered in blankets and a record sleeve left on the cabinet: *Boulevard*, St. Germain. 'Hello?' I called. 'Where is everyone?' My holdall was half on the threshold, half on the porch step. It seemed lighter when I picked it up. I remember hoping they'd gone off without me—feeling the relief of it like medication. So I walked out to the garden thinking there would be no Volvo waiting on the gravel. But I saw the bonnet's rusty blue, and all the blood went heavy in my legs.

Something had changed. I knew it.

QC was in the driver's seat, hands on the wheel, stiff-armed. Coming through the gate, I caught his eye and got nothing back—not a blink, not a crease, not a sideways glance. Glazed is not the right word for how he looked. It was as though he'd been suspended in formaldehyde.

Passing the windscreen, I could see my father in the back-seat with Chloe. They were packed in close to one another—weirdly so, I thought. As I opened the door to get in, I got a fuller sight of them. She was sitting upright, leaned into the crook of his left arm. Her lips were so pursed they were translucent, and she was breathing only through her nostrils—fast little puffs and gasps. I believe that she was trembling. His right arm was strained across his stomach so his fist could reach the shallow in between her hip and ribs. 'And you claimed you didn't need to go,' he said to me. 'How much of that tea did you drink, anyway?'

I didn't know what to say.

'Well, don't just stand there, Danno. Get in.'

'My bag,' I said. 'It's—'

'Stuff it in the footwell. There's tons of room.'

I did as I was told and put my seatbelt on. QC was already buckled up. After I settled next to him, he finally moved to look at me. His whole face was an apology. 'Where now?' he said to my father.

'That's up to Daniel.'

Chloe's breathing was not getting any slower.

'Are you okay?' I asked her, twisting round.

My father flinched, tugging her backwards. 'She's never been better. Have you, Chloe?' When she didn't respond, he tugged her again. 'Have you?'

And in one broken note, she said: 'No.'

QC turned on the engine.

'Take it slow,' my father said. 'or you know what happens.'

The car rolled back, crunching the gravel chips. We were facing the long steep slope of the road. 'So, it's up to you, Daniel,' said QC. 'Tell me where to drive, we'll go there.'

I didn't understand.

I couldn't think of anywhere.

'Home,' I said. It came out with a question mark.

QC glared at the rear-view. 'You hear that?'

'Yeah, I heard him,' said my father. I had never known his voice to sound so hollow before that moment. His pretence of goodness had diminished. I had the outermost of him and nothing more.

'So? What's the plan? What do I do here?' said QC.

'We're not going home yet. Ask him again. Oi, Danno—' my father kicked the back of my seat. 'Danno.' He kicked it again and I turned. He had the Stanley knife this time, raised up in his fist like a Drifter he'd bought for me and wanted to unwrap. 'You see this? You see what I've been forced into?' Chloe spluttered, trying to angle her cheekbone away from the blade. He dropped the knife back to her side. 'I was thinking we'd drive north for a bit. See a bit of greenery,' he said. 'How's that sound to everyone? Good?'

I was already crying. '*Dad*,' I said. '*Dad*. What are you *doing*?'

But all he had to say to me was: 'Get the atlas out then, son. Go on. Sit back and show QC how well you navigate.'

Of course, stories told at knifepoint are unreliable, and I would be misguided to recount the words she was coerced into saying that afternoon without first stating that I know how much she censored them—for his benefit, and for mine. Except the feeling grew in me, the further we drove, the more he compelled her to speak, that Chloe was telling me a version of events she knew I'd sieve the truth from, maybe not right away, but in the future. She was banking on it, I suspect. And that's why it's important to relay the things she told me in the car—to make it clear how shrewd she was, how brave. I want you to know everything.

For a while, we drove without conversation, just the abject noise of my father's whistling, and my telling QC when to turn, which exit to take. We were headed towards the Pennines. 'Somewhere up there. Anywhere, *I* don't care,' were my father's instructions. Chloe's stuttered breaths went on until we found our way to the A660—I had my finger on the vein of it, but didn't know at what point I was expected to stop tracing the route. Outside, there were rows of houses with nice hanging baskets, drystone walls, and bus shelters, corner shops, opticians, squat yellow boxes of grit for the roads: civilised things, decent things. Inside, was my father and his Stanley knife.

We got as far as ilkley before QC piped up. I suppose he couldn't stop himself. 'Can I ask you something, Francis?' he said.

My father cleared his throat, as though awaking from a nap. 'I think you just did.'

'Look, the least you can do is tell us what you're hoping to get out of this.'

'I don't really know yet.'

'You don't know yet,' QC said. 'That's great. That's fucking great.'

'Proof, I suppose. That'd be a start, wouldn't it?'

'Of what exactly?'

'Of the fact that I've been royally fucked over by the universe.'

'Is that all? Jesus Christ, mate. Join the club.'

'You haven't got a clue what I'm talking about.'

'Oh, I'm sure I don't.'

'No, you don't. They don't teach you it at fancy schools like yours.'

'I got kicked out of mine, but okay.'

'Yeah, mate, you had it rough.'

'It wasn't all plain sailing, trust me. And what d'you call *this*, by the way—a picnic?'

I knew this sort of goading would only make my father twice as determined. I hoped that QC would shut up again.

'I think you need to do this girl a favour and stay out of it,' my father said. 'I'm not sitting here to have my head examined. Especially not by you.'

QC went quiet.

I tried to make a plea of my own. 'Dad, you need to tell us why you're doing this.'

'That's pretty clear, I think,' he said.

'But this isn't like you.' I didn't believe it even as I spoke it.

'I don't know if you're right about that, son.'

Chloe made a tooth-sucking sound, as though he'd pressed the blade a little closer.

'I don't understand it,' I said. 'Any of it.'

'I know you don't. That's part of the reason I'm doing it, Dan.' And I heard the drag of his elbow against the backseat as he hauled her in. I turned to check on them. Her chin was squeezed in his left hand. He was puckering her cheeks like a kid with a doll, and she was trying not to resist. 'Tell him,' he said to her. 'Tell him what you did to me.'

'She can't speak if you're holding her face like that,' said QC, eyeing the mirror.

'No one's talking to you, Barnie.'

'Then let her go.'

'Are you *trying* to make me hurt her? Shut the fuck up.'

QC went quiet again.

I was still craning my head back to look at them. His hand slid down to her shoulder, and she exhaled with relief, or disgust, or both. 'Turn round,' he said to me, 'you've got a map to read. And, anyway, I want you to listen, not gawp at her. This is the most important conversation you'll ever have, believe me, so just follow orders.'

I was afraid to do anything else.

'Go on,' he urged her. 'Don't leave out the bit where you completely fuck me over.'

After a moment, she said, 'Okay, okay. I . . .' and broke off. Her voice had dried up, and so had her lips. 'I don't know— what you want me—to say.'

'Start with how we know each other. The rest follows from there.'

'I can tell him that,' said QC.

'I told you to shut up.'

'I mean it.'

'I want him to hear it from *her*, idiot. Just drive the fucking car.'

She managed to collect her thoughts enough to speak, despite it all. I was amazed by her. There was something of my mother's attitude in Chloe, a deep-lying toughness. It's doubtful

that they'd ever have been friends, the two of them, but still—
put them in a room without my father, they might well have
found some other common ground. I like to imagine these conversations sometimes. I prefer to dream up words she did not
speak than think of those my father forced into her mouth.

* * *

HIM: Tell him what you do on the show. Go on. That's a
      good place to start.

HER: Make-up.

ME: Dad, please. This isn't right.

HIM: Don't undersell yourself, Chlo. You're an artist.

HER: Assistant.

HIM: She's an Assistant Make-up *Artist*. Tell him whose
      make-up you do.

HER: Everyone's.

HIM: Come on, don't be coy about it.

HER: Maxine's.

HIM: She does Maxine Laidlaw's make-up. Well, she helps.
      You do her scars and everything, don't you, Chlo?

HER: Yes. And her eyes.

HIM: What about her hands?

HER: And her hands.

HIM: What d'you think of that, Dan?

ME: It's nice.

HIM: Nice? You can do better than that.

ME: It's cool.

HIM: It *is* cool. Now—tell him how we met. Who pursued
      who?

HER: On set. I saw you.

HIM: Where?

HER: In the queue. For coffee.

HIM: And who else was in that queue?

HER: A few others.

HIM: You don't remember?

HER: No.

HIM: Declan Palmer.

HER: Right. Declan Palmer.

QC: He's one of the producers.

ME: I know.

HIM: How d'you know?

ME: I watch the credits every week.

HIM: See, Chloe. See how much of a fan my lad is? You thought I was exaggerating.

ME: Dad, you've got to stop this. You're hurting her.

HIM: Hush. We're just getting warmed up. Tell him what you said in the coffee queue.

HER: I said I liked the way you worked.

HIM: And what did you mean by that exactly?

HER: They'd asked you to build something quickly and you did it.

HIM: What was it? The thing I had to build?

HER: I don't remember.

HIM: Course you do.

HER: [. . .]

QC: A step in Cryck's compartment. So Maxine could reach higher.

HIM: Shut up. She's telling it.

HER: I was waiting for them to re-light the scene.

HIM: There you go. That wasn't so hard, was it?

HER: I thought you were nice. I liked how confident you were.

HIM: It's all coming out now. That's it.

HER: You were handsome.

HIM: All right, I'm not looking for compliments. Just stick to the facts. Who pursued who?

HER: I pursued you.

HIM: That's important to remember, Daniel. *She* pursued *me.*

QC: Yeah, skip to the bit where you cheat on her.

HIM: I swear to god, if you don't shut it—

ME: Please. Stop. Keep out of it.

QC: [. . .]

HIM: How long did we go out for after that, Chloe?

HER: Five months.

HIM: No. Try that again.

HER: We were never really—

HIM: What's that? Say it louder so everyone can hear you.

HER: We were never really together.

HIM: Repeat that again.

HER: We were never together.

HIM: Wow. So quick to admit it all of a sudden.

HER: I thought we were, but we weren't.

HIM: You wanted something serious.

HER: Yeah.

HIM: But I didn't. I was quite straightforward about that, wasn't I?

HER: Yeah.

HIM: So, what were we to each other, then—friends?

HER: I don't know.

HIM: Of course you do.

HER: I can't say in front of—

HIM: Dan's a big lad. And he likes to know things, don't you, Dan?

ME: [. . .]

HER: We slept with each other.

HIM: How often?

HER: A lot.

HIM: Eight times. Is that a lot?

HER: Yes.

HIM: Is it really, though?

HER: No.

HIM: You wouldn't say we were an item, then?

HER: [. . .]

HIM: Don't make me repeat myself.

HER: No. Like I said. We weren't together.

HIM: You didn't have any right to think of it that way, did you? We weren't a couple.

HER: No.

HIM: So then explain to Daniel why we couldn't get on set today.

HER: [. . .]

QC: You've missed about ten steps there, Fran.

HIM: Shut up.

HER: That was down to Palmer, not me. I—

HIM: Turn round, son. Keep your eyes on the map.

HER: I made a mistake.

HIM: You made a mistake. What kind of mistake?

HER: I accused you of something.

HIM: How were you sure I did the thing that you accused me of?

HER: I don't know. Because I saw you.

HIM: Did you come and speak to me about what you saw? Or did you just blab right to Palmer?

HER: No, no. I—

HIM: What?

HER: I didn't speak to you. I just told Palmer.

HIM: Yeah, you're pretty good at telling tales.

HER: [. . .]

HIM: So don't be all vague about it. Explain to Daniel what I'm supposed to've done. If you were so positive about it all, you can stand by it now, can't you? Paint him a picture.

HER: [. . .]

HIM: I'll fill in the background, if you like . . . It was back in March. At the studios.

HER: Yeah. Right. It was back in March. Re-shoots.

HIM: QC—this would be the perfect time for you to talk.

QC: What is it you want me to say?

HIM: That you were there with me.

QC: I was there with him.

HIM: Why?

QC: Does it matter?

HIM: Yeah. Quite a bit.

QC: Someone'd lost the main section of the house. We had to build a new one, make it a chimney breast and put in a fireplace. But the designers couldn't find the fireplace—period details and all that. So it took all day, waiting there while they sent out a couple of assistants to get one that looked the same and the scenic painters fixed the colour. We were sitting on our arses. Huge waste of money. Pissed off Declan Palmer no end. These things happen in TV.

HIM: And you were with me the whole day?

QC: Well, I didn't follow you into the bogs or anything. But yeah. I'd say we were together for most of it. I think you dropped me home that night.

HIM: Which is funny, when you think about it. 'Cause that's not what Chloe said now, is it?

QC: No, mate.

HIM: Tell him what you said to Declan Palmer, then. Go on, let him hear it.

HER: I saw you with someone else.

HIM: Come on, *who*? Don't leave out the important bit.

HER: Eve Quilter.

HIM: Eve-Quilter-from-the-show, Eve Quilter?

HER: Yes.

HIM: Which one is Eve Quilter again, Daniel?

ME: Charlotte.

HIM: Sweet, isn't it? He knows the whole cast, even the minor characters.

HER: Right. It's sweet. It's sweet.

HIM: And if you had to guess, Dan, how old would you say Charlotte is in the show?

ME: I don't know. She's the oldest sister.

HIM: Have a guess.

ME: I think she's meant to be sixteen.

HIM: Yeah. I'd say that's about right. Sixteen. So, go on then, Chloe. Here's your chance. Tell him what you said I did to her. Tell him what you think you saw.

HER: Oh, I *know* what I saw.

HIM: You don't know fucking anything.

HER: You had your hands up her skirt.

HIM: Complete and total lies, Dan, by the way.

HER: Eve was on the counter in her dressing room. Her legs were wrapped around him.

HIM: She's making all this up. And let me tell you how I—

HER: His hands were right up her skirt. He was kissing her neck, right here.

HIM: Sit still. I didn't say you could move.

HER: [. . .]

HIM: See, Dan, this is what she reckons. You tell me if this makes any sense to you, and if it does, we'll stop the car and go our separate ways . . . She reckons that I went into Eve Quilter's dressing room—you know, just wandered in there on my own and put my hands on her in broad fucking daylight, with all the fucking cast and crew waiting round on set with fuck all else to do. And she reckons that she saw all this when she was passing through the busy fucking corridor, because not only was I standing in a young girl's dressing room with my hands right in her knickers, I was also so completely fucking stupid that I did it with the door wide open so every jumped-up make-up lady who knew my face could walk right by and see me. That's what she reckons.

HER: I didn't say knickers. I said skirt.

HIM: Same fucking difference.

HER: You'd know.

HIM: Shut the fuck up now. It's time for him to talk. You tell me if that makes any sense to you, Dan.

ME: [. . .]

HIM: Daniel?

HER: [. . .]

ME: Did you really not do it, Dad?

HIM: I can't believe you even have to ask me that. Of course I fucking didn't. That girl is sixteen years old. *Sixteen.* I might be many things, son, but I'm not that. I'm not that. What kind of person would that make me, eh? If you never accept another word I tell you in my life, then please hear this: I didn't go anywhere *near* Eve Quilter. Not once. Ever. And that's the simple truth of it. Tell him, QC. Did you see me go anywhere near the dressing rooms that day?

QC: Yeah. I did, actually.

HIM: That's right. You did. Because we went *together.* And was I in Eve Quilter's room?

QC: Yeah. But she wasn't in it.

HIM: Right. Because she wasn't even on the set that day.

QC: No, I've got to say, as I remember it, she wasn't.

HIM: So why the fuck did we need to go to her dressing room, then, if she wasn't there?

QC: She told you to meet her there. Chloe did, I mean.

HIM: Ah. *Chloe told me to meet her there.* And you came with me. Let's just underline that part. Make sure Daniel knows. Tell him again. Tell him why.

QC: You thought that she was getting a bit obsessed with you. Clingy. You were trying to let her down gently. I was there for—I don't know. Moral support, I suppose.

HIM: Sounds right to me. Does that sound right to you, Chloe?

HER: Yes.

HIM: And what happened in the dressing room, QC? Did you see me do anything?

QC: No. Nothing really happened. She tried to make you go out for drinks with her, after we'd wrapped, and you said no.

HIM: There you are, see. Where was Eve Quilter while all this was happening?

QC: No idea.

HIM: Now, tell Dan what you told me the day before. The day before I met you in her dressing room.

HER: [. . .]

HIM: You know what I'm talking about.

HER: [. . .]

QC: Don't, Fran. Come on. She's admitted it. Stop now. There's no need for—

HER: I said that I loved you.

HIM: More than anyone. That was what you said. More than anyone.

HER: Yeah. More than anyone.

HIM: You said you couldn't concentrate on anything.

HER: Yeah. I said that.

HIM: And what did I say back?

HER: [. . .]

QC: Come on, Fran, you've put her through enough.

HIM: It's not half what she's put me through. Not even close.

ME: Dad, she's terrified. Please.

HIM: I just wanted you to hear it from the horse's mouth, son. Tell him.

HER: [. . .]

HIM: Tell him or I'll slice your fucking ear off.

HER: You said you didn't.

HIM: Didn't what?

HER: Love me.

HIM: I said you meant nothing to me, actually.

HER: Yes. You said that.

HIM: I told you to get over it, didn't I? Move on in a hurry, I said.

HER: Yes.

HIM: And what did you do?

HER: I'd already moved on.

HIM: Nope.

QC: Fran, Fran, come on. Put it down.

HIM: You went to Palmer with your made-up little story, didn't you?

HER: Yes.

HIM: To get me in trouble.

HER: Yes, yes. Yes.

HIM: Your word against mine.

HER: Yes.

HIM: And whose side did they take?

HER: Mine.

HIM: Yours.

QC: Leave her, mate. Come on.

HIM: You see how easy that was? I should've done this months ago. We should've done this right in front of Palmer. Stop moving. Stop fucking moving.

ME: I get it, Dad. She got you sacked. You didn't do anything. I get it.

HIM: Yeah, you're fucking right I didn't. So you can blame her for all this. Not me.

ME: You should've just told me this before.

HIM: I couldn't.

HER: [. . .]

HIM: Apologise, then. Apologise to my son.

HER: I'm sorry.

HIM: I'm sorry *who*?

HER: I'm sorry, Daniel.

HIM: For ruining everything.
HER: For ruining everything.
ME: It's all right.
HIM: What?
ME: You should've just told me.
HIM: [. . .]
HER: [. . .]
QC: So now what, Fran?
HIM: You're going to pull over.
QC: Here?
HIM: No. When I say.
QC: You're going to let her go, right?
HIM: [. . .]
QC: Fran, you're letting her go, right?
HIM: Shut up. I'm thinking.

The road became undulant. A few miles back, we'd started to encounter farm vehicles: tractors towing rotary tillers that engulfed the lane and caused regular traffic to bunch and overtake on half-blind bends. The land was mostly fields studded with sheep. Now and then, a clutch of woodland would rise and disappear, and we went by so many grey-brick cottages and farmsteads that I stopped noticing them by the time we reached Giggleswick. There was a train station there, set back from the main road, out of view. I watched the rusty steel tracks emerge from the hedgerows as we passed, and followed them in parallel, over the lush green pasture till they vanished. There was a bright blue 'P' sign on the verge just after that, and my father said: 'Here. Park up when you get to it.' A few hundred yards and there it was: a sliver of track the length of a swimming pool, the width of a supermarket aisle. QC slowed and steered us into it. For a while, we sat there in the empty lay-by, waiting. Cars flashed by on the road, heading south, heading north. 'We'll leave her here,' my father said. 'She can walk to that station we passed.'

'Okay. That's good,' QC replied. 'That's good.'

'I don't have any money,' said Chloe.

'What?'

'For the train.'

'I'll give her some,' said QC. He started fishing in his jeans. My father stopped him. 'Hands on the wheel.'

'I'm just getting my wallet.'

'She doesn't need your money.'

I blurted out: 'I've got some. In my shoe. A twenty.'

My father snorted. 'Oh yeah, since *when*?'

It was what my mother called my Safety Money, a little insurance just in case I ever found myself in need. A year ago, she'd written on it—CURRENCY OF AOXI—to prevent me wasting it on sweets, and would inspect it every now and then to make sure I still had it. I never had the heart to tell her that the only currency on Aoxi was a handshake. She liked parental tricks like this, ways of preparing me for serious things without me even realising. I think that she'd expected I would use it in a lesser crisis—something to pay for a taxi to my grandparents' house after school if she got stuck with overtime at work. Instead, it would supply the train fare for a woman my own father had been holding hostage. 'Go on then,' he instructed, 'let's see it.' I had to dig it out from underneath my insole. When I held the note out for my father, he squinted at it for the longest moment: 'Toss it down there on the mat,' he said, so I dropped it into the footwell. 'A lot of money for a lad to keep secret.' His eyes were still on it. 'We could've used that before now.' He let the twenty sit there. 'All right, I've changed my mind. QC, you're getting out.'

'What?'

'You're going to leave the key in the ignition and get out the car. Then you're going to walk all the way out there into that field, as far as that tree—you see it?' QC stooped to gaze out my window. Where the rutted seam of the land met the low-hanging clouds was an oak tree walled off with grey stones. 'As soon as you reach it, I'll let her out, too. She's going to walk over and meet you. You're going to buy her a train ticket to wherever. I don't care what either of you do after that, but if you don't do exactly what I just said, then it's you who's responsible for the wounds I give her. Do you read me?'

QC sniffed. He sent a resigned look in my direction. 'Yeah. What about him?'

'He'll be going home.'

I tried to gauge the distance to the oak tree. It was something like five hundred yards, about the same as the path from my front garden to the nave of St. John's church. I could walk it in six minutes, run it in just under three.

'I think you've made it pretty hard for me to trust you, Fran, I've got to tell you,' QC said. 'How do I know you'll keep your end of this?'

'You'll think of something.'

QC jounced his legs by the pedals. 'No, sorry, you're going to have to give me more than that. I want the knife. I'm not leaving them in here with you and that knife.'

'I'll give it to Daniel. You get out of the car, I hand it over, you walk to the tree. Fair?'

QC deliberated. 'All right.'

Chloe writhed in my father's grip. Her nostrils jetted sharply.

'*Shshhh* now.' He kissed the top of her head as she bucked against him. '*Shshhh*, settle down.' If I hadn't known better, it might have seemed like tenderness. 'Let's not take all day about it, eh?'

QC unclipped his seatbelt and it spooled back over his shoulder. He patted the steering column, glanced down at me, said: 'Good luck with the rest of your life, lad.' And he opened the door, stepped onto the bitumen. He stood at the back window and banged on the glass.

My father lifted the knife from Chloe's side, his other arm constricting her. 'Dan, hold out your hand,' he said, and I watched the Stanley knife approach the platform of my palm in near slow motion. It was hot, hefty, sweat-soaked. Afterwards, he spread his empty fingers on the window, and QC started walking.

I watched him step over the low steel barrier, into the thistles and brambles. He stood on the barbed wire sheep-fence and hurdled it awkwardly. Then, with a quick look back, he trudged through the tall grass into the open field.

'He forgot about the child lock,' my father said. 'You'll have to let us out.'

The bodily smells of the car were more present than ever: sour perspiration and breath. By now, I thought, my mother might have heard my message. I wondered if she would glean the trouble I was in from the dejection in my voice; I always thought that she could read my thoughts before they had occurred to me, so perhaps she was already on her way with the police.

Now his grasp on Chloe's neck was double-tight and she was whimpering. Such grave and quiet sounds. I wanted to comfort her, but I didn't know how. I studied the knife blade for traces of blood: there was nothing. I turned to her and saw there was tiredness in the white space of her eyes, a corruption of the colour. 'Whatever you did, it doesn't matter,' I said to her. I was trying to raise her spirits, but it only made her cry. 'You'll be okay.'

'It shouldn't have come to this,' my father said.

I didn't acknowledge him.

QC was still striding for the tree.

'The real shame is, I loved that job. I was fucking good at it,' my father said. 'I was fucking good at what I did. Palmer didn't even bother talking to me, just cut me out the picture. *He's not even on a contract? Simple then, he's gone.* I bet he never even spoke to Eve about it, either. If he'd just come to one of us and said, *I've heard this rumour going round*—we could've told him what was really going on. I could've got back to doing what I'm best at. But who's going to believe someone like me over *her*? Look at her. Look how she acts. Butter wouldn't fucking melt, would it? Pretty little make-up lady minding her own business. Well, no, actually. Actually, she's not like that, she's petty and vindictive and she's—' He stopped. I don't know if he caught a reflection of himself in the window and saw what I saw—the absurdity of a man keeping a woman in the backseat of a car against her will and trying to moralise about vindictiveness—but I was simply glad that he had finished. He started on a different tack: 'You're right, it probably doesn't even matter. I should've just told you about it and faced up to things. But the more punches you take for no reason, the harder it is to feel nothing. They all add up. Like I said before, it's like the universe is up against you, it doesn't want you to have the things you want. Not ever. It's hard to keep dusting yourself down and keeping on. I'm not an idiot— I know all this was my own doing. But I've done it now, and I wish I could say it hasn't made me feel a whole lot better.'

'I don't believe you, Dad.'

'Yeah, well,' he said. 'You and the rest of the world, eh?'

That acid taste was in my throat again.

My father peered out at the green of the fields. 'I can't let her go now—you know that, don't you? If I let her out this car, she'll just go straight to the police and blab on me again, and they'll come after me. And that'll be it. Well, I'm not taking any more punches. I'm not going to be like Pascoe, banged up just 'cause no one ever thought to stop and ask him *Did you do it?* I'm going to see this out. All the way. I have to.'

'You need to let her go, Dad,' I said.

'No. I can't.'

'For me. You can.'

He shook his head. 'Sorry. Can't do it.'

Chloe was biting down on her lip just to keep herself from speaking. There must've been so much she wanted to let out, but she was no more than twenty of QC's strides away from safety. Nineteen, eighteen. Her jaw was shaking.

I tried again: 'But, Dad, this isn't right. It isn't right. Even if you didn't do the thing she said, all *this*, what you're doing now, it's *wrong*.'

Twelve, eleven, ten.

My father cleared the phlegm out of his throat and gulped it. 'Soon as QC makes it to that tree, you're going to get out and follow him. Do you understand what I'm telling you? Just step out and go. No looking back.' Maybe he was not dispassionate—somewhere in the blankest recess of his mind, there might've been regret and pain and sadness, but he'd partitioned it so well that there was just one tiny indication of it: a twitch of his face, as if trying to shift a pair of glasses higher up his nose.

'I'm not leaving you alone with her.'

'Then you'd better learn to drive in the next thirty seconds,' he said, 'because I'm not letting her out.'

When QC reached the tree, he turned and started semaphoring. He was just a distant shape flapping its arms, indiscernible to anyone who wasn't looking for it. I wished he could've kept walking forever, in a permanent state between the here and there.

'We see you, Barnaby, we see you,' said my father. 'All that money on his education, not a bit of sense.'

There was nothing else that I could think to do: I leaned and pressed the horn. A hidden crowd of birds darted up from the grass. I hit the hazard warning lights.

'What the fuck are you doing?' he shouted at me.

QC stopped waving.

The drone backwashed in my ears.

'Turn those fucking lights off.'

Cars approached but didn't slow down.

QC began to walk back, getting bigger by the tiniest of increments.

I felt a thump against the back of my seat. Another.

Chloe's feet.

He was choking her. She was bent up in the V of his arm, his right hand smothering her mouth, pinching her nose. 'What's it to be, Dan?' he called to me. I was still blaring the horn. She was thrashing her feet. 'You can run away or you can try and stop me, but you can't do neither.'

I got out of the car. 'QC!' I shouted into the fields. 'QC!'

He was running but gaining no ground.

The back of my father's head was cushioned on the window-pane before me. I opened the door and he almost dropped out. He hinged himself upright, Chloe still kicking.

'Let go of her,' I said, chewing on the words.

The indifference he showed for me then was so familiar, the same attitude that overcame him when my mother used to beat his chest in arguments. He had seen the knife in my hand but was sure it wouldn't trouble him. His brow hardly tightened.

'QC!' I called again.

Chloe's skin was getting bluer.

'I don't think he'll make it, Dan. Running's never been his strength.' He squeezed. Hard. Chloe sagged like paper under water. 'Come to think of it, he's always been a little—'

I slashed him—I had no choice. High on the meat of his arm. Every bit of it felt shameful: the easy way the blade took to his flesh and split it open, how the gash oozed straight away (not like nicking yourself with the point of a compass), how he didn't so much recoil in pain as judder with it. The sheer speed with which blood permeates a woollen sweater is something you don't expect.

'Ow, jesus *fuck*!' my father was seething. 'Dan, you fucking —you cut me!' As he clutched at the wound, Chloe gasped and filled her lungs. She managed to scramble halfway out the door, her hands touching the kerb right by my feet. But he heaved her back in, shrugging the sting off. His blood smeared and flicked all over her. She reached for the other door, found the handle, but it wouldn't open. The car was bouncing.

'QC!' I called. He was still too far away.

Cars went by in a flurry. They didn't heed the hazard lights or the rocking suspension. If I'd been thinking straight, I would've tried to flag them down.

My father kneeled with her shoulders pinned beneath him. But she was strong, and buffeted him enough so that he swayed. She bit the inside of his thigh. Her teeth must really have sunk in, because his howl of agony was strident. It enraged him. He forced her down again. His hands surrounded her windpipe. Blood was leaching from his sweater, dribbling from the cuff.

I tried to jump on his back. I didn't want to cut him any more, so I struck him with the butt end of the knife. Somewhere in the middle of his spine. He threw his head back to resist me. I struck him again, and nothing.

'QC!' He was getting closer. 'Hurry!'

I dug the knife handle into my father's gaping wound. He winced and toppled forwards, reaching down into the footwell. My fingers came back printed with his blood. Chloe thrashed and kicked. He pushed up with his knees and shoved me out onto the kerb again. There was some object in his fist. And he glanced at me, panting, tightening his grasp. As she tried to sit up, he lunged at Chloe and hammered her three times with it. The first impact made a thud, the next was like a splintering, the last was like the dropping of wet clothes. I saw her feet convulse and then go still.

I must've screamed something, I don't know what. My legs collapsed underneath me. I sat there, jellified.

My father slid out of the car with the object still in his grip. When he tossed it back onto the seat, I realised what it was: the ashtray he had pilfered at the Little Chef.

He went to smack the hazard lights off, sweat-drenched and bleeding. Any traffic that there was fizzed past us—other people's problems are invisible at sixty miles an hour.

QC was coming; he was at the barbed wire fence. I could hear him shouting, 'Fran! Fran! Fran!' I should've run to him, but instead I hurled the knife into the verge, as far as I could make it go; it landed somewhere in the thistles. My father snickered. He walked to the boot and raised the lid. I heard him digging for the bucket. He was so cold and nonchalant. The boot clunked shut, and he came round with another Stanley knife and a roll of duct tape. He'd removed his sweater and bandaged his wound with an old black shirt. I sicked up acid mucus down my front, then. He took me by the collar, reeled me in. Our backs were pointed to the road, our movements hidden by the car's dumb bulk.

What was it that I felt while this was happening? A fear greater than words have the capacity to evoke. But more than that, I think: depravity. An evil that belonged to me by association.

QC came rushing through the brambles and skipped over the barrier. 'Fran, leave him alone. What the fuck have you done?' He saw the way my father was holding me and stopped. He was doubled over from the sprint, hacking the spit up from his lungs. 'What the fuck are you doing?'

My father just glided up the knife blade. He scraped it softly on the cartilage of my ear. 'Here's what you're going to do now,' he said, and we shook with the velocity of traffic.

SIDE THREE

CAMPION GHYLL

D o you want to know the moment it occurred? It was just after the fuel gauge needle sank into the red as we were coasting on the A590 and I said: 'We're going to run out of petrol soon. Shouldn't we stop?' My father didn't answer, so I nudged forward to get his attention, rocking against the binding of the duct tape till it gave a little at my waist. It happened then—I saw the apathy in his expression. A look of sheer estrangement—from me, from himself, from reason. I glimpsed capabilities I never knew he had. He was no more than a brute and he seemed comfortable with the fact. And when I heard him say, so cool and undisturbed, 'You mean diesel. We've got plenty,' I understood that he had finished being my father, as he had finished being a husband, and a stage carpenter, and a painter-decorator, and a council maintenance worker, and a labourer, and a tomato picker, and a student, and a sheep farmer, and a son. He was so serene it chilled me, as though this was his resting state, his factory setting, to be unburdened of the people he was meant to care about, each slow grown relationship, each held aspiration, each great and small responsibility that makes a life worth living.

* * *

We were in the South Lakes, heading west, driving through a landscape I had never seen before: crags of ash-grey rock bearded with conifers and liverwort, roughed-up grazing land

and hay meadows, swathes of rhododendrons, disused stables, ruined barns, and distant bonfires—a pastoral inbetweenland. I had watched the dales of Yorkshire flow into the pale brown hills of Lancashire and reconcile with Cumbria. At Newby Bridge, he'd snatched the road atlas and dumped it in the quiet space behind us. 'I know the way from here, don't worry.' Now the carriageway had merged into an overpass above a shining river. I couldn't stop shivering. 'I told you—*cut that out*,' he said. 'You're being pathetic.' There was a petrol station in the next little town (Greenodd—how could I forget a name like that?), but the forecourt was occupied (two Land Rovers and a motorbike—why do I recall this, too?) and my father just kept going. The road ascended. The tree cover thickened and the light became spasmodic, strobing on the tarmac. We emerged onto a skinny level track. There was a row of weathered cottages and a farmyard where small gangs of Friesian cows were lounging on the grass. The sky was vast and barren, the hills divided by a hundred walls and thorn dykes. And, under different circumstances, all of this could have been breathtaking. But no amount of scenery could distract from what he'd done.

Behind me, across the footwells, Chloe's body lay under a mound of dustsheets.

QC was unconscious on the backseat, gagged, his wrists and ankles bound.

It seemed like hours ago that we had left the lay-by, but the clock said different—every second in that car was torturous. My father was not racked or haunted—he did not even look shaken. Nothing he had done appeared to shock him. Nothing he'd resolved to do was weighing on him, either. He was in a strange repose. But less than fifty minutes ago, he'd forced another man, supposedly his friend, to get into the backseat of his car and tape up his own ankles. He'd shut the door on him and locked it. He'd steered his own son to the boot at knifepoint, made him fetch an unlabelled plastic bottle and douse a rag with acrid chemicals. He'd compelled the man to scroll his window down partway so he could take the soaking rag and stuff it in his mouth and wind the tape around it—*no, tighter than that, tighter.* He'd waited for the man to retch until the vomit dribbled from his nose. He'd watched the man grow woozy and pass out. He'd pushed the boy into the passenger seat, coiled the duct tape round his midriff, one loop at a time, until the roll was spent. He'd stepped out to unhitch the off-cuts from the roof rack, ditched them on the kerb. He'd used the bungees as restraints, tying the man's hands behind his back and coupling them to his feet. He'd shoved the woman's body off the seat, into the footwells, covered it with heavy cotton dustsheets specked with white emulsion, snicks of wallpaper, tiny lumps of filler. He'd got into the driver's seat and fastened the boy's seatbelt, of all things. He'd turned on the engine and said, 'Don't make me gag you, too. Not a word, you hear? Not one fucking word.'

* * *

Someday you might see the Lake District. I've only been there once, but I suppose that I could claim it's in my blood. There's a special part of it that I remember from the trip, a sight that I'm ashamed to say I reminisce upon as though it were a postcard sent to me by someone else—I try hard to envision it sometimes without the context. It is the point when, leaving the brooks and streams of Ulpha, coming up the scrawny pass through Santon Bridge, the trees suddenly disperse, and up ahead there is a congress of high fells—among them, Scafell Pike, the highest of the English mountains, whose face is textured with as many shades of green as there are permutations of the stars. These rocks reflect a certain quality of light I've not experienced in any other part of the world. That someone could be born into a place like this and end up with a heart so dark is inconceivable. The sense it gave me, when I first saw it framed inside my father's dirty windscreen, was the closest I have ever felt to God. It was only as we drew nearer, winding up the stone-walled road and coursing through the heaths, that I realised this mountain land wasn't just part of him but part of *me*—and we had not lived up to it. We were changing it with every last rotation of our tyres, making it complicit.

* * *

My father drove by memory. His eyes were heavy and faltering. His limp hands made the slackest gestures with the wheel to steer us beyond Nether Wasdale, where one side of the wooded track began to lean into a gully. The dark mass of the fells loomed beyond the trunks of pines. Until the road dipped suddenly to give a clearer view, I didn't notice that the gully was in fact a lake. The water was glaucous, troubled. It spread along the fellside where the scree inclined at an acute angle, an accumulation of black rocks and moss that looked ready to spill. We drove along the bank, almost at the level of the shore. Strange grey sheep were roving in the craggy pasture on my side. They were Herdwicks like my grandfather reared, but I didn't know it yet. There was no cause for pleasant conversation about the local fauna. For once, my father didn't take the opportunity to regale me with the things he knew—I suppose he must've recognised that everything he knew was insignificant.

I stared at him, his profile, the whiskery bulb of his Adam's apple. He was pungent with white spirit. His skin had an unctuous sheen, a rawness at the creases. If he felt that he was home, he didn't show it. There was not even a glimmer of remorse about his attitude. Wherever we were going, whatever happened next, the only map was in his head.

He seemed to want the quiet and it was not hard to uphold. There's a state of mind in which all sound gets muted. Maybe you've experienced it by now. I don't mean meditation. I mean a despondency that overrides even the noise of your own thumping heart. QC had begun to moan on the back seat as we were leaving Grizebeck, kicking his heels up, writhing, but I had tuned this out. Because I couldn't help him. I couldn't even lift my arms. So I had to blank the noise.

Further on, we started to encounter people. A few hikers on the fringes of the road moved aside to let us pass. I hoped that they might catch a glimpse of me and see the cargo we were hauling, but their backs were turned to us as we sped by.

The track rolled on, hugging the shoreline, the fuel tank getting emptier, the fells getting taller, reigning over us. A cyclist struggled up the slope as we were coming down it, his face haggard and purple, and I held my breath as he wheeled by the window where QC's legs were hinged up, wobbling, and I thought this was my best and only chance. I screamed until my lungs ached.

The cyclist looked, but I suppose he was too tired to gauge what he was seeing, and we were going at such speed I'll bet he couldn't gather his own thoughts in time. My father smacked the button on the stereo, blasting the end of a song. The dissonance of Cocteau Twins at such a volume was so jarring, the cyclist swerved away. He must've thought it was a joke—silly kids misbehaving, showing off—so he kept on pedalling.

My father let the music play until the lake vanished from sight. He slowed for a cattle grid, shut off the stereo. 'Do that again and you're going in the back with them,' he said. The last word was emphatic, meant to frighten me.

The fells were bunched together now in the windscreen. A line of static cars revealed themselves—makeshift parking spaces on the gravelled fringes of the road—but no people. Here, we took a right, crossed an iron bridge over the rocky river. The surface of the track became less certain. The lake spread out again before us, lapping at the scree. My father arced around it, down a lane almost too slender for the car— it was less a road than two long tyre-tracks worn into the grass.

A farmhouse sat low on the hillside ahead, its chimney funnelling smoke. There were several buildings in fact: a set of crooked outhouses with rusting farm machinery, a hay barn stuffed with yellow bales. We approached them at a crawl. The car bounced over ruts of hardened mud impressed by tractors. I heard QC bucking on the backseat, his nostrils wheezing.

My father turned into the driveway, where a carved wooden plate on the gatepost said: CAMPION GHYLL. 'Stop whinging back there, Barnie. No one's listening,' he said. The farmhouse faced uphill. He pulled up close enough so that whoever was inside could see us walking up the yard from the rear windows, and far enough that no one could survey the human mess on our backseat.

I found the voice to ask, 'Where are we?' It was confirmation I was seeking, not an explanation.

He gave me an agitated look. 'Don't ask questions you already know the answers to. It makes you sound needy.' He yanked the key from the ignition and stepped out the car. There was an instant smell of fresh air spoiled with sheep shit. Dogs were yapping nearby.

He came around and opened my door. 'Keep still while I do this,' he said, and leaned in with his Stanley knife to slice the duct tape from the seat. I felt some warmth returning to my arms. 'You're going to do exactly what I tell you to in there.' He ripped off the tape and let it hang. 'Kick up any sort of fuss and all you're going to do is make it easier for me. I don't need a good excuse to hurt your granddad. Do you get what I'm telling you?'

I nodded.

'And no crying either. You're as bad as he is.' He motioned at QC.

I wiped my eyes and sucked my lip.

As I got out, an old black dog came limping at us, growling, baying, followed by another. My father made a hoop with his fingers, took it in his mouth and whistled—a wavering toot like a birdcall. The dogs paused, queried him a moment, then sat down. 'See,' he said. 'Just act like them and you'll be fine.'

* * *

We didn't use the front door. He led me through a gate to a back porch where every window pane was gunged. The rubber doormat looked as though it could have lain there for a century. Lifting its corner with his shoe, he exposed an imprint in the dirt where a key should've been. He tried the door anyway, found it locked. 'All right, let's think about this,' he said. The dogs had followed us. They were sniffing at my heels. When I patted them, he told me not to. 'I wouldn't, if I were you.' Then something occurred to him. He wagged his finger at the thought. He stood on the crumbling timber of the window ledge at one side of the porch and reached up to dislodge a roof tile. Jumping down, he had the key. It slotted neatly in the lock and turned. He pushed the door back. 'After you,' he said, thumbing at the space.

It was clear no one had used this back entrance in a while. I had to trample over strung-up stacks of newspapers, cardboard boxes full of empty cans, dismantled fishing rods and wicker baskets. The door on the other side was open to a dingy kitchen. The range was radiating heat, but the only light came from the corridor. A loaf of bread lay part-sliced on the table with a jar of pickle and a hard nub of white cheese. There was a portable radio, a half-finished crossword, and an unguarded tin of Wintermans. The dogs were scratching at the porch door, whimpering.

My father came in behind me, sizing up the room. 'Stay

there. And I mean *there*.' He brushed past, striding to a pantry at the far end of the kitchen. A lightbulb stuttered on when he pulled the cord. He collected a bag of dry dog food and a big metal dish from the floor, which he filled with pale kibble till it ran off the sides. From a high shelf, he took a bottle of old Navy rum and poured most of it into the dish; the dry pellets soaked it up, grew plump with the booze. His shoes crunched on spilled kibble as he went back through the kitchen, passing me without a word, and out again through the porch door, marshalling the dogs with one outstretched leg, laying the food down. 'What d'you think of the place?' he said, coming by me again. When I didn't reply, he said, 'Yeah, it used to look a lot nicer. Cleaner, anyway.' He went back to the pantry, shoved a wooden step-stool out from underneath a shelf, and stood on it. Fumbling at a panel in the ceiling, he unhitched it, slid it back. He stretched an arm into the recess, rummaging inside the way someone might explore behind the cushions of a couch: eyes down, groping blind. As soon as his hand found what he wanted, his expression changed. Not a grin as such; more like a tweak of satisfaction. I thought I heard the rattle of loose screws. But when his arm came out it held a long leather pouch with carry-handles, like the case for a snooker cue.

'Who the fuck are you, you little toerag?' said a gruff voice behind me. 'Get out of here before I fucking skin you.'

I turned to find an old man in a tattered, baggy jumper. The wool around the collar had a scattering of bread crust. He was coming at me, wielding the crook of his walking stick. 'There's no money here, if that's what you're after. What've you done to my dogs? Where are they?'

'Nothing. I'm just—I'm—' I staggered back against the worktop.

'Whose kid are you, Aiden's?'

'No.'

'You are. I've seen you before. You're one of the step-kids. You can fuck right off.'

My father stepped out of the pantry. 'Leave him alone, you old fool. That's your grandson. That's Daniel.' He was carrying the cue-case over his left shoulder as though it were a spade he was about to dig with. A canvas satchel hung from his right. 'Where are you keeping the cartridges now? There were only two left in the bag. You must've done for a few grouse since I was here last.'

'*Fran*. I had a feeling it was you.'

'Oh yeah?'

'Yeah, I had that nasty taste come over me when I was eating.'

'Ah, it's so nice to be home,' said my father.

The old man seemed to lose his balance. He lowered the stick and leaned on it with both hands. 'Waste of breath telling you not to come back again, isn't it? Might as well be talking to the ewes.'

'Yeah, but this time I've brought Daniel as a sweetener.' My father laid his palm on my head and gave my hair a gentle tug. 'An awful lot of Hardesty in him, don't you reckon? He's got your scowl, look. Poor lad. We're hoping he'll grow out of it.' He set the cue case down on the worktop. 'Say hello to him, then. Give him that warm embrace you're famous for.'

The old man peered at me, not unkindly. 'Hello, son.' Then he said to my father: 'You're in above your head with something, I can tell.'

'Nothing gets by you, Dad.'

'Your arm's in pieces, and you're lugging that thing like you're planning on using it—doesn't take much adding up.' My granddad turned to me, his face tormented. This was the first time I had ever seen him outside of a photograph—at home, there was a single faded print of him in a water-stained album, posed by a fireplace with my father as a teen. I had been told at least three times that he was dead, so his heavy presence in the kitchen was unsettling and miraculous to me. I didn't even know his name—Paul Martin Hardesty—until I came to read it in the paper. He was a frail and weather-beaten version of the man in the picture, hardly recognisable. His skin was dry and dulled-out at the cheekbones, and the patchy brownness of his neck was baked on by a life of summers on the fells. 'What's he up to?' the old man asked me. There was a murmur in his tone not dissimilar to my father's.

'We were meant to be in Leeds,' I said.

My father glared at me. 'Oi. What did I tell you in the car?'

'What's in Leeds?' said the old man.

'Nothing you'd be interested in.'

'I asked *him*.'

'Well, did you hear me say it was all right to start a conversation? No. Sit down.' My father heaved a chair from the table, pushed it across the tiles. 'You're looking a bit wobbly these days, Dad. Your knees finally give up on you, or what?'

The old man just stared at him. 'What are you doing here, Francis?'

'Either sit or be sat. Up to you.'

After a moment's thought, my granddad sank into the chair: a slow, indignant movement.

My father went about unzipping the lower end of the cue-case. 'You didn't answer my question about the cartridges.' From the guts of the case, he slid out a shotgun as shined and brown as a horse chestnut. I gasped at the sight of it, but my granddad hardly blinked. 'You do keep all your things in decent order, Dad, I'll give you that,' my father said. He admired the dark varnished stock before snapping it open. The barrel swung down. He took two orange shells out of the satchel and slotted them into the gun with the indifference of a man loading new batteries into a remote, then hasped it shut. Aiming it right at the old man's forehead, he said: 'Cartridges?'

'You're going to have to shoot me for them.'

'If that's how you want it.'

The old man lifted his chin. He extended his arm across the table, grasped for the Wintermans tin and the lighter. The way he flipped back the lid with his thumbnail was so familiar. The way he lit the cigarillo with his hand cupped round the lighter flame was not. A cloud engulfed his head, the fragrance like a coffee pot boiled dry. 'Want one?' he said.

My father lowered the gun, placed the butt against his toes. He snatched the whole tin and pocketed it, then took the cigarillo from my granddad's smoking mouth and dragged on it. 'Cartridges,' he said again, snorting out fumes.

The old man regarded me with an obvious pity. 'At some point,' he said, edging forward on his chair, 'at some point I hope you and me get a chance to do this properly. So much of life is better when your dad's not in the room, in my experience.'

'Can't disagree with you on that one,' my father said. 'Are you going to tell me where they are, or am I going to have to turn this place completely upside down?' He lifted the gun again, trapping the cigarillo in his scabby knuckles. The muzzle was almost touching the old man's cheek.

I sputtered, snivelled.

'Are you going to tell me why you need them?' said my granddad. 'Two isn't enough, I take it.'

My father dragged serenely.

'That's always been the problem with you, Fran. You think every plan you make's a good 'un.'

'Is that right?'

'Seems to me.'

'I'm not sure you've picked the right time to lecture me, Dad. You comfortable in that chair?'

'Not really.'

'Well, I'd start making friends with it, if I were you.'

The old man sneered, canted his head at me. 'What happened to his arm?'

'He sliced me open with a Stanley knife,' my father said.

'That true?'

I shrugged.

'Must've had your reasons,' said the old man. 'You don't seem like a lad who goes round cutting people up. I've known a few bad seeds and you're not even half of one.'

'Cartridges,' my father said. 'Now.'

'He never even told us you were born, you know. Nine years, it took. Nine years. He let his mother die without her knowing. What sort of man does that?'

My father paced towards him with the shotgun. 'I want those fucking cartridges.'

At this, Paul Hardesty grew irritated. 'How'd you know I haven't run out of them?'

'You wouldn't let that happen.'

'I'm seventy-four years old. I've forgotten more than you remember.'

'Yeah, right.' My father must've noticed some brief shift of the old man's eyes, then, because he lowered the gun and turned to scan the space above the corner kitchen cabinet. 'What? Up there, are they? That's a new spot.' Gripping the shotgun, he knelt on the counter, swiped his arm over the top edge of the cabinet. 'Christ, it's lucky those Germans never caught up with you, eh? You'd spill the national secrets in ten minutes, you would.' I heard him shake the box. 'That'll do it.' He sprang down, upturned the brass-capped cartridges onto the worktop, and stuffed fistfuls of them into the satchel.

'You've blood all down your trousers,' my granddad said to me.

I bowed to check them. 'Yeah, I know.'

'So does he.'

'I know.'

'All right, enough,' my father said. He came and grabbed me underneath the armpit. 'We're going to ring your mother.' My heart brightened at the thought. He nudged the old man. 'You still got that ancient thing in the hall?'

'No, I put in a cordless.'

'Look at you, embracing the twentieth century.'

'Well, I can't be going up and down the stairs for it all day. Ground like this'll do for you eventually—you wouldn't under-stand what that feels like.'

My father jerked me forwards. 'Go and fetch it.'

I hurried off, then stopped. 'Where from?'

'It's in the front room, son,' said Paul Hardesty. 'On the set-tee.'

'What's a settee?'

'Are you joking?'

'He's a pure-bred, this one.' My father laughed, and called to me: 'The sofa.' He hopped up on the worktop, knocking his heels against the cabinets below. A grey maggot of ash dropped to the tiles. And bringing the sights of the gun up to his eye, squaring it at my granddad, he said in the weightiest tone: 'No insubordination, Dan. Remember?'

I went through the hallway, not sure of my direction. There was a lamp on the sideboard with scorch stains on its shade and, on the peeling olive wallpaper above it, a gallery of small oil paintings of the lake and fells in basic wood frames; in among them was a picture of a black-haired woman in square glasses I assumed to be my grandmother. She had the same bony nose as my father. I reached a junction of two doorways and went right, into the living room. A modest fire was burn-ing in the hearth. The little TV set had shaky reception and the sound was turned down low: I could make out a uniformed vet on the screen, examining a hedgehog on a padded table. I col-lected the phone from the arm of the couch and went back.

My father didn't move from his perch on the worktop, just

held out his hand for the phone and told me to sit. He had prepared a chair for me beside his father. As he dialled, beeping
the numbers, my granddad whispered to me: 'How much trouble is he in?'

I flashed him all ten of my fingers and he nodded gravely.

'It's ringing,' my father said, setting the phone to his ear.
The gun was pointed somewhere in the hinterland between my
granddad's chair and mine. 'Kath, it's Fran, just checking in.
Before you go off on one, I—oh, then who am I speaking to?'
He pursed his lips, listening. 'Look, you need to calm down for
me, Janet, okay? You've not even heard what I've got
to . . . Hang on, is this really necessary?' He was laughing now.
'I mean your attitude. Relax. You don't even know me, love.
I'm just trying to reach Kathleen and you're giving me an ear-
ful. Where is she?'

She was in pursuit of us—I was cheered by this thought
until I remembered the message I had left for her. My father
would not be pleased to learn about it.

'No, just tell her I rang, Janet, okay? I'm not calling that
thing, it'll cost me the earth. I'll phone back again later . . . No,
we're not staying here long. There's no point. She's getting
worked up over nothing, as usual.' There was a backlash in the
receiver; he pulled it away from his ear, letting her shriek at
him. Then: 'What are you on about? Daniel's here with me.
We're having a great old time.' His eyes narrowed at the reaction. 'Did he now? I see. Well. That was a while ago. D'you
have kids, Janet? It's hard to keep up with their moods sometimes . . .' He threw the stub of his Wintermans into the sink
and it fizzled in the washing-up bowl. 'Tell you what, let's put
him on now. You can ask him yourself.' His arm was flapping,
beckoning me.

'Just do what he says,' Paul Hardesty instructed. 'Don't
worry.'

I walked over. My father dropped from the worktop and

kneeled to hold the phone against my left ear, his dry lips itching my right. The bitter cigarillo smell was fresh on him. Janet
had a tendency to talk to children as though all of them were
deaf or slow-witted—she was a close but fairly new friend of
my mother's who would turn up at our house sometimes
around six thirty with red wine and a video, her hairstyle as
intricate as sugarwork, her bassy laugh resounding—and this
only made it simpler for my father to direct our conversation.
Extemporising lies over the telephone was his speciality. He
murmured the script into my ear, and I followed it.

* * *

HIM: Say hello.
ME: Hello.
HER: *Dan? Are you all right?*
HIM: You're fine. Why?
ME: I'm fine. Why?
HER: *'Cause your mum's been frantic. She'll be so relieved you
      called.*
HIM: Tell her not to worry, you're all right.
ME: Don't worry. I'm all right.
HER: *There's a bit of a delay, Dan. Is your dad on the line with
      us?*
ME: No. It's just me.
HIM: Good lad.
HER· *Promise he's not telling you what to say?*
ME: Yeah, I promise.
HER: *Swear on your mum's life?*
ME: [. . .]
HIM: She doesn't like you doing that.
ME: She doesn't like me doing that. It's tempting fate.
HER: *Okay, you're right. But I need to know he's not there
      telling you what to say to me.*

ME: He's not, Janet, I promise. Why would he do that?

HER: *You don't sound very convincing.*

HIM: Tell her you're fine but you're bored of me. You want to come home.

ME: To be honest, I'm fine and everything, but I'm getting kind of bored. My dad can be a pain sometimes. I want to go home.

HER: *Oh yeah? How come?*

HIM: He only cares about himself.

ME: He only cares about himself.

HER: *Yeah, he's as selfish as it gets. We know.*

HIM: His idea of fun is playing pool. You hate pool.

ME: His idea of fun is playing pool. I hate pool.

HER: *Where've you been playing that, Dan? In a pub or something?*

HIM: Yeah.

ME: Yeah. More like a hotel, really. It wasn't so bad. They had a good jukebox.

HIM: Good. Keep that up.

HER: *Where?*

HIM: In the countryside somewhere. You're not sure.

ME: Somewhere in the countryside.

HER: *Where in the countryside, Dan? I'm going to tell your mum to pick you up.*

HIM: You're not there right now.

ME: We're not there any more. That was yesterday.

HER: *So where are you now? Where are you calling from?*

HIM: Somebody's house.

ME: Someone's house.

HER: *Oh yeah? Whose?*

HIM: Maxine Laidlaw's.

ME: [. . .]

HIM: Go on.

ME: Maxine's. You know—from the show?

HIM: Good.

HER: *What you doing there?*

HIM: She invited the whole crew. To watch the first cut and celebrate.

ME: She invited us to watch the first cut. And celebrate.

HER: *The what?*

HIM: The first cut of episode one.

ME: The first cut of episode one.

HER: *Oh . . . And where is this house then exactly? I'll let your mum know.*

HIM: Berwick-upon-Tweed.

ME: Berrick on Tweed.

HER: *Blimey. Isn't that in Scotland?*

HIM: You think so.

ME: I think so, yeah.

HER: *Have you got the address, then?*

HIM: No. Why?

ME: No. Why?

HER: *'Cause you seemed a bit funny, Dan, earlier. Your mum played me the message.*

ME: Oh that. I was just . . . bored.

HER: *She's been tearing her hair out since she heard it. She's on her way to Leeds now, took your grandpa's mobile just in case. Let me give you the number so you can ring her. Don't worry about the cost, we'll sort that out.*

HIM: Take the number.

ME: Okay. Let me get a pen.

HIM: Nice.

HER: *[. . .]*

ME: Okay. Ready.

HER: *It's 0958 . . . 256 . . . 457. Got it?*

ME: Yeah. 0958 256 457.

HER: *I've been sitting here manning the house phone in case you rang, but now you've got the mobile, you can phone her whenever. Are you really telling me—God's honest truth—that you're fine?*

HIM: Tell her yes.

ME: Yeah. I'm fine, Janet, honest. I'm ready to come home, though.

HER: *Okay. Will you ring your mum on that number then?*

ME: Yeah. I promise.

HER: *All right, good. Put your dad back on. I want to tell him something.*

ME: Okay. Bye, Janet.

HER: *Bye, Dan.*

HIM: [. . .]

HER: *[. . .]*

HIM: Hi, Janet. You satisfied? . . . Nah, don't bother . . . Well, I could, but why? . . . Yeah, but why does she need me to? . . . In about ten minutes, I reckon . . . Just a pub. And it was only for a night . . . Thing is, I'm needed down in Wales tomorrow for a shoot. Last minute thing, so I'll have to bring Dan with me now, unless she wants to come and get him . . . Well, I don't know, we could meet somewhere halfway. How long ago did she set off? I'll get her on the mobile, if I have to. What's the number?

First he gave me duties to perform. I was instructed to bring the medical kit from the cupboard underneath the stairs—it was a lidded wooden box with a hand-painted red cross, stocked with enough curative material to treat a decade's worth of minor farming injuries. Some of the crusted tubes of ointment must've been in there since before my father was born. He rinsed his arm under the kitchen tap, keeping the shotgun trained on my granddad, and then he made me pad the wound with paper towels, apply a glob of Germolene and two square cotton dressings, and wind a bandage tight around it, sticking it all down with a giant fabric plaster. I had to retrieve one of the old man's cardigans from the airing cupboard and help my father put it on, an arm at a time, while he held the gun. Next, he told me to unplug the telephone connectors from the wall sockets, and I did—I went into the living room, where the TV was playing adverts about accidents at work, removed the wires from the base unit of the cordless phone and, just to demonstrate my full commitment to his orders, detached its warm 9v adaptor from the mains. When I came back in, he was pushing the gun's muzzle to my granddad's temple. The old man was tilting at the sharpest angle to relieve the pressure. My father threw me a roll of parcel tape and commanded me to coil it round the old man's ankles and the chair legs twenty times, one foot then the other. I looked at my granddad in apology, and he gave a long blink in acceptance. Once his feet were secured, the old man put both hands behind his back and I was ordered to tape them at the wrists.

'Don't argue with him, Daniel,' my granddad said. 'I've always known this sort of thing was coming. His mother used to tell me different, but I knew.' For this, he got the steel nose of the gun stabbed hard against his ear. 'Ach, fuck you, Francis, you ungrateful rotten bastard. I take it back. She never even talked about you once.' For this, he got the butt-end to the face. The old man's head sagged.

'Don't, Dad! Leave him! Please!' I said.

When my granddad straightened up, his mouth was a cluster of split flesh, bilging with blood. He spat out a tooth. My father kicked at it until it skittered to the baseboard. 'Nothing ever came out of that head worth a penny,' he said. He brought the gun down, one hand on the forestock, and went to plunder the cupboards. Underneath the sink, he found a blue plastic washing line. 'That's about right,' he said. It was still in its packaging, still bore the price tag. He bit off the wrapper and tied the blue line round his father and the chair, tugging it so tight it dug into the old man's chest and arms the way that butcher's twine indents a joint of beef. 'Whose hay is that out in the barn?' my father said. 'Don't tell me you mowed and baled all that on your own.'

Paul Hardesty glared at him. 'It's mine for now,' he said.

'So nobody's coming to shift it?'

'Not that they've told me.'

'You sold the sheep but not the hay?'

'Didn't have the hay when I sold the sheep.'

'Then why'd you mow it?'

'It needed mowing.' My granddad spat a clod of blood, wincing. He tried to straighten in the chair. 'If you think I'd let good hay spoil and go to waste, you're even more stupid than I took you for. It only adds more value to the farm now. You wouldn't believe the price I'm getting from these incomers. It's more than twice what—' The butt of the shotgun shattered his nose. He let out a guttural noise from his belly, an agonised roar.

'You never used to talk so much,' my father said. 'I liked you more that way.'

* * *

The dogs were curled up on the path when we came out. I had to step over them. He made me walk two yards ahead, directing me. The shotgun was back in its case and he carried it with both hands across his chest like gathered firewood. I could hear the zips tinkling against the leather as he strode. When we reached the drive, where the Volvo sat with its windows fogged up, he told me to stop. He scuffed a line into the gravel with his shoe. 'That's your mark. Stand there and don't move,' he said. 'I'm going to check on Barnaby.' I waited while he traipsed towards the car and peered in through the boot, his face right up to the glass, eyes blinkered by his hands. He went around to the driver's side and looked in through the back window for good measure. It seemed he was contented. He came marching back along the gravel. 'Follow me,' he said, going by. I didn't pursue him right away, so he turned and glowered at me. 'Come on.' And as I caught up with him, he gave me a soft little shove up the slope.

He guided me around two outbuildings—they were large stone sheds, empty but for scatterings of straw and sawdust, metal gates and hurdles with no livestock in them. The next building was more like a corrugated iron hangar, full of mechanised equipment: rusted shafts of metal, spiral blades, wheeled trailers, forked apparatus with curling tines. We walked beyond them, through an in-bye of tired grass that inclined up the fellside, towards a long stone wall fringed with pink-headed flowers. The earth was dry and solid underfoot but the dirt cleaved to my toecaps. 'Keep walking,' he instructed. 'We're going just up to that wall.'

By the time we got there, my calves were sore, burning. The wall was not much lower than my eye line. He made me sit down next to it, then did the same, placing the gun-case onto the grass and weeds. 'I wanted you to see this before we get out of here,' he said.

'Are you taking me home?' I said.

He shrugged off the question and my eagerness. 'Have a look at this, first.' He touched the face of a mossy grey stone in the wall, brushed it with his thumb. A daub of red paint, long-faded, was visible under the muck. The stones above and around it all had the same marking. I told him I didn't under-stand, and he said: 'That's becoming a catchphrase of yours.' I didn't know what this meant, either.

He leaned back against the wall and huffed out a breath. Out came the Wintermans tin from his jeans. He lit one and sat there drawing on it thoughtfully, the smoke trailing off in the breeze. 'When I was growing up here, your grandma liked to paint,' he said. 'It was just a hobby, nothing she thought she'd ever do full time or anything, but I used to like watching her. Everything she painted was outside her window, you see—she never had to go far for inspiration. Down to the lake or some beck, looking up at Scafell or Great Gable. This place was all she needed. She used to pick all these campions and fill up the house with them, but foxgloves were her favourites.' He sipped on his Wintermans, sighed at the landscape before us. 'Anyway, I've always felt like I never quite belonged round here, I don't know why. It's like some people say they're born into the wrong skin or whatever, or they're a man when they're really a woman, but for me, I don't know, I just felt like I was meant to be somewhere else. All the time. It used to bug me, this little voice in my ear the whole day. I tried to ignore it, get past it, but no. It wouldn't leave me alone. And everything your man in there asked me to do for him, I just wasn't very good at it. I always fucked it up, or fumbled it, broke it. Do you know what that feels like? I hope that you don't, I really do. 'Cause it's horrible. You get a what's-it-called, you know, a *thing* about it. Nothing you do's ever good enough. Nothing works out. I was useless with the sheep, couldn't gather them if my life depended on it. I was even bad at mucking them out. I put diesel in the elevator once and it exploded. It made me feel like a curse. I hated this place so much, and I'd go complaining to her all the time. And my mum, bless her heart, could only stand so much of me whining—I mean, after a while, she must've started to think I was complaining about *her*, what she did for me. But that wasn't it. I went to her one day to whinge about something the old man had said to me— this would've been around clipping time, when he was at his narkiest—I think he called me a waste of space, or something like that. You sort of forget the particular insults after a while. Now—' He held his finger poised, inviting me to wait for him to ash his cigarillo. 'Now, this time, my mum was out painting in the meadow here, and she doesn't say anything at first, just hands me this tube of red oil from her box, and I ask her what it's supposed to be for. So, d'you know what she tells me? She says, *See that wall up there? Your great-granddad built that wall, did you know that?* And I said that I knew, though I don't think I was sure about it. And she goes to me, *Here's what I want you to do, Fran, okay? Instead of running to me every time you get a thought in your head about not belonging here, or wanting to be somewhere else, I want you to go up and put a spot of red on one of those stones. It'll be like you're writing your name on it. And when it gets to the stage where you're coming back to me for another tube, well, then we'll have a serious conversation about it, and we'll see how you feel about that wall. Does that sound fair enough to you?* My father stubbed the Wintermans out on the sole of his shoe and flicked it away. 'So that's what

I did. I suppose she wanted me to feel connected to this place somehow, and that was just her way of doing it. I was marking my territory, I suppose. But d'you want to know how quickly I finished that tube?' He gestured to the entire wall. 'I painted every stone along here before it got to clipping time again. If you don't believe me, check.'

I got up, because I didn't trust a word he'd told me and wanted to be proven right. But there was no doubting what I saw when I inspected that wall. The face of each stone bore the same red disc of paint, almost washed out but perceptible. There were hundreds of them, thousands even. I must've walked half the length of the meadow before he whistled me back. When I turned, he had the gun-case over his shoulder. The sun was purpling on the crags beyond him, and he was just the same Fran Hardesty as ever. As I returned to him, he said: 'You believe me, then?'

'Yeah,' I answered. But I understood those paint marks were just more tricks of perspective, another thing that he'd appropriated for effect. Maybe he had lied so often to himself he couldn't tell the difference any longer.

My father started down the hill. 'Problem is, we never had that conversation like she promised, and I still don't feel connected to this farm or anything round here. But that's not the point. The point is that she *wanted me* to. It was important to her. It's never meant anything to my old man, though, what I want. Selling up without even asking—well, it doesn't hurt, 'cause I expected it, but it's like another lump of shit the universe has kicked at me, another thing I probably fucked up somewhere along the way. So there you are.' He cleared his throat. 'I've got nothing I can give you any more, son. That's it.'

'I don't care,' I said.

'Yeah. Well. I care.'

We passed back through the field in silence. I had not eaten since the dire English breakfast at the White Oak—I felt hungry and ashamed of it. He must've thought that I was walking crookedly down the hill and needed to relieve myself, because he called: 'Oi, you'd better make use of all this space while still you can. Go against that gate here. I'll wait.'

'I don't need to,' I said.

'Trust me,' he said.

I stared back at him.

'Go on. I'm not asking, I'm telling.'

He lurked behind me for what must've been five minutes, until a line of dry dirt fattened beneath my feet, steaming. 'See,' he said. 'There's always something in the tank. I knew it.'

We came around the back of the machine shed. One of the dogs was staggering on the path, rebounding from the flank of one outbuilding to another like a fly with half a wing. 'Hang on, we're going a different way now,' he said, when I went right.

We crossed the front yard of the house where the old man's clothes were airing on a whirligig and a congregation of old wellingtons sat upturned on a rack by the door. I could see the flicker of the TV in the living room. Around the side, across a gravel path, was the hay barn. My father urged me forwards, through the vast open entrance.

This is where I tell you something I have never let escape my mind before. There aren't many people who have heard my explanation of what happened at the farm that day: five or six police officers, three social workers, ten different psychiatrists, a close friend, and a partner I've kept near enough to broach my past with. They've all asked me the same question: Did I ever think that he was going to kill me there, too? I've grown used to saying no. I've always said that if he'd planned to do me harm, he would've done it earlier, in the lay-by where he ended Chloe. But I think I've only remained steadfast to this answer for so long because the police inspector seemed so satisfied when I uttered it the first time. There's never a good reason to expose more avenues of your mind to scrutiny than necessary.

But if you want the truth, I thought that he was going to kill me in that hay barn. I had a premonition of it. When he said, 'See that big conveyor belt on wheels? You're going to switch that on for me,' I saw that old hay elevator and thought it was my doom. I imagined he was going to send me up the slatted chute of it until I dropped and hit the concrete twenty feet below, then make me do it again and again until I couldn't get up any more. That a well-raised boy could conceive of such a thing at such an age is what has kept me from admitting it all these years. I hope you will appreciate exactly what I mean. Where does a forecast of violence like this come from if it isn't from some natural capacity I have within me to envision it, something intrinsic to my make-up? It's important that you contemplate this, when the time comes.

'Don't look at me that way, you've got it easy,' he said. 'Used to have to start it like a lawnmower. Now there's a proper motor on it.' He instructed me to carry the dusty lariat of cable to the mains and turn it on. Nothing happened. 'All right. Flick that green switch. And cover your ears.'

Every night, the hum and clatter of that old machine invades my sleep. Have you ever stood beside a generator on a building site and felt the tremor of it in your eardrums, that deep protracted rumble? Have you waited at a platform and listened to the scrape of train wheels as they brake upon the rails? It is both those sounds at once, forever. I often hear it faintly clamouring throughout the night. Chugga chugga *clank*. As though someone is still working that machine ahead of me, just out of view. In the kitchen, my granddad's head was hanging slack. There was a syrupy track of blood on the front of his jumper. 'This is where you get off, Dan. I've things to sort out on my own.' Chugga chugga *clank*. Chugga chugga *clank*. Fran Hardesty planted a strong hand upon my shoulder and steered me past the sink. 'There's a bucket in there you can use if you need. And plenty to eat on the shelves. There's even a few cans of Coke—drink them all at once, why not? No one'll know.' I was guided to the open pantry. Chugga chugga *clank*. Chugga chugga *clank*. 'Sit down there.' He shunted me onto a box of tinned tomatoes. Removed the step-stool. 'Back in a minute.' A pull of the cord and the light clicked off. He shut the door. 'Dad, where are you going?' I said 'Where are you going?' He clattered the key in the lock, and I heard the bright thump of it latching. Chugga chugga *clank*. I waited in the near-perfect dark.

'You'll be all right in there, lad . . . Keep your head down,' my granddad called to me, slurring.

'What about you?' I called back.

Chugga chugga *clank*.

'Don't you worry about me . . . I'm not afraid of him . . . I've seen a lot worse.'

I shouted for him, but he didn't answer. Then the blackness thickened as the key slid back inside the hole. The door creaked open. Chugga chugga *clank*. Chugga chugga *clank*. My father stood in the waning daylight with my holdall. He delivered it into my arms as though laying a wreath. 'You can switch the light back on, you know,' he said. 'The cord's right there, look.' Chugga chugga *clank*.

I held that bag like a friend. 'I thought you were taking me home.'

He stood there, nodding at the floor. 'You're better off here, son, believe me.' This was his petition right to the end: believe me, believe me, believe me, *believe me*. Chugga chugga *clank*. He sniffed. 'I wish I had more for you, Dan. I never meant all this to happen.' And he stepped away, locking me in. Through the hairline gap under the door, I watched the conformation of his feet dissolve to nothing. Chugga chugga *clank*. 'I was born in this kitchen.' Chugga chugga *clank*. 'You think

I don't know that?' Chugga chugga *clank*. 'Just something that crossed my mind.' 'Do it, then, if you're going to. What are you waiting for? Finish us off. Pretend I'm a dog, if it helps you.' Chugga chugga *clank*. Chugga chugga *clank*. Chugga chugga *clank*. Chugga chugga *clank*. 'Not as easy as you reckoned, uh? Typical.' 'Shut up. I'm thinking, that's all.' 'What's so funny?' Chugga chugga *clank*. Chugga chugga *clank*. 'What the fuck—?' Chugga chugga *clank*. 'I said, what the fuck are you laughing at?' Chugga chugga *clank*. 'Nothing. You're just . . . Oh, I don't know, Francis. It's a bit late for thinking.' Chugga chugga *clank*. 'You can't even do *this* right, can you?' Chugga chugga *clank*. 'Well, I tell you what. I'm done with thinking now. I'm done with listening as well.' Chugga chugga *clank*. Chugga chugga *clank*. 'Thanks for nothing, Dad. Thanks for absolutely nothing.' Chugga chugga *clank*. Chugga chugga *clank*. Chugga chugga *clank*. Chugga chugga *clank*. 'Open your mouth. I said *open your mouth*. Bite my fingers and I'll make it ten times worse for you.' Chugga chugga *clank* . . .

The locals had become accustomed to the din of the old man's elevator in the summer and were used to hearing backfire from his tractor's engine now and then. My granddad also had a reputation for impatience when it came to foxes roving on his in-byes—he'd been known to shoot the air to scram them on occasion. In fact, sudden cracks of shotgun fire were not unusual in farming country, where lambs sometimes went lame with scald or foot-rot and needed to be euthanised humanely: most farmers in Wasdale Head preferred the firearm method to the stunbolt or injection, and kept guns mostly for that reason. So the shots that killed my granddad and QC raised no alarm. They might as well have been two rocks cascading on the fellside.

If I was the only one who noticed them, it was because I had my ear pressed to the keyhole of the pantry door in expectation. When they came, they sounded far away—two brisk smacks without echoes, ten seconds apart, contained within the chugga chugga *clank* of the machine. I remember sinking to my knees after I heard them. A feeling of certainty coursed through me: he had done it. My guess was that he'd shot them both front on, through the forehead: first QC and then my granddad. This was as much as I could picture—the lead-up to the act. The fluttering strip lights, the thrust of the barrel in my father's hands, the kiss of the steel against their pleated brows, his finger on the trigger, but nothing else, nothing that came next. Because I had no precedent by which to imagine such brutality. I had boys' adventure novels. I had barely watched a film above a PG rating. I didn't know the mess a shotgun makes of the human skull at close range, how it explodes the planes of bone into so many uneven pieces—particles so small they'd have to tweeze them out of hay bales at the opposite end of the barn. I didn't know the blast was strong enough to send a man careering backwards in a chair five yards. Details like these would reach me afterwards, and cling.

* * *

Of course, I looked for ways, but the pantry was not easily escaped. It was roughly five feet square, with shelves on three sides starting at the level of my nose, running up to meet the render and the farmhouse beams. Below them, wholesale goods: drums of cooking oil, crates of wine, enormous paper bags of dog kibble and potatoes, cartons of orange juice, giant plastic bottles of blackcurrant cordial and malt vinegar, packets of salt and sugar, rice, lentils, barley, pasta, a vat of lard, boxes of tinned fruit and vegetables, nets of red onions. Sundries from the kitchen packed the space: aluminium foil and baking sheets, a tray of cutlery, food mixers, Tupperware, unbranded breakfast cereals, jars of pickled cucumbers and mayonnaise and piccalilli, stacks of plates and dishes, bowls, vases, and baskets. I tried to smash the doorknob with a can of skinned tomatoes, thinking it might improve my chances with the lock, but the tin buckled and punctured, trailing juice all over me. I jammed a fish knife, then a skewer, then a dessert spoon handle into the doorjamb and jimmied them for so long they left my hands welted and calloused, and I succeeded in displacing the bolt inside the latch by not one centimetre.

All attempts to reach the ceiling hatch were useless: my fingertips fell short of the panel by several feet, and when I tried to boost myself by standing on a shelf, it collapsed under my weight—I dropped and cracked my elbow on the tiles. (Later, in the hospital, a doctor would explain to me about the olecranon, the bony protrusion I had chipped, and it gave a brief distraction from the pain to hear him speak of it.) I spent what seemed like hours kicking at the door to see if I could weaken it, disturb it from its hinges, punch through the face of it, but made no progress. I resolved to keep on going but was too exhausted to continue. My frustration withered me. And it was when I leaned back against the crates and boxes to catch my breath that I realised the chugga chugga *clank* had finally stopped. There was no sound any more beyond the keyhole. I only heard the scratch of my own cheek against the wood, incidental noises from within my own body. He wasn't coming back for me—I understood that much—but I didn't know what he expected me to do. Wait to be discovered? Keep myself alive with canned produce and Coke? Pacify my quaking guts by defecating in a bucket—until when, exactly? It seemed as though the only option was to hunker down.

When I turned the light off, there was unremitting darkness, not even a faint glow from the moon beneath the door. For the first time in my life, I felt entirely alone—it wasn't just the kind of loneliness that I'd become attuned to as a boy, when Saturdays came around and I had no other prospects for companionship besides my mother and the sporty, rough-playing neighbourhood kids; this was a comprehensive separation from everyone and anything I loved. It was getting colder and colder in the room, and I was growing nauseated by my hunger. So I yanked the light back on, unzipped my holdall, rummaged for a sweatshirt and a cleaner pair of jeans. I pulled at the sleeve of something woollen, and Karen's walkman dropped out with it. The headphones were still attached but anchored deep within the chaos of the bag. I found the box of tapes right at the bottom, all four cassettes inside, out of sequence. And while I ate my way through a whole pack of stale cornflakes, one dry handful at a time, and washed it down with orange juice, I realised that Maxine Laidlaw's voice was my protection—she could help me through it. I tried to calculate how long the batteries would last, if I should ration my listening over time, or if I should listen in one clear stretch until they drained. The sugar satisfied my insides and upset them all at once. I would need the bucket soon. My elbow hurt. I didn't like the silence, didn't like the bright light or the dark, didn't like the cold, didn't want to think about my father, what he'd done, where he was going next. The tapes, the walkman, my World's Best Aeroplanes Top Trumps, a camera without film, three books from the Joe Durango series, and a collection of six moulded plastic war figurines that I'd collected through subscription to a partwork magazine named *Men of Glory*—these were my connections to the world, the life I wanted to get back to. I decided I would listen to one section of the story and then stop, preserve the batteries. But as soon as the headphones were on and I pushed play, I felt that I was in the company of friends and didn't want to leave them.

* * *

[. . .] A carpet of wild garlic had grown over the conducer site since they had been there last. Cryck had axed a path through all the scrub and hawthorn in the night, but it seemed that not one flower had been trodden on the way between the outer edges of the forest to the clearing where he found her. She had been working there for twelve straight hours. 'When you have the chance to leave a place like this,' she had told him, heading out of camp, 'what good is sleeping?' After all this time, he still found it hard to tell when she was tired—exertion was not something that impaired her.

The morning of departure she was standing at the face of the conducer with the slats of her old khav held to one eye. The sky was causing her great consternation. He assumed that she was simply calibrating to the exit frame position. But, as he got closer, she said gloomily: 'Something's wrong here, something's out of sync. The paraxials are running evenly and all the readings are within the normal range, but I'm not getting any permanence from the quorhs. I think perhaps those last two aren't as stable as I hoped. We might need more.'

'Where from?' They had already walked most of the country, or so it seemed to him. Though he would gladly walk as many miles with her as she required, he was starting to lose faith that she could engineer a way back to Aoxi through their salvages alone. If the materials they had left on Earth were not enough, then Cryck would be marooned. She would die in her compartment like a prisoner, and he would never get to see Aoxi, as she promised. How could he ever make his father understand his need to reach Aoxi without Cryck? There would be too much to explain. He would be better off living in the woods.

* * *

It was summer everywhere except the kitchen pantry. The tiles absorbed the cold and spread it through my bones. I had to stop the tape and put on every layer of clothing I could find in my holdall. By the time I'd finished I was padded like a mattress but I felt no warmer. I unfurled a cardboard box and laid it on the floor as insulation. I braved two sips of supermarket brandy, recalling what my grandmother used to say it did for cockles, and the point of trivia she liked to amuse me with at Christmas time about the barrels on the collars of St. Bernard rescue dogs. But nothing took the chill away. The coldness was too deep to remedy. It was a draught in my marrow. It was all the grief lying in wait for me, frozen in the pipes. I climbed up on a crate and caged the lightbulb in my hands so I could feel the heat close to my skin; and I suppose this is what kept me going. The warmth in my fingertips travelled to my heart, gave me the sensation back, enough to believe that if I stayed patient, occupied, I would be found. But the only thing that stopped my mind from shutting down was *The Artifex Appears*. If I hadn't had those tapes and the ability to play them, I think I would've lost what matters most: the facility to remember who I was before my father left me there.

* * *

[. . .] *The manifold conducer was a soundless apparatus, but it resonated at a frequency that charmed the bats at night—Cryck preferred to call them birdrats, and that always made him laugh. Albert had never thought of them as vermin until the evening of departure, when the treetops pullulated with the creatures and their constant swooping and affray so near to the equipment made him anxious. For such a large contraption, the conducer was still sensitive to the vibrations of his footsteps, which Cryck said were unusually heavy for a boy so young, and whenever she permitted him to enter its internal chamber, she made him put on special plimsolls that were three sizes too big for him. That night, she was evidently mindful of the birdrats overhead but didn't have the time to worry. She was already busy in the chamber when he got there, running through her final checklist. She saw him waiting at the door and waved him in. 'Shoes,' she said, meaning the plimsolls. He slipped them on.*

'Have you seen what's happening out there?' he asked.

'As long as they stick to the trees they shouldn't disrupt the calibrations too much,' she said. 'We'll keep an eye on them, though. The more of them gather, the more I'll worry.'

'What if they fly in here?'

'They won't.'

'What if they do, though?'

'If they do, they'll destroy everything. Now please—you're distracting me.'

He had never seen anything quite as remarkable as a manifold conducer in full working order. The quorhs were primed and they emitted such a pleasant light. The outer mechanism was blue-green with pulsing strings, which ran through the entire instrument from the groundlings to the shell, from the tower to the cable trunks and the paraxial mounts. The awe he felt for it, standing inside, was even greater than the time he'd visited St. Paul's Cathedral with his father and his sisters, when they'd looked up at the spire just as the morning bells began to toll. 'Magnificent,' his father had said, then. 'Quite marvellous,' his sisters had echoed, and they had lifted him up the steps, one arm each. He would miss them all when he got to Aoxi, but he would write to explain his reasons. He knew they would be happy for him.

* * *

A boy at school had told me about rubbing batteries to revive them when they faded. So when Maxine Laidlaw's speech began to drag and deepen, I stopped the tape. I removed the flagging Evereadys from the walkman and buffed the ends of them against my thighs. It gave me only a few seconds' worth of extra charge at first, and I thought I'd have to add the boy's name to the list of people I would never trust again. But then I wondered if the effect of rubbing them could have more to do with temperature than friction. So I held the batteries in my fist until the metal casings were no longer cool when touched against my lip. I was lacking body heat, so it took a while to warm them, and I could already feel my mind starting to shift to other places, other people I didn't want to contemplate. Still, the change of temperature was all it took. Maxine Laidlaw's voice returned to normal, lasted to the end of the third tape. When the walkman clicked off after Cryck's bungled departure, I knew I had a choice to make. If I listened to the final tape from the beginning, I might never hear the end. If I skipped ahead, to the middle of the next side, I might reach the resolution of the story on the strength of the remaining charge, but what else would I miss?

If this sounds like a trivial problem, given my situation, I can assure you that I've come to view it as one of the most important choices of my life. Because the more power I could eke out of those batteries, the less I had to be alone with my own thoughts. While I had those words, I had their goodness. I had peace. I had normality. I could keep my life intact. Without them, I had memories of lay-bys and thumping traffic, broken skulls and blood. I had burgeoning ideas of where Fran Hardesty was headed in the car. I had the kind of helplessness that chokes.

So I pulled the last cassette out of the box and wound it forward with my little finger. This was as much as I got:

[. . .] positive, but when the doctor laid the photograph upon the table, Albert could not keep his voice from quivering. He felt the room closing around him. 'No,' he tried to say, 'that isn't her. You've got the wrong person.' So what if the woman in the picture had a hefty, slumping carriage like Cryck's? And so what if her eyes appeared to have the same pale irises? And so what if she had the stumpy neck, the bean-sized nostrils, and the groove above the lip? There were still a lot of differences. He might even call them doubts. For one thing, this woman had a complete set of white teeth. Her hair was so much cleaner, straighter, pulled back off her face. The downward angle of the cheekbones was a fraction too obtuse. Her lips were fuller and her earlobes shorter. And then there was her skin: immaculate. No scars across her brow, or crackling patches, or blisters round her nose.

'Look again,' said Doctor Wendell. 'She'd be twenty years younger in this picture.'

'I don't need to.'

'You're absolutely sure this isn't her?'

There was more falseness to the doctor's smile than he had ever sensed from Cryck.

'That isn't her,' he said again.

S ome nights he stayed out so late my mother would surrender. She'd abandon her vigil at the bottom of the stairs and slump to bed, leaving the hall light on for him, and when she came into my room to check on me, straightening my duvet, brushing my fringe back with her thumb, I would say, as if I didn't know, 'What time is it? Is he not home yet?' On the good nights, she would shush me, tell me everything was fine, now go to sleep. On the bad nights, she would perch beside me with the mattress warping, asking me to recount exactly what I knew about my father's movements before he left the house: what he'd been wearing, if he'd eaten, if he'd taken his keys with him, if he'd put on aftershave, if he'd pinched the window cleaner's money from the drawer. She wouldn't let me rest until I'd answered all her questions. Then I'd hear her in the bathroom, clattering the lotion bottles in the cabinet for a while, running the taps to cover her weeping, and I'd lie awake imagining what he was doing out there in the world without us.

At that age, I didn't know what adult misdemeanours looked like. So I pictured him in smoky pubs where drinkers gathered round to hear him telling stories—he'd have them spellbound, chiming in with counterpoints and friendly patter. In my head, he was a well-liked man, appreciated for complexities and traits my mother didn't know he had. I suppose I couldn't help but attach my own desires to the situations I created for him. I needed there to be extenuating reasons for his disappointments, something to redeem him in my mother's

eyes. And so I thought of him driving through the night to collect a special necklace he'd ordered from a craftsman in a
workshop many miles away. I thought of him picking tulips
from a local garden for a bouquet, having to explain himself to
the disgruntled members of the household when they caught
him in the act. I thought of him standing at the top of his painting ladder at the lamplit window of a cottage in a distant village—a rundown property that he'd been secretly restoring. I
thought of him with two flat tyres on a dark road in the countryside. I thought of him waiting in the A & E department with
a stranger he'd discovered lying in the street on his way home,
an epileptic or a homeless woman. I thought of him sitting in a
veterinarian's consultation room with a cat he'd run over. I
thought of him stuck in a lift. I thought of him working the
night shift as a security guard in a fancy office building, an
extra occupation he'd been too proud to divulge to us.

None of these thoughts came close to being the truth and
they only reveal how little I understood him. But I got so used
to imagining his whereabouts it almost compensated for his
absence. What the mind cannot experience, it can project. I'm
sure you'll figure this out for yourself some day. Happier lives
can be lived outside reality. Not in dreams or hallucinations. In
brighter reflections on things past. Scenarios that we invent
because the facts alone are just too hurtful. Sweeter flesh we
eat because the sharp, dark pit cannot be swallowed.

* * *

For instance, Friday 18th August, quarter to six or thereabouts. I'm in the pantry, emptying myself into the bucket.
Ammonia of my boyish piss becoming froth. All that orange
juice escaping. The walkman batteries are done and I can't settle. But my elbow's still electric, pain is crackling down my side.
I look up at the ceiling hatch. The shelves won't take my weight.

Maybe if I stack the boxes and the other junk then I can build a platform high enough, try again to reach. It only needs to hold me for ten seconds, twenty at the most. So I make a base out of the boxed-up cans, the oil drums and crates. Add the baskets and the Tupperware, the bowl of the food mixer. Add the kibble bags, the wooden tray, the plastic bottles, and the jars. It's holding steady but it needs more ballast. I see a small brown parcel on the middle shelf, behind a hardened pack of demerara sugar. Square enough to fit between the jars and stabilise them. I bring it down, but something on its flank catches the light.

Silver ink.

Addressed to me.

My father's upright scrawl.

Daniel Owen Hardesty, c/o Campion Ghyll Farm, Wasdale Head, Cumbria, England.

Fives stamps in the corner showing the same image: a woman in a bonnet walking in a copse with geese. One word printed in the sky above her: Eire. A broken circle of a postmark but it's smudged: Dublin 13 Feb 93.

The paper doesn't rip. I have to bite the edges to unwrap it. A jewellery box. Grey velvet. Thin and square. The gold motif has worn away. I lift the lid.

A tarnished key.

I hold it up to my right eye, point it at the naked light bulb. It looks to be the perfect size. I try it in the pantry door. It opens to reveal a different evening, brighter sunshine. My father frying sausages and eggs on the kitchen range. Two dogs fussing at his heels. He turns to me, ambivalent. 'I thought you'd never work it out,' he says. 'Fetch your plate. It's almost done.' He gestures to the empty table where a place is set for me beside my granddad and QC and Chloe Cargill. 'We can't stay till morning, so we'll have our breakfast for dinner. I promised you the royal treatment next time, didn't I?'

* * *

For instance, Friday 18th August, six thirty or thereabouts. He's driving south, alone, depleted. In the Volvo with its tank refuelled. Every drip of diesel pilfered from the jerry cans in the machine shed. The twilight lingers over Nether Wasdale. An orange-purple glister on the fells. The lake is fading in the rearview. Another Wintermans scorches his fingers. White smoke eddies in the car. The smell of burned coffee. He can't get a radio signal. Music's up loud just to keep him awake. *Garlands*, Cocteau Twins. Fretless bass and synthesisers. Voices singing underwater. He's keeping to the limit. Beyond Eskdale, beyond Ulpha, beyond Grizebeck. Bloody thumbprints on the atlas. Gawthwaite and Lowick Green, Spark Bridge and Penny Bridge. Back to the roundabout in Greenodd. The A590 all the way to Kendal and onto the M6. He's driving with a private purpose. South. And she's driving with a different purpose. North. They're meeting at the halfway point, determined on a phone call with a faltering connection. One hour earlier.

'No, Fran—Rugby.' She was on the mobile in her car.

'Rugby? You're still miles away.' He was on the cordless in the farmhouse.

'*Where exactly are you going?*'

'It's for a shoot. Last minute thing.'

'*No, I said where.*'

'What?'

'*I said where. Which part of Wales?*'

'South. Near Abergavenny. Look, you should get off the M1.'

'*I know that, Fran.*'

'Get straight on the M6.'

'*Don't start giving me orders. This is your mess I'm sorting out, not mine.*'

'Either way, you'll want to get on the M6. There's a service station at Sandbach. You know it?'

'Why the hell would I know it?'

'All right. Jesus Christ. Just find it on the map, then. It's halfway. And it's easy.'

'Fine.'

'You've got a decent map?'

'I've got a map. I don't know if it's decent.'

'I'm sure it'll do.'

'Put him on now, would you?'

'I told you. He's sleeping.'

'Go and wake him up.'

'What d'you want me to do, throw a brick? He's in the car. I'm in a phone box over the road.'

'Well, hang up. Wake him. Call me back.'

'I'm on my last bit of change here.'

'I'll call you back, then. What's the number?'

'No idea. Doesn't say.'

'Fucking hell, Fran. You're useless.'

'How am I useless?'

'Oh, if only we had time to count the ways.'

'I'm telling you that lad's just had the best day of his life, and you're calling me useless. Typical.'

'You'd better not be lying to me.'

'About what?'

'I don't know. You're acting funny. I know that much.'

'I'm telling you, he really hit it off with Maxine. He got signed photos, little trinkets from the show. You want to see the haul he's coming back with.'

'It didn't sound like he was having fun to me.'

'Yeah well, you know Danno. King of the understatement.'

'I'm so fucking mad at you. What the fuck were you thinking?'

'Calm down. You're acting like I took him on a tour of Wormwood Scrubs.'

'*That's not the point and you know it. You should've phoned.*'

'Yeah, all right.'

'*I mean, Berwick, for crying out loud! That's fucking ridiculous. It's not what we agreed, Fran. Not even close.*'

'Yeah, but come on. Sometimes you've got be spontaneous, don't you? Maxine's got a cinema in her house up there. She was making a thing of it, and Dan wanted to go. What was I meant to do, say no? She's a knight of the realm.'

'*What was that? I lost you for a second.*'

'It's a bad line. I said I didn't have a choice. Dan wanted to go.'

'*I can't hear you very well. What's that clattering noise?*'

'Lorry parking up.'

'*Your voice has gone all tinny.*'

'Let's just make sure we get our plans in order, otherwise—'

'*Sandbach Services, you said. What time?*'

'About nine.'

'*Nine?*'

'Yeah.'

'*Okay. Got it.*'

'We'll see you later, then.'

'*Make sure he's belted in.*'

'Yeah, yeah.'

It's dark when he passes through Lancaster. His headlights puncture the gloom. An intermittent sheen from the motorway lamp posts. Not quite enough to read the atlas, spread out on the passenger seat. He clicks the interior light on. His finger tracks the throat of the M6. Which junction is it?

The radio begins to grate. Voices far too merry and self-satisfied. Every song is bubblegum. He opts for silence. The hymn of tyres on bitumen. He's exhausted. Hard to tell one concrete walkway from the next. Which junction is it? Overpasses and footbridges. Hard to keep his lids from dropping. Are they headlights or cat's eyes? The verges are becoming

girders are becoming traffic cones. Where did the road markings go? Which junction? His wheels creep towards the slow
lane, the hard shoulder. A sudden judder perks him up. Clock
face jounces in the dashboard, all a blur. The shotgun slides on
the backseat.

He turns the radio back on. Searches for a station. Talk
show. Opera. Reggae. Club tracks. Adverts. Talk show. News.
News. Weather. News. Adverts. Adverts. News. Adverts.
Classical. News. Enough.

The hymn of tyres on bitumen. He reaches for the glovebox. A bit of *Treasure*, maybe. The shotgun slides on the
backseat. He hunts for the cassettes. Right hand on the
wheel. He peeps above the fascia. Road is clear. Not in the
mood for *Blue Bell Knoll*. Not in the mood for *Louder than
Bombs*. Tired of *Garlands*. Tired. He should've brought more
tapes along.

A leftward creep to the hard shoulder. Tired. That sudden
rumble. Tired.

Glovebox bounces shut. Too late to correct it. His eyes
blank out. He doesn't think about the hay barn. Doesn't think
about the pantry. Only thinks about himself.

The car scrapes up the banking. Flips. Drops to the
ground like a fumbled cassette. Skates across three empty
lanes and smacks the central reservation. The shotgun hits
the ceiling, fires. Windows shatter. Hits the floor and fires
again. Roof is crushed. He hangs, ensnared by his own seatbelt. Still breathing. Still breathing. The backed-up traffic
waits for him to finish.

* * *

For instance, Sandbach Services. 18th August, ten past
seven. The place is a temple for transient life. A mirror image
of itself.

She comes in from the northbound section of the road with the unnerving feeling that the same facilities are offered on both sides. He didn't say which one he meant: northbound or south? There's an Esso station and a low brick building promising fast food and toilets. A footbridge like a stranded train across the motorway. Futuristic, probably, when it was built. The rest is car park. A segregation system. First, the HGVs with all their colourful containers, the coaches, trucks, and caravans. Then the cars and motorbikes. Not many spaces left for her. She circuits, prowling for an empty bay. Spots one near the boundary fence, where constant traffic shakes the chain-link, where passing headlights saturate the hedges. In she goes, between two vans: a plumber and a carpet layer.

She steps onto the tarmac, locks the car. Smell of chip fat, smell of petrol. Cold summer evening, rain on the way. Hardly anyone outside. Driver underneath a lamp post with a newspaper. Teenagers by the atrium with cigarettes. The automatic doors slide open. A whir of hand dryers from the toilets. Hours to kill in this ungodly place. She goes to get a cup of lemon tea, but they don't have it. Just normal tea in polystyrene. She carries it to a bright corner of the seating area. A vantage point from which to check the car park. Puts her father's mobile on the table. Gets the book out of her handbag. *Snow Falling on Cedars*. Hard to concentrate above the chorus of those hand dryers. Hard to quiet her thoughts. She settles in.

She reads five chapters and absorbs none of the words. Drinks three cups of mediocre tea for comfort. Visits the ladies' twice and browses magazines in the newsagent's. By ten to nine, she's standing in the atrium, observing the incomings. By quarter past, she's outside in the spitting rain with folded arms, treading the kerbside, scanning every row of cars in case she's missed him pulling in. At twenty past, she sees an old blue Volvo and her spirits lift. But the number plate isn't the same. It's driven by a white-haired woman. Small dogs in a cage inside her boot. Still no sign of him by half past. She decides she's on the wrong side of the services. She looks up at the covered footbridge, all its dismal portholes, and understands she'll have to cross it.

The metal stairs are flecked with fag ends. A fragrance she can't place. Body odour? Fox piss? What? But she's the only person in the long chute of the bridge. Walking over traffic. The oceanic wash of it below her feet. Her steps are noiseless.

She emerges on the southbound side. The building is a duplicate. Same atrium of tinted glass. Same fast-food promises. Esso signage looms above the rooftop. But no whirring hand dryers. No sounds at all. Even the rain has abated. And her first sight of the car park locks her knees. She almost trips.

Every bay is vacant but for one. Streetlamps shine at the perimeter.

An old blue Volvo Estate.

Alone in the lot.

She knows the number plate by heart.

On this side, everything is closed. The automated doors are all unmoving. Not a soul around.

She heads towards the car, trying to catch a glimpse of them behind the windscreen. It feels like an ambush. There's something odd about the car. Has it been cleaned? The paint is glossy, fresh. The bumpers polished to a gleam. Not a speck of rust. Is that a brand new roof rack? The closer she gets, the stronger the intuition. No one's in the car. She peers in through the driver's window. Empty.

The grey upholstery is pristine. The *Ordnance Survey Road Atlas of Great Britain* is laid upon the passenger seat. This can't be right. The car looks better than it did the day she bought it. She tries the handle, knowing it's pointless. But it clicks, it opens. She gets in. A showroom model scent. Only noughts on the milometer. The key in the ignition. Dealership fob hanging down. What is this? Where are they? She sits there, considering. She wonders at the footbridge. She listens to that oceanic wash.

The new-car smell is making her eyes water. She's allergic to the chemicals. Her lashes start to sting. Mascara comes off on her fingers. She flips the visor. No mirror. Instead, she notices a blemish on the vinyl. Somebody has written on the beige with biro. An upright lettering in green. *Dear Kath*, it reads. *Change of plan. Follow the map to Vicarage Lane. We'll wait for you.* Signed *Francis,* with three kisses.

The atlas opens at a page he's folded down for her. A route is highlighted in yellow: it takes her off the motorway, ends somewhere called Audlem. Cheshire. What the fuck is he thinking?

She leaves her own car on the northbound side and takes the Volvo south. Sticks to the route he's charted. Onto the A500. West. Past Barthomley, past Chorlton. Quaint names on the map she's never encountered before: Hough, Walgherton, Hankelow. Eighteen miles on the clock now. It's five to ten or thereabouts. She's almost arrived. He's circled the junction. That's where they'll be waiting. End of this long village road.

Three paths merge up ahead. A cast-iron lantern stands on the verge, spreading a warm downy light. A medieval church on a hill: St. James the Great. Shadowy Anglican cross in the yard. Cottages and shops both ways she looks. A pub to her right—maybe there? No. To her left, there's a street sign under a window: Vicarage Lane. She follows it.

When she comes down the track, she passes allotments and boarded-up premises, ivy-clad fences and gardens. Next thing, he's there in the beams of her headlights. Fran Hardesty. Perched on a plain wooden cattle gate. Wearing blue overalls. Smoking. There's a wedding marquee set up in the paddock behind him. Dirty white canvas. No guy ropes. He tosses his Wintermans, hops to the ground. Nonchalant wave. A gesture that says, *Wind the window down, Kath.* So as soon as she pulls in beside him, she does. And before he can lean in and utter a word, she confronts him: 'What's with the treasure hunt, Francis? Where is he?'

He plants his hands on the roof, smiling in. A face like a riddle he wants her to solve. His hair has grown down to his neck, tied back with elastic. His skin is tauter in the darkness. He looks more like the man she used to know. The man she met. 'You can park up there, by the old folk's home.' Even his voice is rejuvenated—warm and lower-pitched. It could persuade her of anything once.

'*Fran*,' she says.

'What?'

'You know what.'

He's still smiling in at her. 'Hold your water for a few more minutes. You'll see him soon.' He backs away, a finger to his lips. This is how he used to be, this is how he used to influence her, this is what she's missed. His quiet authority. Inscrutable thoughts. The confidence she used to have in him. 'Leave the car there and I'll take you in.'

'In where?'

He nods at the marquee.

A long time since she's felt so little anger in his company. What's another few minutes? She takes the car ten metres down the lane. There's a grassy collar to park on. An old brick building just over the way, leaded windows gleaming on the lower floors. The air is lush and warm as she climbs out. A second weather.

He's waving at her from the gate, beneath a lamp post. Giving her the hurry-up. She bounds along the lane. His fists are in the pockets of his overalls. He's not himself tonight, in the best way possible. The loyalty is back. The kindness he mislaid has been returned to him. It's in his stance, the partial listing of his head each time he looks at her. Southbound Francis. So much better than the northbound Francis.

In the paddock, the marquee is glowing amber from within. The night is perfect. There's a clarity about the stars. How has he managed this? Tricks of perspective. Everything made to look real from afar. He extends a hand for her. 'Show won't start until we go in,' he says. 'It's okay. Trust me. This is going to be something you'll remember for the rest of your life.' Her palm closes round his thumb. It's not a mistake. She lets him lead. He swings back the gate with a pleasant low squeak. Tows her across the nubby old grass like a kid. Into the heart of the field. The tent brightens as they near it. He parts the canvas ingress. She steps inside, believing. No more disappointments from now on.

When I heard the invocation of a woman's voice outside the door, I thought that it was hers. 'Daniel? Daniel, if you're there, love, say something.' She rattled the handle again. My mother had arrived at last with all her calmness and gentility. The soft pitch of her speech was just the same. I had watched the skinny blades of daylight come and go beneath the door three times. My elbow wouldn't bend and I had gut-cramp. But here she was, calling. Her old self. I spoke back: 'Mum. *Mum.*' There was an exalted cry after this. She shouted through the kitchen: 'In here! I've got him! He's here!' I recognised the difference in her then. Another accent. 'It's all right, my love, you just sit tight,' she said. There was a scratching and chirruping. Radio noises. 'Are you hurt, Daniel? Are you feeling okay in there?'

'I spilled the bucket. I'm sorry.'

'Don't worry about that. We'll clean it up.'

'I think my arm is broken.'

'Can you move?'

'Yeah. I'm cold, that's all. I can't stop shivering.'

'We'll have you out of there soon, my love. Can you breathe okay?'

'Yeah. But everything stinks. I spilled the bucket.'

'All right, Daniel. That's all right.' One more chirrup from her radio. She had a murmured conversation with another voice outside. 'You still there, love?' she said to me, getting closer. A sliver of her face gaped in at me below the door.

'Yeah.'

'My name's PC Millen. I'm with the Cumbria police. You're going to be fine now, Daniel, I promise you. We'll get this open and we'll see about that arm of yours. You're going to be all right, I promise you.'

The lock was crowbarred from the latch. The door swung back. The brightness of the afternoon teemed through the farmhouse, into me. And it was PC Millen I saw first, her quick, determined body bounding forwards with a blanket. She wrapped me up and scooped me off the sodden cardboard. I was drenched in my own piss. She didn't mind. I felt the safety of her uniform against my cheek, its padding and its warmth. The radio crackled by my ear. She didn't speak, just carried me. I watched her face from underneath. The tension of her jaw. There was a birthmark like a tea-stain just below her hairline. Her strength was extraordinary. The longer she held me, the more I seemed to gain her energy. She was not my mother but, in that moment, she was good enough.

* * *

I wasn't let outside until the hay barn had been sealed off. PC Millen sat me at the bottom of the stairs and waited by the bannister, eyeing my grandma's paintings. 'The paramedic's going to come and check you over in a sec,' she told me. 'They're just finding somewhere for the ambulance. Bit of a traffic jam out there now.'

I nodded.

'Anyway, it doesn't look to me as if it's broken, but my X-ray eyes aren't working at the minute, so you never know. Hey, that'd be cool, though, wouldn't it? X-ray eyes. I used to have those X-ray specs when I was your age. Ever have a pair of those?'

I shook my head.

'We all had them in my day. Used to have to send off for them out the catalogue. They were just paper with a bit of coloured plastic. Rubbish.'

I knew that all her small talk was to shelter me. She was trying to uphold a semblance of normality, and I was grateful for it. But I needed more than that. When I asked her what had happened to my mother, she tugged a few times at the baluster. 'I'm not sure about that, love. They haven't told me anything. We just have to sit and wait here for a minute or two, okay?' She sniffed and gulped. 'They'll want to take you to the hospital. Check you over. They might even put the siren on for you, if we ask.'

I tried to stand, but my legs wouldn't raise me.

'Woah, woah, steady on,' she said, and came to sit beside me. 'Let's just wait and see.'

I spoke up: 'He was going to meet her.'

'Who?'

'My dad. Have they found him?'

'Honestly, Daniel, I'm not clued in with all the details. There's an investigation going on, that's all I can tell you. But I'll ask for you, all right? I'll ask my sergeant.'

'He was going to ring her on the mobile and arrange it.'

'I'll make sure my sergeant knows that, too.'

'Couldn't we just phone her now, though, from here? I've got the number in my head. I need to know that she's all right. I need to know if she's—'

PC Millen squeezed my knee. 'Right now, my love, it's best if we just sit and let the officers do their jobs, okay? Leave it to us for the time being.'

The paramedics had no answers for me either. They checked my vitals and my injuries and asked if I felt strong enough to walk to the ambulance, and I said no. But they deflected all my questions ('Oh, I'm only qualified to put your sling on, sunshine. I can't help you with that, I'm sorry') and deferred to the constabulary ('The police are taking care of it, I'm sure'). I was helped into a wheelchair and pushed along the hallway, out of the front door, along the gravelled path between the outbuildings. The dogs were dead in the yard with their tongues hanging out, wallet-size number-plates laid at their feet. I was taken right past them. Uniformed police were busy taping up the animal sheds. Others in blue coveralls were heading for the hay barn with enormous cameras. Bald men in shirts glanced down at me as I wheeled past. The driveway was empty, but a line of marked cars formed a cordon at the gate, lights pulsing blue. Beyond them, the ambulance. 'I'm going to leave you with the medics for a minute, Daniel,' said PC Millen. 'But I'll follow in the car, okay? Let me see what I can find out for you, love. I'll do my best.' She stroked my shoulder and went off towards the other uniforms.

The next time I would see her was an hour later, in the hospital. She came into my cubicle, trailing in the footsteps of a slender man with glasses. He had his blazer slung over his shoulder, hooked to his forefinger like a schoolboy showing up for an obligatory detention. He took a seat at the end of my bed and introduced himself as Detective Chief Inspector Barber from the Cumbria Constabulary. 'But you can call me Graham,' he said, smiling. 'And PC Millen you already know.' He smiled at her, too. 'Why don't you sit down as well, Daisy? Makes me nervous when folk stand over me.'

As she went and got herself a chair, she motioned at my cast. 'How long did they say you've got to keep that on for?'

'Six weeks,' I said.

'Ah, that's not too bad.' She winked at me.

Barber watched her settle into the chair. He crossed his gangly legs and rubbed his shin. 'So,' he said, engaging my eyes. '*So.*' Then it seemed as if his confidence escaped him. He gave an inward cough. 'Okay, I should start by saying that I'm the Senior Investigating Officer on your father's case—that means I'm the one they've put in charge of sussing out this mess. And so far there are lots of things we know and a lot more things we don't, and to be honest with you, Daniel—is it Daniel, or d'you like Dan better?'

I shrugged.

'To be honest with you, Dan, the things we know are quite upsetting and hard to understand, so I'm really going to need your help with all the rest.' He looked away, considering my cubicle, the bedframe, the melamine furniture, anything but me. 'I spoke to the doctors. Seems you got a bit dehydrated and obviously you've chipped your elbow, but no major damage done. We're all so relieved about that. You had a lot of people worried. I think your grandma's on her way up now. And we'd really like to get you discharged and home as quickly as we can. But PC Millen seems to think—' He paused, looking down at her shoes. His eyes glassed over. 'PC Millen tells me you've been asking where your mum is, and I—' He exhaled. His fingers reached under his lenses. 'I'm sorry, Dan. In the police, we're trained for things like this, but it's hard to keep all your emotions under wraps sometimes—forgive me. It's the worst part of my job.' He wiped his glasses with his handkerchief, slotted them back on his nose. PC Millen was shaking her head at him, pursing her lips. 'Anyway, I'd better tell you that your mum and dad were found in Audlem late last night. That's a fair few miles south of here, in Cheshire. A cleaner at the nursing home phoned 999. He'd seen them in the field over the road, you see, and heard some noises. He reckons half past ten, or thereabouts. And when the local officers arrived, well, I'm afraid they found two bodies in that field. I'm very sad to have to tell you this, Dan—your mum and dad are gone, son. They were both found dead. I really am so sorry.' And he went silent, as though giving me a moment to wail out all my anguish in a single flume, but nothing came. It wasn't that I hadn't processed what he'd told me—I'd known the moment he sat down. I think it was because I wanted to possess the pain and isolate it, hold it deep within me so that it wouldn't spread to other people. Maybe I could smother it before it multiplied. 'Dan, are you okay, love?' said PC Millen. 'Do you understand what's happened?' I should've let it out, right then, but I didn't.

* * *

All that my fixation on the details ever gave me was an understanding of how many things can never be undone. There was a point in my late teens when I obsessed about the inquest, scrutinised the transcript from the coroner's court in search of consolation. At this time, I felt some lingering resentment towards my grandparents for not letting me attend the hearing—they had cheated me of something, I believed, though I couldn't quite say what. Closure, maybe. The opportunity to hear my father exposed for what he was: a man of cruelty without mitigation. So I requested all the paperwork that I could access. I went back to consider the summation of the evidence the police submitted (two separate counties had jurisdiction on the case but the inquest was convened in Cumbria—more bodies equalled greater responsibility). I went through all the in-court testimonies and written statements, including my own—the words seemed to belong to someone else, paraphrased in procedure-speak, an adult register I didn't recognise—and the accounts of other witnesses were just as difficult to read. Declan Palmer had a lot to say about my father's 'uncontracted' role on *The Artifex* and the cause of his dismissal from the crew, much of it misleading; Kelly, our waitress at the Little Chef, confirmed where he'd acquired the ashtray; the two security guards from Yorkshire Television explained my father's strange behaviour and the revocation of his access card; his 'affair' with Chloe was revealed by her best friend; the cleaner from the nursing home told of the gunshots and the cries he'd heard and the strange car that was parked on Vicarage Lane. And there were several others. I thought that if I focused on the where, when, how of everything, I might gain some comprehension of the why. But the more I read, the more I realised: a person's actions can't be quantified by facts alone.

My mother's body, for example, was discovered 3.7 metres from my father's body. He walked her to the centre of the field at gunpoint, made her kneel, and shot her in the forehead (*why?*). Then he took a few strides backwards (*why?*), kneeled down and shot himself below the chin. He'd still been close enough for the forensics team to notice splinters of his cheekbone in the mincemeat of her facial tissue. Neither were identified from pictures in the usual way: my mother was distinguished by her dental records, my father from his fingerprints. West Midlands Police had matched them with an ante-mortem sample they'd obtained when he was twenty, after he'd been taken into custody for affray (*why?*) in Coventry city centre in November, 1979—the only time he'd ever been arrested in his life. Truths like these are what you learn from inquests. There is no comfort to be gained from them.

* * *

It's the closed-circuit camera footage that I'll never find a way to blank out. I was shown the video on the fourth day of the police investigation. DCI Barber drove four hours to my grandparents' house in Bradenham to play it for me. He brought PC Millen with him, knowing—calculating, you might say—that her supportive presence would make me more amenable to talking. I was too destroyed to speak to anyone at that stage, but I'd taken a particular objection to the Family Liaison that had been assigned to us, a quiet male officer called Dudgeon, because he dressed in the same half-hearted manner as my father: always a shirt beneath a crew-neck with cord trousers.

My grandmother showed the inspector and the constable into the front room and made them tea in the fine china. There was some preliminary chat about my grandpa's health and general prognosis while everybody sipped Earl Grey and took a biscuit from the tin. My grandmother explained that I had barely said a word to anyone since I'd been home. (She used that word, 'home,' as if it were a label she could unpeel and restick to anything she wished.) She was staying strong for my benefit, she said, but I recognised the weary vacillation in her voice.

Soon, the inspector rose and asked where he might find the television and the video recorder. He stood at the cabinet and told me what I should expect to see: pictures from the car park cameras at Sandbach Services, black and white, no sound. 'It might be very difficult to watch. I'm sorry. But it's necessary.' There was a delay while he fixed the tracking. 'I don't want to say much else about it,' he told us, picture wobbling on the TV behind him, 'I just want you to let me know if there's something I'm missing.'

'If this gets too hard, Dan, you just say so, and we'll stop,' said PC Millen.

I nodded.

The video started. A line of grey crackled mid-screen. At first, all I could see were two rows of parking bays. Then I noticed the roof rack of the Volvo near the right edge of the frame, its rear end towards the camera. There was an awful stillness to those first few seconds. I watched them, feeling powerless.

A few more seconds.

A scratch across the screen.

And there he is.

The dire grey image of my father climbs out of the car and

comes to lean against the boot, one heel on the tow bar. He waits for half a minute with his fists stuffed in his jacket, doing nothing. No sign of his bandages. A complete change of clothes. The sure-footedness of him is haunting, so much worse on film. And, soon enough, he spots her. He waves as if she's just a taxi with its light on somewhere out of shot. She breezes in, a grainy ghost in slacks and blouse. Her work attire. She rushes at him, motioning, motioning. He pats the air— *Calm down, Kathleen.* They stand a yard apart in argument. She shouts right in his face. Two bystanders turn to look, amused. She prods my father's chest. He stands, impassive. She's trying to see beyond him now, into the back windows. She kicks his shins. He doesn't move. She strikes his chest four times. The bystanders lurk, top right. He steps aside for her. She clocks the empty car: where am I? Her arms go up: *Where is he, Fran? What've you done with him?* He leans against the bumper. The Wintermans are out. She slaps the tin away. The bystanders edge closer. Maybe they'll protect her. He isn't moving. She shouts at him and walks away. Her face towards the camera for the first time, burnished by the streetlamps, changed. Where is she going? Out of sight for now. He lets her go. Waits. Keeps waiting. A little longer. Then a dark hole opens in his face and shuts. He's calling after her. Two more gawkers creep inside the frame: fat heads, bare arms. She returns to him, motioning, motioning. What did he say? Her mood has changed. She's cowed. They're back within a yard of one another. His palm lands on her shoulder. She shrugs it off. He tries again. She shrugs it off. They face each other. Seconds pass. A minute. Then a sudden move: his hand goes to his pocket. A Stanley knife, a soaking rag, an ashtray. No—what *is* that? Something harmless pinched between his fingers. The camera barely picks it up. She snatches it. She holds it to the sky. What is it? Paper? The streetlights white it out. She smothers it inside her fist. Her body sags. And then they're done. He passes her the car keys. She's contemplating something now, but what? He goes to the passenger side, taps his watch. She goes to the driver's side, gets in behind the wheel. It almost looks cordial. The disappointed bystanders have seen enough. An entertaining tiff. All over now. The car reverses out. An easy arc. The headlights beam. And off they go. To the edge of the frame, then further. Further. Until there's nothing left of them except these final motions captive in the tape.

'That's it. That's all we have.' Barber pushed eject. The video whined out of the machine.

I said nothing. My grandmother said nothing. My grandpa in his chair said nothing.

'We've been trying to identify those witnesses, but nobody's come forward yet. That's making things more difficult.' The inspector slipped the tape into its sleeve and sighed. 'We've cross-checked every number plate of every car in the vicinity and spoken to the owners of those vehicles. Nobody saw anything.' He went back to his seat, refilled his teacup from the pot. The clink of his spoon against the saucer felt impertinent somehow. Was he only here to remind us all how dead she was?

Eventually, my grandmother leaned forward. 'I really wish you hadn't talked me into that.'

'I didn't want to have to play it, I assure you, Mrs. Jarrett. But, as you know, I'm trying to make this case as watertight as it can be.'

'What exactly are we meant to say?'

'Nothing. You're not meant to say anything. It's just a discrepancy in the chain of events, and I hoped that Daniel would be able to offer me some insight.' The inspector stared at me.

'How d'you mean, discrepancy?' My grandmother said.

Barber scratched his forehead with his thumbnail. 'Well, you saw it. She got into the car of her own free will. At least, that's what it looks like. We expected there'd be evidence of some coercion. You know, a weapon of some kind. That would fit with the previous . . . Well, that would fit with how he treated all the others.'

'Why does it matter?'

'Because the court will need to take this video into account. And it makes his actions look more questionable.'

My grandmother recoiled at this. 'You mean they don't *already* look that way?'

'Excuse me. I misspoke.' The inspector set his teacup down. 'What I meant was, his *intentions*. This footage makes the whole thing look a bit spontaneous. Do you understand? Premeditation is what the coroner will look for. I don't want there to be a whiff of doubt about it. For your daughter's sake.'

'She's . . . dead,' my grandpa said weakly. 'Who . . . cares?' He had pulled the tubing from his nostrils. He was breathing gravel.

'I do, Mr. Jarrett. And the coroner will, I can assure you of that.'

'Not going . . . to jail . . . either way.'

My grandmother rose. 'Philip, get your air back on, you fool—I'm not burying you, too.' She went and worried with his oxygen canister. She vented at the inspector: 'You lot should've warned me how upsetting this would be for everyone. What good does it do to go back through it?'

'If we've upset you, Mrs. Jarrett, we apologise,' said PC Millen. 'We weren't trying to make this worse.' She looked at me, her lips pulled tight. 'It's just, we thought we might be missing something Dan could help us with.'

'What did he give her there, at the end?' said Barber, angling his head at me. 'That's what I'm interested in. What should we be looking for?'

I didn't know. I was too numb to think. It was easier to focus on the quiet snowstorm of the television screen, the fluctuating grey.

'No, no,' my grandmother said, 'I think you need to be going.

Daniel's been through too much as it is. I want you out now, please. My husband's very unwell. And you lot should've told me you'd be doing this—I would never have allowed it.'

'Yes, well, I can see it was an error. I do apologise if I've distressed you all.' The inspector stood and brushed crumbs from his shirt and tie. 'Thank you very much for the tea, Mrs. Jarrett. We'll leave you to get on with things.' He collected his blazer and the video. 'I'll just use your loo, if that's okay?'

'Across the hall,' my grandmother said, and he went.

PC Millen was still on the lip of the sofa. 'I'm sorry about him. He's under quite a bit of pressure and it's making him a bit, you know.' She got up and straightened her uniform. 'The last case like this he worked on ended up a mess—a man got off who shouldn't have—and, well, you should know he's doing everything he can to make sure he gets this one right for you.' She glanced at me with an expression I mistook for pity. 'If there's anything you can think of, Daniel, you just give me a ring, okay? You have my number.'

The next afternoon was honeyed with the kind of full, enticing sunshine that no person wants to see projected on his curtains when he's trying to forget the world. My grandmother appeared at my bedroom door to persuade me out of bed to have some lunch with her on the patio. 'Just a few minutes of fresh air, a bit of daylight, Dan, that's all I'm asking. You need to eat.' Hers was the only voice that I still paid attention to. I knew that she was giving me the best of her affection, devoting every bit of energy she had to looking after me, and I felt guilty that I couldn't yet reciprocate—I couldn't even rouse the impulse to feed myself or wash. All I wanted was to lie in bed with the curtains shut and my headphones on, letting myself be hypnotised by Maxine Laidlaw. 'I tell you what,' she said, coming in, 'I'll get everything ready, all right?

I'll put your clothes out for you. All you have to do is put them on and come downstairs.' I let her rattle through the dresser, rummage through the stiff new clothes she'd bought for me (I couldn't stand to wear the old ones that were in my drawers at home). And then she went into the corner cupboard, sliding metal hangers. 'What've we done with your shoes, Dan? I can't see them anywhere. If they don't fit you, we can always change them. I didn't know what kind you liked—all trainers look the same to me, but I thought I couldn't go wrong with Nikes. You should say, though, if they're not right. I don't mind going out and getting you a different—Oh, you're up. That's wonderful, Daniel. I'm so glad.'

My feet were on the floorboards for the first time since the early hours. 'They took them,' I said. 'The police.'

'Oh no, I don't think so. They'll be downstairs somewhere, in the shoe rack.'

'Not the new ones. The old ones. They've still got them.'

When I'd been admitted into hospital, I'd changed into a gown and blue pyjamas. The police had taken all my filthy clothes in evidence at the DCI's request, including my blood-spotted trainers. I'd watched PC Millen put them into plastic bags before she left my cubicle. She'd told me I could get them back whenever I wanted, but I hadn't replied. I would've been content to let her burn them where she stood.

My grandmother was looking at me oddly. She came and felt my forehead with her palm. 'Well, I suppose we could ask Dudgeon if they're done with them.'

'No, I don't care about the shoes. I hate those shoes.'

'Oh. All right. Well—'

'I need to speak to PC Millen.'

'Oh, my darling, I don't know if that's the best idea. Maybe once you've eaten something. I could get her on the—Daniel?'

I was up and out of bed already, heading for the landing, where Millen's direct line was scribbled on the jotter by the telephone.

It took a few rings to connect with her. She answered with

an enervated tone, then heard my voice and changed immediately. '*Okay, okay, I'm all ears, Dan,*' she said, '*you tell me what
you think you know, and I'll make sure I pass it on.*'

I explained that underneath the insole in my trainer I had
kept a twenty pound note. Safety money from my mother.
Maybe if they checked my father's car, or searched the field
again, they might find it there. *Currency of Aoxi*, I told her. It
had to be what he'd shown her in the car park.

'*Okay, spell that last bit for me. What was on it, Eyoxi?*'

'A-O-X-I . . . It's where Cryck's from. In the show.'

'*Your dad's show?*'

I went quiet.

'*Dan—you there?*'

'It's not *his* show. He just worked on it.'

She breathed a moment. '*Yes, you're right, love. I don't
know why I put it that way. Stupid of me.*'

'Will you tell Graham?' I said.

'*Of course I will. As soon as we're done here, I'll get right
onto him.*'

My grandmother was on the landing now. She came and
covered my shoulders with a dressing gown.

'She knew I wouldn't have told him about the money,' I
said. 'Not unless something was wrong. That's why she got in
the car.'

'*You're saying she thought he'd harmed you?*'

'I think so. Maybe. I don't know.'

Millen considered this. '*No sound on the tape, that's the
problem. We know he said something to change her mind, but if
we can't hear it, we can't prove it.*'

Six days later, at the inquest, DCI Barber would say different. He would outline to the coroner what he felt the evidence
suggested: that she had got into the car and driven nineteen
miles with Francis Hardesty to Audlem for the simple reason
that he'd told her I was waiting for her there. I was the incentive

she was following, Barber said. The banknote was the lure. It was a premeditated plan, devised by Francis Hardesty before he arrived to meet her. The shotgun wasn't brought out from its hiding place until they'd left the services together, when the road was dark enough for him to threaten her, unnoticed.

Let me tell you one important thing I've learned: presentation of the facts is not the same as exposition of the truth. There are fissures in the substance of what people say. As we speak, we omit. It's purposeful sometimes, a self-preserving measure. At other times, it's accidental, a failure of memory, a lapse in awareness. Either way, it's inevitable. I have tried to be as open with you in this version of events as I have ever been with anyone. But I'm certain that, for all my efforts at transparency, I've left things out that are significant. That's why it's difficult to look back at the inquest and ascribe much blame to Declan Palmer and the others who gave testimony. Because even when we try our best to let the truth out, there is always a remainder. When a story is told, it is changed.

Had I been at the hearing, I would've been the only person in the room who could've told the court that Declan Palmer's statement was inaccurate. Nothing he withheld bore any consequence to the verdict (four unlawful killings and a suicide), so you could say it didn't matter. But what he left out of his testimony made my father into something he was not—it bothers me that I'm the only one who understands this. Palmer's version:

'I wouldn't say I sacked him as such, no. He was on an hourly rate with us, uncontracted. I just decided not to keep on paying for his services. We had a chargehand carpenter on a pretty good wage already, and another three casuals—Barnie Seddon being the best of them. I needed to make room in the budget, so I got rid of the one my chargehand said was the most dispensable, whose work wasn't as good, and that person, unfortunately, was Fran . . . Oh no, he wasn't happy. There was a bit of a scene in my office—well, I call it an office: it was just a trailer out in the car park the directors shared with me . . . He knocked over a filing cabinet, that's all. Ranting and raving, mostly . . . I honestly couldn't say for sure. I was told that he and Chloe had been seeing each other, and it hadn't ended very well . . . I think it's possible that he was jealous, yes. She'd started going out with someone else, is what I heard . . . If that's who it was, I'll take your word for it. I honestly didn't pay too much attention to the love lives of the crew. I just tried to keep the shoot running on time and within budget. That's my job as a producer. But I can say that Chloe was extremely talented, and very well liked.' And so the public record shows my father was a lesser carpenter, released from the crew for his sub-standard work. I know this to be wrong but I can't prove it, and I hate that I still care. There was not a single mention of the name Eve Quilter at the inquest. No talk of what happened in her dressing room. No reports of gossip on the set about the two of them. No acknowledgement of Chloe Cargill's allegations whatsoever. At first, I wondered how this could've been allowed to pass unchecked in Palmer's testimony. Even Chloe's friends didn't remark on it when they spoke about the end of her involvement with my father. Does this mean they weren't aware of it? Or does it mean it never happened? All I know is, when I looked through my own statements to the police, I found no mention of Eve Quilter either. I checked through the recordings from my interviews with the inspector, hoping it was a mistake, but they confirmed it was my fault. I hadn't broached the subject once. I'd failed to get across the detail. Maybe I was lost and muddled in my grief. Maybe I was still trying to protect his reputation in some unconscious way, I can't be sure.

You see? Omission.

Omission begets more omission.

Omission leads to maybe after maybe.

Such as, maybe Declan Palmer had no reason to admit why he'd dismissed my father, since the police never asked him about Eve Quilter specifically. Maybe he was acting in the show's best interests. Maybe he was acting in his own best interests. Maybe he was trying to spare Eve's reputation. Maybe he was telling the truth. Maybe, in the years gone by, I misremembered everything that Chloe told me in the car. Maybe some involuntary process in my brain planted the memory of Eve Quilter there in the aftermath. Maybe I can't trust my own recollection any more. Maybe you shouldn't trust it either.

You see?

There are other facts I have to question now, because of this. Like all the documents submitted to the court. Divorce papers, drafted by my mother's solicitor four months prior to our trip.

Eviction threats, found at his last registered address, demanding payment of rent arrears. Deeds to my granddad's farm, signed over to a family of strangers. My granddad's will and testament, from which the name of Francis Hardesty was expunged in 1990. A letter from my father's GP: 'Mr. Hardesty was in good physical health, but he was palpably depressed.'

The implications of these things are quite persuasive. They seem to indicate his motives. Except my father was more complicated than these facts report, and I can't reconcile them with the man I knew, the equanimity he showed on our drive up to the farm, the easy-breathing comfort of him in the lay-by with his Stanley knife.

Another oddity: when the contents of the plastic bottles in his car were tested by forensics, they found that one contained a brew of toilet bleach and acetone—homemade chloroform, they said, which toxicology had shown to be ingested by my granddad and QC. At what point did he decide to make this concoction? After the divorce papers came, or before? Was it the day my granddad sold the farm? The night we spent at the White Oak in Rothwell? The day he picked me up? Or was it just a blend of chemicals he found effective in removing gum and varnish, which he happened to have with him from the start?

The coroner's verdict spoke of a man driven to murder by rejection, jealousy, humiliation. A man whose separation from his wife and child, whose escalating debts and thwarted aspirations, whose failed relationships with others pushed him—and I quote—'to the verge of despair and then off the edge.' But I don't believe his crimes were born of any pent-up rage at all the disappointments of his life. I believe that they were born when he was born. I believe the problems that he had were merely the excuses he'd been gathering over time, the licence he'd been saving up to use.

* * *

It would be just as false to claim that Chloe Cargill's life is represented by the facts reported in the newspapers. They might as well have printed her CV. Twenty-six years old. Assistant make-up artist (credits: *The Artifex*, *Singles*, *Demob*, *Stay Lucky*). Former pupil of Pudsey Grangefield High School. Member of the Roundhay running club. 5' 3". Blue eyes, brown hair. Blood type: AB. If you believe what they wrote in the tabloids, she and my father had a 'doomed romance,' 'a sex-fuelled affair,' 'a torrid five-month fling.' Was this really the extent of her? For some reason, I expected better from the television news. The main networks covered my father's crimes for a fortnight, and they regurgitated the same details about Chloe. They showed them as graphics, bullet points on screen. They played slideshows of her happy and alive in photographs, one of which I recognised from her toilet wall. Sometimes a

reporter summarised her in dramatic tones, standing in the
partial darkness of Vicarage Lane with a logoed microphone
and hair stirred by the wind. Sometimes she was mentioned in
the voiceover to a montage of images: quivering police tape—
front door of her house—plain-clothes officers in conversation—lay-by—ashtray—farm and driveway—field in Audlem
with coroner's tent. They reran her parents' anguished statement outside court after the inquest. They held cursory, in-
studio discussions with criminologists and other experts,
Chloe's bereaved friends and colleagues: a make-up artist from
a show she'd worked on, a man she knew from the running
club, a woman she'd been at school with. It's taken me this
long to realise I have no right to know any more than this
about Chloe Cargill. Those few hours I spent with her are all
that I deserve, these images are what I get to carry with me.
The rest is for the people who loved her.

* * *

My mother will not be reduced in the same way. I have
twelve happy years with her to cling to, the privilege of wit-
nessing her life in motion. I have the small things no one else
perceived. I have her heart. At any time, I can recall the struc-
ture of her face and all the pretty imperfections that defined
it—the pores, the lines, the marks, the moles. If you want me
to sketch the tight arrangement of her teeth from memory, I
can show you every angle, gap, and intersection. I can recreate
the sound she made when she bit an apple, the hollow clamour
of her mouth upon it like a horse's. I can describe to you the
slightly scalded colour of her skin whenever we went swimming, how the chlorine dried it out. I can tell you how her
stance was different from the other mothers at the school gate:
upright as a stake with both hands pleated at her stomach. I
could list for you each piece of jewellery that she ever wore,

from the opal brooches to the nacre pendants, from the cheap unwieldy beads she bought at market stalls to the pure-gold heirlooms locked inside her dressing table. I can explain the curlicues of hair that stuck to her forehead when she boiled pasta at the stove. I can identify the point at which her voice would split when she got angry, how it deepened when she got suspicious of the speed at which I'd done my homework, how it shifted up two octaves whenever something pleased her. I can reveal her maddening habits: the way she licked her thumb before she turned a page, the way she would remove her clip-on earrings and put them in her sweaty shoes when she lay down to watch TV, the way that she would squeeze the hoover bag to check for coins before she emptied it. I know the books that she read twice (*Wild Swans*, *Hotel du Lac*, *Doctor Zhivago*) and the ones that she pretended to have finished (*The Bonfire of the Vanities*, *The French Lieutenant's Woman*, *The Sea, The Sea*). I can tell you that she always had a first-class postage stamp inside her purse. I can recall the dresses that she wore on my tenth, eleventh, and twelfth birthdays (floral, pale yellow, stripy blue). I can tell you that she never stopped surprising me with things she knew, like how to make lined curtains from two rolls of basic fabric, how to play the chord of D on a guitar, how to defragment a hard drive, how to mend a puncture in a paddling pool. I could always glean her mood from the weight of her footsteps on the stairs and the sharpness of the clatter when she laid the dinner table. I could divine her thoughts from what she doodled while she talked to people on the phone: a shaded pyramid or square meant she was bored of listening, a cartoon boy with bug-eyes meant she was excited to be sharing news. I can remember everything about her, good and bad. The dear and disagreeable. But what I cannot do is capture the full splendour of her personality in words: there simply aren't enough of them.

* * *

Progress is accepting that I'll never know their conversations. Somewhere in between the Sandbach Services and Audlem are the reasons why he killed her, and I have no way to access what was said. That thirty-minute car ride is a vacuum. In the weeks after she died, I did everything I could to make myself imagine it. I tried to put my mind there like a hidden camera. But all that I could see was blankness and the only things I heard were ricochets of older arguments: *useless worthless idiot don't have to explain myself to you I can do what I want why don't you shut your fucking trap for once always blaming someone else for your mistakes don't you ever have a plan I mean where's your self-respect you've always wanted me to fail you love to see me fall down on my arse don't you there's nothing you like better than humiliating me god I wish I'd never met you nobody can stand you always whining at me always whinging you don't know you're fucking born your parents dumped you even your own son has no respect for you I can't stand to be around you any more I never loved you anyway oh yeah and what you going to do about it eh yeah right that's what I thought all talk.*

As more time passed, that car ride became easier to see. Unwanted images would drop into my head in idle moments. When I was unpacking the textbooks from my school bag, they would come to me. When I was lathering my face with medicated soap at bedtime, they'd come to me. When I was standing in the cafeteria line, while I stood at bus stops in the rain, when I was helping my grandmother clean the fish tank, when I was lacing up my shoes, when someone else was pondering a move at chess club. Fragments of my parents' old discussions would resurface and I'd let their voices play, trying to make them fill the shapeless space within me.

I would hear my father bleating to her about Pascoe: 'And

it was probably the only time I saw my old man teary-eyed, the day he left the farm, but when I bring it up with him today, oh no, he denies it ever happened. And I'm not ending up that way, no chance, I'm not gonna be another Pascoe he can wipe away like shit he trod in and won't speak about, so yeah I let him fucking have it, didn't I? Right in the head. And you know what? It felt good. It was a fucking relief.'

I would hear her trying to divert him from his purpose: 'Like those weekends in the caravan. We were happy once, that's all I'm saying. And it never really leaves you. I mean, we can fix this. Whatever you've done, we can fix it.'

I would hear her making promises: 'Just tell me where he is, Fran, please, just tell me where he is. I swear to god, I'll give you anything you want. Everything I have. I'll empty my account. I'll give you anything. The house. My car. I've got diamonds in my dresser drawer worth thousands. You *know* that. You can have them. Anything you want. Just, please, Fran. Tell me where he is and this won't matter.'

I'd imagine him goading her: 'Maybe we should go and meet that headmaster now, eh? Let him see us at our best. I'll bring the gun in with me. We can have a chat and see if he can overlook that maths mark. We can talk about what cartridges are best to use. I'll bet he's shot a thing or two in his time, posh fella like him. Yeah, we can talk about that seventy-six and see if he changes his mind.'

I'd imagine her goading him: 'If you're going to kill me, Fran, for god's sake change this music, will you? I'm not dying to this awful noise.'

I'd hear her dreaming up escape plans: 'You could drop me here and catch a ferry into France. You've got your passport in the back, right? All your other stuff is here. I wouldn't say a word. No one'd be chasing you. You'd have time. And once you've made it there, you just keep going. Anywhere you want. Find work. Do anything. Take a train out to Bulgaria. You've got friends there, haven't you? Let them help you out. Go there. Work in a vineyard or something. I wouldn't say a word. It's got to be a better plan than what you're doing now. Fran, listen to me. *Fran.* You can do it. You can go.'

I'd hear his validations for the place they ended up: 'My mother was christened at St. James's, did you know that? Yup, this is where they wet her head and told her she was saved. I always thought it would be bigger, the way she used to talk about it. But you know how it is. Everything's so disappointing in real life.' / 'Does there have to be a reason? I was looking at the atlas and it caught my eye.' / 'Yeah, I know it doesn't look like much. I mean, it's just a paddock. I used to have this big idea that I could buy the plot one day and build a house on it, and that'd be my start in life. But my old man wouldn't lend me any money, so it just sort of fell away, the whole idea. I've kept coming back to visit it, to see if it's been snaffled. And here it is, look. Still a fucking paddock. What a waste.'

These conversations loop and overlap.

They start but never finish.

I haven't found a way to stop myself creating them.

I've spent so many years inventing explanations for what cannot be explained that I can barely differentiate the real voices from the phantoms in my memory. The worst part is, I know that my imagination was inherited from him. My father could construct a frame of lies in less time than it took a better man to shrug his shoulders, and it frightens me how much I share this capability—their speeches bloom inside my head so readily when I permit them. I cope with the problem. I stave it off. I occupy myself with enough work that I can bypass all the idle moments of the day. At night, I gulp down Ambien— sometimes I need two of them to mute the chugga chugga *clank*. Treatment of the symptoms. It doesn't seem sustainable, but I'm yet to find a medicine for the cause.

She was six years older and her hair was shaved so close that when she stepped in from the rain she only had to run her hand across her scalp to dry it. She no longer had the gangling posture of her television days, no slump, no cradling her other elbow while she stood. Instead, she had the feigned disinterest of someone who'd grown used to being looked at, examining the restaurant with a blank expression while the waiter hung her coat. I was sitting in the deeper reaches of the place, where it was emptiest. The serviettes and breadcrumbs of the late-departed lunch crowd were being tidied all around me. She was escorted down the aisle towards my table. Her rubber clogs made bright gymnastic squeaks on the parquet. The embroidered pattern of her blouse shone as she moved. When she noticed me, she slowed her strides so much the waiter had to turn and check she was still following. I stood up to greet her, and the first words she said to me were: 'Oh my god, I thought you were—I mean, you really do look like him, don't you? I actually had a weird feeling for a minute there.' My smile must've seemed uncomfortable. '*Shit*, is that completely the wrong thing to say? Oh god, it is. I can tell from your face. Okay. You know what? Let's wind that back and start again. Agreed?' She held out her hand across the table. 'I'm Eve. Nice to meet you.'

'It's nice to meet you, too,' I said. 'Thanks for finding time for me.'

'Oh, not at all. It's good to get out and do civilised things. They're keeping the reins pretty tight at the minute.'

The waiter pulled out the chair for her. As she sat down, her eyes still scrutinised me.

'You're not even allowed out for lunch?' I said.

She took her menu. 'Sure, but once it gets to dress rehearsals they try and keep you within a mile radius. Close enough to send the AD out to get me with a lasso. The trouble is, round here, there's—'

'Can I get you anything to drink?' the waiter said.

'Tap water is fine. How fresh is that jug?'

'It was here when I arrived,' I said.

'Then maybe let's refill it,' she told him. 'And could I have a few slices of lemon? Just, you know, on a little dish or something. Don't put it in the jug, is what I'm saying.'

The waiter nodded and went off.

'I hope this place is okay for you,' I said. 'I don't know London very well.'

'Actually, I was just about to say you picked the ideal spot. There aren't really any good places to eat in this neck of the woods, so if I absolutely have to stay in Waterloo, then I usually come here. It's the best of a bang-average bunch.'

'Oh good. I think.'

She grinned, lifting her menu. 'Are we going to be eating, like properly eating, or should I just order some coffee and a massive slab of tiramisu?'

'I don't mind. Whatever you've got time for.'

'Well, how hungry are you?'

I was too nervous to be sure. 'Fairly, I suppose.'

'Come on. Are you an eight? A six?' She studied the first page, screwing up her face. 'Because I'm about a four. There was a tub of mini-donuts doing the rounds backstage and I must've had about a hundred of them. I eat such crap when I'm nervous, and I'm terrified about this play. I might just get a cappuccino or something—but you get what you want.'

'All right.' I decided to order what she ordered. It was

important to me that she didn't sense any inequity between us or feel the pressure to uphold our conversation longer than she wished. The waiter returned with the water jug and her lemon slices. She asked him for the hottest cappuccino he could make, then told him: 'Drown the froth with chocolate. You can hold the shaker thingy over it for twenty seconds. And I'll have some of those little italian biscuits on the saucer, you know the ones I mean.'

'And for you, sir?'

'That sounds good to me as well.'

'Nothing to eat for you today?' He gave me a slow blink of disapproval, as though he'd personally hand-picked each item on the specials board.

'No, sorry,' I said.

Eve laughed. 'Don't apologise. You're not obliged to order food.' She watched the waiter traipse off with our menus. 'If you went to a gallery, they wouldn't make you buy a Giacometti, would they? They'd be happy if you bought a postcard. So don't let them guilt you.' Then she turned to study me again, thinning her eyes. 'I didn't know London much when I was your age, either. First time I came down here on my own I nearly wet myself just looking at the tube map. I still feel that way some-times and I've been living here ages. You reach a point where you forget how big it is.'

'Yeah. It's not like I don't come here, I just try to stay away from theatre land, if I can help it.' A dryness came to my throat.

'Of course,' she said, 'I get you.' And she offered me a top-up from the water jug, filling both our glasses. I took a sip. 'In case you're wondering about the hair, it's for the play. I don't usually go for the hooligan look.'

'I think it kind of suits you.'

'Ah, you're sweet. It's really just a gimmick they came up with. If the script is bad, do something drastic. That seems to be their thinking. We'll see if it works.'

'Is it a decent role? The character you're playing, I mean.'

'I dunno. I'm still trying to suss her out.'

'I thought the show opened soon.'

'Yeah, the previews start on Thursday. Bad of me, I know, but here's my problem: I really hate the play. It's corny and I want to rewrite all my lines. I'm meant to be this woman who leaves prison and can't get herself together. This local gang thinks she's a snitch and they take over her whole life. They move into her flat and won't leave her alone, so she has to sort of prostitute herself to get rid of them. It's like, what do they call it? A sting operation. I wouldn't waste your money on a ticket—trust me. It's just the kind of thing some old Etonian writes so he can look more urban and humane. Don't get me wrong, I'm glad for the work. I need it. I'll take the lead in *any-thing* in my situation. And, you know, I *had* been looking for a good excuse to get my hair cut for a while.' She laughed self-consciously, picked up a lemon slice and began to peel the rind from it. 'I'm jabbering at you, aren't I? I'm sorry. I wasn't sure what to expect today, and—it's just, *Christ*, you remind me of him. It's so hard to look at you and not feel—*you* know what I mean.' The lemon flesh was dropped into her glass, the residue was sucked clean off her fingertips. 'I'm finding it all a bit spooky.'

'You don't have to explain,' I said. 'I'm just grateful that you're here.'

'Yeah, well. I wouldn't be too grateful. I can't remember all that much about him, if I'm honest. I think I tried to banish him from my memory—we all did, right? But I'll do my best.' She de-rinded the next lemon slice with her teeth, spitting the pith out. 'And then maybe you can stop pestering poor Richard, eh? He's pretty weird about his inbox.'

She was referring to her agent. I'd sent him fifteen emails in the course of eighteen months, each one 'FAO: Eve Quilter.' The first of them was typed up on a slow computer at the local library; it had taken weeks to draft because I couldn't find a way of mentioning my father without undermining the whole message, and everything I thought of made me sound revengeful. I'd settled in the end for something earnest and confessional: 'Really I just want to ask you a few questions about my dad, that's all, because I'm finding it quite hard to move on with my life, and hearing small details about him is the only thing that seems to help.' A month passed with no reply, so I'd sent another, and another. I'd changed the message every time, becoming more and more apologetic. The last was sent from an internet café near school, where kids from chess club went to play their networked games of *Half-Life*. While I was typing, someone at the terminal beside me was shooting indiscriminately at US Marines with a bolt-action rifle:

> Dear Eve, I hope you will forgive my perseverance. I haven't given up on the idea that some day we might get a chance to talk, but I understand if you'd prefer to forget about my father entirely (I would do the same, in your position). There are so many things he ruined in my life that I'm still trying to understand how to move past them and be happy. I feel that speaking with you, even just for a few minutes on the phone, would help me so much. Please write back and let me know if you have any time to spare. I'm sorry for troubling you again. Kind wishes, Daniel Jarrett

At this stage, I'd stopped expecting a response. Writing to Eve Quilter had become habitual. Even if it wasn't fruitful, it had made me feel like I was doing something, and I thought of it as an equivalent to my grandmother's Sunday churchgoing: I was dispatching prayers into the ether. But then, one afternoon in January, I was home alone, revising for a Physics mock exam, and the telephone rang. When I answered, the voice that came back was American and rather forthright. He said his name was Richard Beck, the talent agent, and was I the Daniel Jarrett who'd been emailing him? 'You're persistent, my friend, I'll give you that. I've never forwarded so many emails in my life.' He was calling at Eve's urging. 'Look, she just wanted me to reach out and test the ground a little, check you're not some grown-up wacko living out of his garage—the internet is full of loons who want to meet a pretty actress, so you can't be too careful.' I had answered all his questions and told him that I had some questions of my own about Eve's time on *The Artifex*. 'I don't think she'd have a problem with that. She feels bad for ignoring you this long, so let me run it by her, okay?' The next day I'd received an email from her Yahoo address, saying she would like to meet and talk. She was in the last rehearsals of a play at the Young Vic but she could 'pinch an hour' on certain dates 'anywhere in Waterloo.' I did an online search for restaurants and we arranged a time.

Now there she was at last, a table-width from me, and all that I could think about was how to introduce the question without scaring her away.

The waiter appeared with a tray of cappuccinos and our biscuits. He set them down and fussed over the placement of the sugar bowl. Eve rubbed at her brow as though it were a carpet stain, one-fingered. 'You can just leave that,' she told him. 'I don't take sugar.'

'Me neither,' I said.

Off he went again, tray under arm.

'What was I saying?' said Eve.

'You were telling me you don't remember him that well.'

'Right. Right. I don't.' She stared down at her coffee and turned the cup round on her saucer—she was left-handed, like my mother. 'Mostly, thinking back on it, the clearest memory I have is how quiet the set was afterwards. They cancelled filming for about a week, I think, then everyone just came back into work and, *click*, tape was rolling again and no one was prepared.

You could tell that no one wanted to be there. I mean, especially the people in make-up, right? Chloe was like proper family to them, and they were just bereft. Everyone was going
through the motions, trying not to get upset with everyone else.
But there were still so many scenes to shoot, it was so difficult
to focus. How that series got finished I'll never know. We
fucked up every single take, I swear. It was a wreck.' With this,
she slid her hands across the tablecloth and gazed at me, as
though to read my fortune. 'Listen, if at any time I sound self-
pitying, throw something at me, okay? I mean it. I know our
problems were pathetic in comparison to yours, but I can only
tell you what I went through at the time. And basically the
show was done the moment the news broke. I remember
Maxine took it hardest. I mean, if you watch those later
episodes, her whole performance is so ragged. It was tough to
watch her act that way, because she'd poured her heart into
that role and made it something brilliant—but she just lost
belief, I think. Not in the show, as such. In her reasons for
doing it. She spent a lot of time with Chloe in make-up every
day. And I remember her saying to me after we wrapped—you
know that voice she had—*Enjoy the party, my love. There's no
chance in hell we're coming back next year.* And, of course, she
was right. Because she wouldn't sign up for it. Which I understand, I guess, but I was young—it wasn't like I had a load of
other projects lined up at the time. I think she went straight off
and did that film about Lord Lucan—did you see that? It was
sort of trashy. But, yeah, I mean, it hit the rest of us quite hard.
I haven't done any TV at all since then. Did you know that?'

I shook my head.

'It's okay. Bring out the tiny violins, eh? I'm just saying how
it changed things.' She'd been slurping at her coffee while she
talked, pausing now and then to dab the film of milk from her
top lip, and I let her go on speaking. It would be wrong to say
I had a strategy—I wasn't there to extract the information from

her in the way that DCI Barber might've done—but I will admit that I gave thought to my approach. I allowed her to find a certain comfort level with me. She steered the conversation where she wanted it to go, and in moments when it seemed appropriate, I nudged it back in the direction of my father. I know that this was selfish of me, perhaps even a little callous. You might say it was an affectation worthy of Fran Hardesty himself. I'm not proud of my behaviour, and I wouldn't act the same way now, but I was eighteen then and still re-learning how to be.

'Do you remember why they sacked him in the first place?' I said, not looking at her.

'No,' she said. 'I mean, well, there were rumours.'

'Oh yeah? Like what?'

'I'm not sure if I should say. You might not thank me.'

I put my cup down a little too heavily. I sighed. 'Have you ever had a filling?'

'What?'

'Have you ever had a filling? Dental work. You know what I mean.'

'Sure.'

'Well, they inject you with that stuff, don't they? To numb you.'

'Novocain.'

'Yeah. That's it.' I brought my eyes up to meet hers. 'I've basically been Novocained all over since it happened. You can't say anything to hurt me, Eve. I wouldn't even feel it.'

She ran her hand over her scalp. 'Okay, but I'm not saying it was true. It's just what I heard. I'm just the messenger.'

'I know.'

'All right then—' She was fidgeting with her necklace now. 'Some of the crew—I guess it was the people who knew Barnie Seddon pretty well—they said that *he'd* told them something.'

'What?'

'They said your dad got Chloe pregnant twice while they

were going out. And he'd made her get, *you* know, I don't like
to say the word if I can help it.'

'An abortion?'

She nodded. 'Well, two of them, actually. Both times. Is
what I heard.'

'Okay,' I said. 'That's news to me.' My voice barely lifted. It
was not what I expected her to say, of course, but I gave her
the chance to explain herself. 'Why would that be a sacking
offence, though?'

'That was my question, too. But apparently—and I'm just
repeating what I heard here—apparently she was crying one
time while she was taking Maxine's make-up off, so she asked
her what was wrong. And when she told her, Maxine was like
stomping round upset about it. Totally enraged. She rings up
Declan Palmer saying she wants your dad gone by the end of
the day. So that was it. Palmer called him into his office, and
your dad kicked off at him, big time—I remember that. I
mean, I didn't see it 'cause I wasn't on the set that day, but
everyone was saying how he'd chucked a chair and nearly
smashed a window.'

I'd been watching her face closely. How the philtrum of her
lip began to moisten. How her lids withdrew into her sockets
and her pupils darted left to right. I thought that, after everything I'd been through, I'd be able to detect an outright lie the
next time one was spoken to me. But Eve had always been a
subtle actress, and I couldn't read her. It made me lean on her
too hard, too quickly. 'How much contact would you say you
had with him on set?'

'Oh, I don't know.' She smiled at me uncertainly. 'Depends
what you mean by contact, Monsieur Poirot.'

'Sorry. That came out wrong. I didn't mean to sound like I
was—sorry.'

'Don't worry about it, really. I guess you must absorb the
way they speak after a while, eh?'

'If I never see a policeman again, it'll be too soon.'

'Right.'

'I just meant, how often did your paths cross? That's all.'

She went quiet for a moment. 'Look, I don't recall his every movement or anything. But I saw your dad around a lot. My scenes were filmed quite early in the day, and he'd be there fine-tuning pieces of the set for us, or making something for the next day's schedule. I'd see him quite a bit between takes, 'cause he'd be off in a corner building something in a rush, like a box for the DP to stand on, or a ramp they'd asked him for, or something they needed fast to get the shot they wanted without, like, the boom op getting in the way or something. He was good at all that stuff, I've got to say. He always seemed to be the one who found the right solution. It's—I was going to say it's sad, but it isn't. It really isn't.' She took a full intake of breath then quickly puffed it out. 'I just liked him—I think that's why I ignored your messages for so long, because I *did*, I liked him. He would make me laugh sometimes. And, I'll be straight with you, okay—I fancied him a little bit. I used to flirt with him. Which is why this conversation is particularly . . . you know what I'm saying. This is pretty uncomfortable.' She gulped down the last of her coffee. 'I was sixteen and he was in his thirties. It's bad.'

'Thirty-six,' I said.

'Yeah.'

'I'm not judging you, or anything, I just—sorry, I interrupted you.'

'It's okay.' She blinked. She rubbed her scalp. 'I think that's really all that I can tell you, Daniel. I flirted with him like a teenager, which is what I *was*. And obviously I feel sick about that now, but—I can't have been the only one, right? I mean, I don't want to sound like I'm praising him, but he *was* a good-looking man. And there were plenty of other girls around who thought so at the time. Chloe included—and she was gorgeous.

She could've had anyone . . . Christ, I wish I'd ordered food now. My stomach's burning.'

'Did he flirt back?' I said.

'What?'

'I'm saying, did he ever try it on with you?'

She held her stung expression long enough for it to pass as genuine. 'No. Why? Is that what you heard?'

'I've heard a lot of things. I'm asking you.'

'Who told you that, anyway?' Her eyes were glistening.

'Does it matter?'

'No, but if someone's been spreading it around, I want to know who.'

I lowered my voice, made sure it came out evenly. 'I heard it from Chloe.'

'Jesus, that's—are you serious?' Her jaw hung open and revealed a silver stud set in the pillow of her tongue, which struck me as unusual (if only because my grandpa used to say that piercing anything except an earlobe was what a woman did to get attention or to punish herself). 'You've got to know that isn't true. It's one hundred per cent *not true* at all,' she said.

And I believed her. There was nothing in her attitude or her body language that incited any doubt. She moved to pad her lashes with her wrist. 'I mean, fuck—is that why he did it, d'you think? Because she thought something was going on between us? *Fuck.*' I hadn't foreseen that she would ask this and it panicked me. I'd wanted to meet Eve because I thought that she might bring me closer to appreciating why, to filling out the landscape of unknowns I lived in. But all that I was doing was redistributing the guilt, creating pain for other people. I could've told her so much then—all the things that he'd extracted from her in the car at knifepoint—but I didn't. I said, 'I don't know, Eve, I don't know why he did it. It's just what I was told.'

'He flirted back with me sometimes, I guess. But he never *did* anything. I was sixteen.'

'Yeah, I know. I believe you.'

'I hope so. I really do, because—look, I'm not defending him, but he wasn't like that.'

'That's something, I suppose.'

'Yeah,' she said. 'It is. It should be.' She pushed her cup aside with such a force the spoon dropped from the saucer, off the table. Bending to gather it, she said: 'I probably shouldn't admit this, but I didn't like her all that much. Chloe. She could be weird with me and other girls on set. She was kind of a head-worker. A bragger, too. Like, always telling us about which club she'd been at, how drunk she was, what this man had whispered in her ear on the dance floor, that kind of thing, as if it was supposed to be impressive. I mean, I don't want to speak ill of her or anything, god rest her soul, and it's just awful what he did to her. And I'll probably burn in hell now or what-ever, but, since we're being honest, I just think you need to know that Chloe had her issues. I mean, who the fuck doesn't?'

'I appreciate you being straight with me,' I said.

'But you know what I mean, though, right?' She angled her head at me, trying to gauge my reaction. 'Everybody's got their problems. I'm not sure why Chloe told you that. It never happened.'

'I can see that now.'

'Is that what you've been trying to ask me all this time? All those emails?'

I shrugged. 'It's not an easy thing to bring up. We don't know each other. We're just connected.'

'Yeah. But still. I could've saved you the train fare.' She leaned back in her chair, waving to the waiter. 'I can pay for the drinks at least.'

'No, don't, please. I think I'm going to order something else. I'm at least a seven now.'

She smiled.

By the time the waiter came, the restaurant was brighter.

Phony chandeliers had been turned on, glimmering above the neat white tables. A placid opera was playing in the bar. Eve glanced at her watch and told me her allotted hour was almost up, as though finishing a consultation with a tiresome patient. 'If I'm not back in there by three fifteen, they'll get the impression I don't care about the play, which, come to think of it, is not a bad incentive to hide here for a few more minutes.' She regarded the waiter. 'He's going to need his menu back, and I'm going to need another cappuccino.'

We stayed there together until I'd eaten half my cannelloni. Our conversation settled back into the mode it started out in— a curious civility—while she spooned off the froth and chocolate from her drink and left the coffee. I asked her what was next for her, after the Young Vic, and she said she had a second audition for an indie film in a few days: 'My first one was a shocker, but the director took pity on me—Richard convinced him I had gastroenteritis, if you don't mind, which is the sort of thing you pay your agent for. He's been great for me.' After the play's run was over, she was taking some time off, seeing an actor friend of hers in San Francisco who was trying to convince her to move out to LA with him: 'It's just a reccy. I'm always like *this close* to doing it, but something always stops me. Probably the thought of being another walking cliché. At least if I'm a failed actress here I can move into my parents' bungalow, work at a bookies or something. Over there, I'd have to join a cult or maybe pole dance. That really American sort of failure terrifies me. I could handle something more low-key.' And she wagged the spoon at me and said, 'Anyway, what about you? What are your plans for the rest of your life?'

SIDE FOUR

NEGATIVE PEACE

There is a plaque I keep on my desk now, here in Manhattan. My wife had it specially engraved and mounted on a rosewood base to match the furniture in my office: *The small man lives his life outside disaster.* It's a line by Sophocles I came across when I was sorting through my mother's books some twenty years ago. She'd underlined it neatly with a pencil and, in the margin next to it, she'd written: *Yes!!!* I used to have a plan to get it tattooed on my arm. I went as far as researching the best London parlours where I might have it done, phoning up to ask how much that sort of thing would set me back and making an appointment for the afternoon of my eighteenth, but when the day arrived I lost my nerve. As meaningful as the gesture was to me, I knew a tattoo would upset my mother. She used to say that they were loutish, a sign of an uncultured mind, and even though she wasn't there to disagree with any more, she still had the authority to overrule me.

The plaque was a perfect compromise. About nine months into our relationship, Alisha and I (still dating then) had been in bed together and I'd fallen into my routine of stroking the tattoo on her right shoulder—a tiny ace of spades, about as plain as it is pointless. She'd asked me what I thought of it. I knew that it meant something to her, despite the fact that she dismissed it as a vestige of a drunken misadventure, so I told her it was part of her and, therefore, beautiful. 'Yeah, right,' she'd said, 'smooth talk. You hate it.' This had led me to explain about the Sophocles tattoo that never was. Afterwards, Alisha had said, 'Well, I still think you should go ahead and do it, but I understand your reasons,' and we'd moved on to discussing something else. It was a few months later that I found a gift-wrapped parcel waiting in my briefcase when I got to work (I'll be damned if I know how she unpicked the combination). She'd had the plaque made at a trophy store three blocks from our apartment. This is the type of thing Alisha did for me back then, and still does after nearly three years of marriage: she thinks about me, apropos of nothing, and has no expectation that her thoughtfulness will ever be reciprocated. Now, every morning, I see that plaque and feel a sense of purpose. It reminds me of the stable life I've managed to accomplish. It anchors me to my desk and sends me home with the resolve to be a better person. If the small man lives his life outside disaster, then I'm hoping to become the smallest man on Earth.

I function in the world these days, and this is an achievement in itself. Still, I can't help wanting more. Not material effects, you understand—I'm fortunate to own a small apartment in the East Village and my grandparents bequeathed me enough money to stay free of the survival worries that most people have to cope with. I know that this is one aspect of my life in which I've been extremely lucky. The company I work for, Vaillant Stack Kinnear, pays me a good salary and I find the job I do sustains the part of me that needs to be continually engaged with unimportant duties—when I'm with clients, I can persuade them that there's nothing more significant to my well-being than the efficiency of their investments, and I'm valued by the partners here at VSK because they continue to mistake this tirelessness of mine for dedication to the cause. Of course, there are fulfilments that a role in corporate finance cannot give me, but I've found these by other means, through volunteering. Two nights a week, I teach free bookkeeping and accounting courses at a community centre in Queens, and I've met people there who have worse histories than mine to tell. As well as this, I give free maths tuition to adults preparing for the GED test, and I've exacted such a thrill from watching these discounted men and women grasp the rudiments of algebra that I plan to scale back on my hours at VSK and devote more time to tutoring over the next few years. What I have, right now, are the constituents of happiness, and I'm trying every day to make these good things aggregate to something like the happiness I had before. This is what I mean by wanting more. There is such a thing as negative peace, I think: a settled state in which so little has been gained and too much has been lost. I'm striving to restore the sense of wholeness that I used to take for granted as a boy.

It's important to have targets. One summer, I would like to drive up to the coast of Massachusetts with Alisha, spend the whole of August in a quiet house with views of the Atlantic, and be with her entirely—no backsliding into other Augusts of my life, no measuring our interactions against my parents' interactions, no recognition of the calendar dates as things to be endured, surmounted.

But the prospect of me lasting anywhere outside the city thrum for longer than an afternoon remains a distant hope—I still need the wakeful patterns of New York to steady me. I still don't have a driver's licence, and I won't be a passenger—if I ever get a cab, I have to be too drunk to notice (Alisha tells me that we took one home after a wedding in the spring, and I threw up each installment of the seafood buffet on the seats). my sleep is now so conditional on Ambien it likely qualifies as drug addiction. I won't claim this nightly ritual of mine doesn't concern me. It certainly perturbs my wife: 'I'm not saying go cold turkey, honey. I'm saying maybe just take *one*, like you're supposed to.' But I'm frightened that a reduction of the dose will amplify the volume of the noises I hear—I don't want them to carry forward into daylight. So if a doctor ever cuts off my prescription, I simply find another one to write me up. The practice I am registered with today is out in Westchester, a decent train journey into the suburbs. This is probably a sign that I'm not coping as well as I pretend.

In my adult life, I've seen more therapists than I've seen clouds, and they've been so entirely useless in such a wide variety of ways that I almost gave up on the idea of therapy altogether. But lately I've been going to a grief support group in my neighbourhood, run out of the basement at the 10th Street Church. It was recommended to me by a doctor as kind of consolation prize in lieu of sleeping pills. I went along one night to see if it had anything to offer, and it surprised me just how comfortable I felt inside the space. The counsellor who hosts the meetings is a man called Dennis Alma, a retired police psychologist. He has a manner that reminds me of my best teachers at school—forthright but avuncular—and he can fill a silence with as moving a soliloquy as you're likely to hear from the mouth of a shrink (the stories he has told us about his life have helped to place my own in context, or at least to position it along a spectrum of guilt: Dennis was responsible for accidentally shooting his own sister when he was five years old). He lets me sit there every other Thursday, cross-armed and silent, without pressing me for contributions. One of the things that Dennis always tells the group is that we must stop viewing the present as the continuation of our past and see it, instead, as the beginning of our future. I know that this is just an aphorism, not an actual solution to the problem, but the same thing could be levelled at the words of Sophocles. I'm getting closer to believing what he says is possible.

Alisha and I met about eight months after I transferred to New York, which constitutes the greatest stride towards contentment that I've ever taken. She was in the very first accounting course I taught in Queens, although she missed a couple of the early sessions. I remember she appeared three weeks in, towing a steel trunk on wheels that she seemed rather nervous about parking in the empty room. 'You can just bring it up to the front,' I told her, 'if you're worried someone's going to pinch it. The others will be here soon.'

She pulled a musing face at me and said, 'Hmm, I don't know. That seems a little far away. My whole life is in this thing.' I couldn't tell if she was being serious or not until she took a desk chair on the back row and set the trunk down next to her, resting her feet on it.

'Is there a pen and paper in it?' I said. 'You're probably going to need to take a few notes.'

'Nah, I got that covered, though.' She brought out an old Dictaphone from the inside of her coat, holding it up as though it were a pocket bible she was about to consult. 'You don't mind if I record this, do you? I just figure it's easier than trying to read my own handwriting later. I haven't studied much of anything since high school.'

'It's fine with me. But you might need to check with the others.'

'They won't care,' she said. 'And if they do, I'll just go ahead and record it all in secret anyway.'

'Like the FBI,' I said.

'Exactly. If it's good enough for the Feds . . .'

I smiled at her and went back to organising photocopied handouts. As I recall, we covered simple balance sheets and cash flow in that session. 'So, I've got a few absentees here on the list, and I'm just trying to guess which one is you. I'm thinking you aren't Rodolpho or Cliff.'

'I'm Alisha,' she said.

'Ah. okay. Welcome to the class.' I ticked the register they'd given me.

'Good to be here. Can I just double-check something with you?'

'Sure.'

'This thing is totally free, right? I mean, you're not going to spring any hidden charges on me.'

'No. It's completely free, don't worry.'

'Good.' She puffed breath at her fringe. "Cause I was sitting here thinking, man, those cashmere pants alone would cost me half my rent. I hope I can afford this guy.'

I had come straight from the office in a tailored blue suit. 'Yeah, I suppose I should've changed into something a bit less—'

'Wall Street.'

'I was going to say corporate, but, yeah.'

'Don't bother. You're teaching us how to be good with our money, right?'

'Sort of. There's a bit more to it.'

'What I'm saying is, if you want anyone round here to follow your advice, you've got to look the part. I'd rather know a guy's got money if he's telling me what I should do with mine. And I'm sure most people in this neighbourhood would think the same as me. So, okay, maybe lose the cufflinks and the tie, roll up your sleeves, but you don't need to come here in your sweats because you happen to earn more than we do. Let it show a little. You're a pro at this, from what I've heard. And besides—' She turned her eyes quickly to the window. 'You look nice.'

Each Tuesday night for the remainder of the course, I resisted the impulse to call on her for answers just to feel the pleasant weight of her attention. I would like to say that I was more concerned with helping her appreciate the fundamentals of accounting than I was with getting to know her, but all Alisha had to do back then was show up with her hair still damp and formless from the shower and I would lose my grasp on numbers, thinking of the freckled incline of her neck and what it would be like to kiss it ('Um, don't you mean, one-sixty-*four*,

Dan?' one of the students would say in my periphery. 'Or is my calculator broken?'). I guessed that she was similar in age to me, though I always got the sense from her behaviour in the class that she was older—there was a candour to her conversation style that I associated with maturity, world-weariness (Alisha is, in fact, a year younger, but I still maintain she has a streetwise quality I'll never possess). Every week, I hoped that she would stop me in the doorway as I left the building and invite me for a drink with her and the whole group; but there was little camaraderie among her cohort—no doubt I'd failed to inspire it—and so the invitation never came. I told myself that it would be unethical to socialise with my own students anyway. I remember thinking it was best if I partitioned my teaching life from my personal life to avoid any conflicts of interest, even though the students were grown adults with their own small businesses and they treated me as their tax advisor.

It took her almost missing the last session of the course for me to change my view on that. With Alisha's seat empty, I got deflated by the idea that I'd never see her again. I spent forty-something minutes of the class discussing straight-line depreciation and recapping my notes on the double entry bookkeeping system, and I couldn't tell you whether or not a word I spoke that night was reasonable or incoherent. When time was almost up, there was a scrape and a shuffle from the corridor, and I saw her peeking in through the window with a face of desperation. I waved her in. 'Is this Time-keeping 101?' she asked, 'because I could use some serious tuition.' The group laughed and jeered, sarcastically—camaraderie at last, I thought—and she came into the room, dragging that steel box of hers across the linoleum. 'Could someone give me a hand here?' she said. 'I lost a wheel getting off the damn bus.' I couldn't run there fast enough. 'Thanks,' she said. 'What did I miss?'

'Everything,' said Rodolpho, in his usual caustic way: he

was a fifty-seven-year-old garage owner who hadn't smiled once in nine straight weeks of teaching. 'But I'm sure Dan can find some extra time to catch you up—can't you, Dan?' Smirks all round the room. I had never felt so utterly transparent.

At the end of the session, I asked the students who would like to get a drink with me to celebrate their official mastery of accountancy, and only Alisha raised her hand: the rest had families to get back to, work to get up for early in the morning, night shifts to show up for. 'No can do,' said Cliff. 'It's been awesome, though. I learned a lot.' I don't know if they were being charitable or if they were especially ambivalent, but I didn't try too hard to persuade them.

'Wherever we're going, we'll need to schlepp this thing,' Alisha said. 'Sorry about that.'

'You take one handle, I'll take the other?'

'Perfect.'

'I'll just have to lock up and give the keys back to the super.'

'Okay. I'll wait.'

That night was our first at the Neptune Diner, the place Alisha and I now return to every year on the same date—her way of consecrating what she refers to as 'our true north anniversary.' Walking down Astoria Boulevard with the trunk swinging between us, I asked her: 'What the hell d'you keep in here, anyway?'

'Man,' she said, 'I don't even know your last name. We've got to be pretty well acquainted before I let that information out.'

'It's Jarrett,' I said.

'See. I didn't know that.'

'You would've done if you'd been at our first class.'

'True. But there's no guarantee I would've listened. I tend to fall asleep a little when you talk. No offence.'

'It's probably my teaching style. Accountancy is too much fun. I have to play it down or no one can sit still.'

She laughed. 'It really works. You're like a shot of Nyquil to the senses.'

'I'm guessing it's equipment of some kind.'

'Huh?'

'In the box.'

'Oh.'

I knew she was a photographer. During the course, she had disclosed it in the preamble to a set of pointed questions about entity—we'd covered the topic in much greater depth than I'd planned to in that session, solely out of deference to her interest in it. 'How expensive are the cameras in here that it takes two people to lug them around?'

'I never said they were cameras. And by the way—*shshh*.'

'No one's going to come and nick it right out of our hands.'

'This is Queens, pal. I'm not taking any chances.'

'You really think we might get trunk-jacked?'

'Shut up,' she said, laughing. 'That's not a word I want to hear you speak again.'

'Well, whatever it is,' I called out, 'it's heavy.'

'Look, you got me, all right.' She was enjoying herself—I could tell from the bounce in her stride. 'My father's pretty well known around these parts. He's in the sanitation business, if you get my gist. I've been chopping bodies up and packing them in here, and now I need a big strong guy like you to help me toss it off the bridge before it really starts to smell, you know?'

I've been told since, by Alisha, that I slowed my walking pace so much, clenching the handle of the trunk, that it nearly slipped out of her grasp. She tells me that my face turned sickly grey, and I stopped speaking altogether for a block or two. There is no reason to doubt that this is true. I have no memory of those minutes, just the chugga chugga *clank* chugga chugga *clank* chugga chugga *clank*. 'Jesus, Dan, I wasn't serious. Are you okay?' she said. 'Dan? I was just kidding around.' It was the sight of the express station that brought me out of it. The N train was shuffling in to the raised platform up ahead and it overwhelmed the sound. I can cope with any noise that I can glean the source of, and I'm often drawn into the subway here for the same reason I used to be attracted to the tube: I know the noise is not *the* noise. 'Yeah, shit, I'm sorry,' I said, 'I spaced out a bit. It happens to me sometimes.'

She looked at me with a sort of pity. 'You want to call it a night?'

'No way. I'm hungry.'

'Oh good,' she said. 'Me too.'

We sat down at a booth (now *our* booth) at the window of the Neptune, with the trunk in the space between us, pressing at my toes. She ordered pancakes and I had a Denver omelette and, while we waited with our beers, she apologised a second time for her line about the bodies. 'I guess it maybe touched a nerve with you or something, I don't know,' she said. 'I was just trying to sound more interesting than I am.'

'There's nothing to be sorry about,' I told her. 'It's not your fault.'

She didn't push me on it. Kicking the trunk, she said: 'Well, I'm still not telling you what's in it.'

'Wait until you've had a few more of these.' I wobbled my glass at her.

'Ah, you're not going to care by then. I need to start lowering expectations.'

'Anything short of plutonium is going to be a disappointment.' I realised it already—the effect she had on me. I felt so much calmer in her company than at any other time during my day. She extracted thoughts from me that I would otherwise have been too mannered to conceive.

'Okay, since you're already losing interest, cards on the table,' she said. 'Here's what it is: a portable darkroom. Cost me like nine hundred bucks, so, yeah, I keep it pretty close. I'm sort of between apartments and I don't have a studio space right now. Can't afford to stop working, and I can set this thing up in, like, a parking lot, so, it comes with me everywhere I go. These last few months have been crazy with work. I've sold a lot of pictures, earned a lot of money, but I've spent way more than I should have. If you saw my balance sheets, you'd cry.'

'I could help you with that, you know. Whenever you want.'

'Shut up,' she said. 'I can't afford you.'

'You know I wouldn't charge you. It'd be my pleasure.'

She planted her elbows on the table, landed the globe of her head on her fists. 'What's with you, Dan? Always doing stuff for free? Are you like some trust fund kid or something, getting his hands dirty with the regular folks?'

'Shit,' I said, and slugged my beer. 'Is that really how I come across?'

'No. Not at all. I'm just curious. I mean, what brings a guy like you out here to teach the likes of me?'

'Oh, you don't have time to hear that story, trust me,' I said. 'And the likes of you are exactly why I do it. I don't get to meet a lot of genuine people in my line of work.'

'Okay.' She narrowed her eyes at me. 'So tell me more about yourself. I mean, how do you keep the roof over your head? I take it you don't live in Queens.'

'Queens is pretty nice. I wouldn't mind.'

'Shut up. Queens sucks. That's non-negotiable. Come on—' She leaned in, lightly scratching at her clavicle. 'You're probably the smartest guy I've ever met. Where did you study?'

'Again, if you'd been there in week one—'

'Get over it. Seriously. Where?'

'The London School of Economics.'

'That's cool.'

'And the Institute of Chartered Accountants.'

'Less cool.'

'Definitely.'

An old couple went by on the pavement outside and she watched them ambling towards the half-lit underpass. 'Must've taken a while, huh? Nine weeks of numbers in my head was bad enough. I only made it through one semester at CUNY. Liberal Arts. I hated it.'

'It's not for everyone,' I said. 'But, I don't know, I've always liked studying for things. Targets are good for me. I can lose myself in them.'

'Now I'm learning stuff I didn't get from sitting in your class.'

I tried to pre-empt her next question, but it only wrong-footed her. 'You ever heard of Vaillant Stack Kinnear?'

The firmness of her 'No' was resounding. This was the same woman who now collects the paper from our doormat every morning, reads through the Finance pages before turning to the Arts. 'Sounds like a girl-band from the eighties.'

'Yeah, well, you asked what keeps the roof over my head. That girl-band is it. I'm in the M and A department there—mergers and acquisitions. I can give you a business card, if you like. I chose the colour myself.'

'Which one did you go for?'

'Cauliflower green, I believe it's called.'

'I don't think that's an official Pantone shade.'

'No. But they're nice. Look.' I took one out of my jacket and handed it to her.

'So what do you merge and acquire?'

'I don't. I just advise people who do.'

'Ah, you're like the guy at my gallery who says, *Photos of the sidewalk are hot right now. Bring me ten and we'll talk.*'

'No, I'm the guy who says, *Here's a pile of data about side-walks. Some of them look good but they might blow up in your face.*'

'Hah. See, that's the kind of gallery guy I need.'

'Well, you have my card now. You know where to find me.'

Our food arrived. Alisha drowned her pancakes in syrup. I attacked the strange coagulation of pale cheese that had been put in front of me. 'So, all right then. What *is* the hottest thing in M and A right now? What are you working on?' she said.

'You really want to know?'

'I really want to know.'

'You don't.'

'Look at my face: I'm serious.'

'But it's so boring. You'll hate me.'

'Wait, have some of this bacon first. I can't eat it.' She dumped two rashers on my plate before I could stop her—another habit of Alisha's I've grown used to, and which feels as charming to me now as it did then. And, while we ate, I told her about the package I'd been compiling to attract investors into aviation financing. Not once did she undercut me, roll her eyes, or feign a coma. Instead, she put her knife and fork haphazardly across her plate and said, 'Well, I've got fifty-three dollars and four cents in my checking account. That's got to get me a piece of something, right? Maybe a bright orange vest and a set of those earmuffs?'

'I'll look into it for you.'

Nodding at the window, she said: 'Do you think you'll stick around here for a while?'

'At some point I should probably start walking to the subway.'

She was beaming at me now. 'No, genius, I was asking if you'll have to go back home some day. You know, to England. Remember England?'

'Oh. Sorry. Dumb of me.' I took encouragement from her question. She had an interest in my long-term future—that had to be a sign that she would see me again, if I asked. 'I guess that all depends.'

'On what?'

'Visa, green card, the usual.'

'Right.'

'But, to be honest, there's a lot of other stuff. Things I need to work out while I'm here. It was meant to be a fresh start for me, and I'm still not sure if it's really what I needed.' This was a conversation we would have another time. We would get to it that August, on a humid Sunday afternoon as we walked laps of Tompkins Square, a featureless blue sky above the trees, a latent sunlight brightening the parapets of buildings far along the seamless strait of Avenue A. I would begin to tell her everything that I am telling you right now. 'Look, can I get us both another beer? Or do you have somewhere to be?'

'Nowhere better than right here,' she said. 'It's still early in my world. I only come alive at midnight.' She folded back her sleeve as though to check her watch, but didn't even glance at it. Time would move at its own rate, and we would let it carry us.

* * *

I'm getting closer to the age my father was that August. It has taken me thirty-three years to find the edge of where I belong, and I'm working my way to the centre. I have needed my mother every day, but I've been without her for so long that I've outlived her example—I remember her from the perspective of a boy who relied on her for every meal, every piece of clothing on his back, every big decision. There's no way for me to know whether her attitude towards me might've changed as I became an adult, what her temperament might've been as she grew into old age. We might've fallen out, become estranged. I might've disenchanted her the way he did. She might've met another man and moved to Kenya, as she'd once dreamed of doing in her teenage diaries. And I wonder all the time if she'd approve of where I live today, the job I have, the company I keep, because there's a greater part of me that understands I wouldn't be here now if she were still alive, that I wouldn't have Alisha in my life or feel this new sense of belonging. I would still be with her back in England, making sure to call her every other night and see her in the holidays, as well-raised men should do.

I suppose it was expected that I'd reach a point of turbulence eventually, when all the hurt that I'd absorbed and grief that I'd blocked out would manifest itself in my behaviour. My grandmother used to say to me, 'Daniel, if you need to go and smash up a few car windows, nobody would blame you, but please don't act like nothing's happened. I'd rather see you angry than unmoved.' She brought me up to meet the aspirations that she knew my mother had for me, and never hesitated to appropriate an opinion if it was useful to the cause of rearing me: 'Think what your mum'd say to you right now, young man. These are *her* orders, not mine.' I don't think she realised how much this helped. It let me channel all my sadness into the pursuit of an achievement that I thought—because I'd been so well reminded of it—was the only thing my mother ever wanted for me.

For years, I managed to repurpose my anxieties like this, directing all my thoughts into preparing for exams that lay in wait—I was terms ahead of other kids at Chesham Park when I first returned to classes, and surprised my teachers with the waltz I took through all my GCSEs (they knew I was a good student but they anticipated a prolonged adjustment back to 'normal' life). After my grandpa died, painlessly, in a still, green room full of chrysanthemums at the Chiltern Hospital, I learned that I could disappear into my education and feel justified in shutting out the world. I hid behind the attitude that if I didn't get the best A-level grades I would disappoint my mother. I hid behind the daunting Microeconomic Principles and Quantitative Methods modules at LSE. I hid behind three years of work experience in financial services and auditing. I hid behind the ACA examinations. I hid behind my exploration of the job market, taking interview after interview after interview until I was satisfied that I was making the right choice (the one she would've made). After I accepted a position in Transactions at the glass Embankment offices of Vaillant Stack Kinnear, there was nothing left to hide behind except the intrinsic need to prove myself to those who'd hired me. And VSK is where I've hidden ever since.

When I look back on this important period of my life, I don't recall much earnest human interaction: a pretty girl I saw across a seminar room once made my heart capsize before she transferred to a different module; another exhausted intern almost made me cry into his blazer one night by the photocopier just by handing me a stapler; a kind librarian and I shared a pleasant conversation once about her love of Joe Durango novels; a temp I slept with told me that I was the least attentive partner that she'd ever had and so I asked—out loud—how I could improve my performance. Somehow, these years feel like a spell of isolation from reality, a slow tour of the confines of myself in which the landmarks of my history were whited out.

Head down and work: it's the only coping strategy I've ever had and I'm grateful that it's kept me upright all this time. I was twenty-four when my grandmother passed away, and I sat in the front row of her church in Bradenham with a hundred funeral mourners bowed in prayer behind me, understanding that I had no family left to tell me how to live, to show me what my standards ought to be.

And so I gave my every breath to VSK. I sweated through my shirts for them. I skipped meals for them. I went without the social niceties that other people had. My only friends were VSK people; I never saw them anywhere except the office corridors and common areas. Every night, when I got back to my flat in Camden, I opened up my laptop and logged in to my

VSK account. I would've given them my last remaining pint of blood if a memo had gone out requesting it. I worked through it, I worked through it, I worked through it, as I always had. My commitment didn't go unseen—by twenty-six, I was made a partner in the M and A department—but I hit that long-expected turbulence soon after.

Women in the office began looking at me differently. I don't know if it was my change in status that attracted them, or if the features that my father gave me bedded in around that time and made me into something worth a second glance. Perhaps the shift came from within me: a boost in confidence, a new assurance in my surroundings. Whatever it was, I saw more London bedrooms, hotel ceilings, kitchen floors, than I had ever thought possible. I went to bed with secretaries, PAs, accounts assistants, HR managers, legal team affiliates, finance directors. Their faces still remain in memory even if their names do not. Some I slept with more than once; some I never saw again; some I made unskilful small talk with in front of clients, in the ascending lift, the lobby. I only sought out women who worked at VSK, but I kept them at a distance. It makes me queasy to admit this. Not just because it shames me that I treated people—colleagues—this way, but because I can't help thinking I was doing it in order to be like him. Or, at least, to gauge how close to being my father I could get if I allowed it.

One night, I found myself on the twelfth floor of a Radisson hotel with a young intern. Let's say, for argument's sake, that her name was Nadine. We had got to talking in the office common area that evening, and she had mentioned she was in the last year of her MSc (I forget which university), undertaking practical experience with the company as part of her degree. I had offered to take her out to dinner, giving no reason other than I hadn't eaten yet and she looked like she could use a meal that wasn't made by Dr. Oetker. We ate, we drank a little wine, we walked to a hotel, we went up to the room. It really was that simple.

She sat down on the bed and slipped her shoes off. Leaning back, she smoothed the duvet with her palms, uncrossed her legs. I went and kissed her, feeling her whole body softening beneath me. Her arms stretched out above her head, and I drew up the high hem of her work dress to see her stomach, the sheer waistband of her tights biting the skin. 'Wait wait wait,' she said, and rolled sideways. 'Just give me a minute. I need to—make us a drink or something, while I go in there?' She went to the bathroom, zipping her dress off. 'Don't be too long,' I said. No sooner had the door closed, the shower started running. I took off my jacket, my shoes and socks. I fetched two beers from the minibar, drank half of one before I lost my patience. The extractor fan was whirring, clattering. The door was unlocked so I went in. I found her standing naked at the basin, a mess of towels at her feet. She was not surprised to see me, but seemed irritated, as though I had intruded on a private argument she was having with herself. 'Well, this is hardly fair,' she said, smirking. 'Now I'm the only one who's—' And I didn't even wait for her to finish the thought. I strode right in and kissed her, walked her back towards the counter. She unbuttoned my shirt and peeled it off. Her fingers roughed my skin. She breathed into my ear and tongued the lobe, pushing hard against me. I undid my belt and she undid the rest. I don't know who decided it—if it was me, or her, or both of us at once—but she turned round in a hurry, bent over the empty basin, spread her arms across the strange blue marble and its ink-blot pattern.

When people ask what prompted me to transfer out of London, I never tell them about this. But I won't hide anything from you—even my ugliest urges. You need to see the ways that I am like him and the ways that I am not.

Because as soon as I had put myself inside her, and I felt the knock of her pale buttocks in the shallows of my hips, the rhythm of her hamstrings going smack smack smack against my thighs, I had no mind to stop. She was making stifled sounds of pleasure. Unusual but familiar. I thought, *Have I been with this girl before? Have I forgotten her?* I paused, pressing my lips against her back. 'What's the matter?' she said. 'Don't stop. I'm not even close.' When I glanced up, I saw our vague reflections in the fogged-up mirror. And I carried on. She leaned into me, her elbows tucked beneath her chest, one temple to the counter. Her breaths quickened and swelled. I looked up again, to watch myself, what I was doing to her. And I saw the woozy outline of him peering back at me, his expression lurking there, stolid and determined, unforgivable. I stopped so abruptly that it irked her. 'No no no, come on,' she said, 'not now. Keep going.' She tried to grab my hands and move them to her breasts. But I was spooked and couldn't carry on. 'I can't, I'm done,' I said. 'I can't.'

'Seriously?' she said. 'But you were—we were—'

'I think I need to lie down.'

She dropped her head back to the marble, aggrieved or plain embarrassed. 'Okay, I guess the bed's more comfortable anyway,' she said.

'No, we have to stop. I'm sorry. I'm feeling a bit funny.'

'You mean like something you ate?'

'No, just strange.'

'Okay. I get it.' Peering back at me, she said: 'Maybe next time.'

'I'm sorry,' I said. 'It's nothing you did wrong.'

'Yeah, I know, Dan. It's cool. I get it.'

While she took another shower, I went and sat on the armchair by the window, looking down at the tarred rooftops of the neighbouring buildings. 'So, do you want me to go?' she said, emerging from the bathroom in a cotton gown.

'I'd prefer it if you kept me company,' I said. 'The room's been paid for. Might as well use it.'

'As long as I can raid that little fridge.'

'All yours.'

'Are you still feeling funny, then?' she asked.

'Yeah, but it's all right. I'm used to it.'

She lay on the bed and flicked the television channels, drinking wine from a bottle for one. I drafted emails on my work phone. 'I don't have anything to sleep in,' she said, and took off her robe, slid under the duvet. After a while, the charmless comedy that she was watching and the alcohol made her drowsy, and I ran out of messages to send. My laptop was still at the office. All I had was this very young woman, dozing naked in the space beside me, the long slant of her shoulder flashing with the TV light. And I had their conversations, pinning me awake again. *Useless worthless idiot don't have to explain myself to you I can do what I want why don't you shut your fucking trap for once always blaming someone else for your mistakes I mean where's your self-respect you've always wanted me to fail there's nothing you like better than humiliating me god I wish I'd never met you nobody can stand you always whining at me you don't know you're fucking born even your own son has no respect for you I never loved you anyway oh yeah and what you going to do about it eh yeah right that's what I thought all talk.*

M y wife's patience is extraordinary. She knows every dimension of my history, so she accommodates the fits of attitude I throw from time to time over the pettiest of matters without appearing to think less of me. She can differentiate between my fleeting sadness and my chronic gloom, and has the sensitivity to realise that there are moments when I need to talk and moments when I don't. She understands why there's a bottle of 'Sunflowers' in our bathroom cabinet, and why the Chesham Library's complete audio edition of *The Artifex Appears* is locked in the top drawer of the bureau in the hall. How is it possible that she has stuck with me for long enough to see beyond my frailties? The outer coldness, the pretence of toughness, the essential oddness: she has breached each layer of me and seems to love what she has found inside. And I have loved her back in such a shambling and unfathomable way that she must wonder—as I do—how intimately I need to know her mind before I let myself accept that she is not a stand-in for my mother. All my prior relationships with women have been ruined by one sad assumption: that I can fix the problems of my parents' marriage in my own life, a gesture at a time, a decision at a time, a sexual encounter at a time. Alisha gets this—she figured it all out within a month of being with me—and somehow she's still here. The forbearance that she has for stupid things I say and do is staggering. Such as when I tell her, 'Look, I know that you want children of your own some day,' when what I mean is: 'Look, I know you'd really love for us to start a family.'

I have let this issue threaten our marriage for much too long. As I told you before, there's a fault line under every forward step I try to make. I don't see how I can ever be responsible for someone else's childhood until I can resolve the problems of my own. It's a mindset that Alisha says I'll overcome with the right help, but I keep resisting her encouragement and sound advice, because she doesn't understand the weight of blood like mine—I work so hard to carry it around as though it's nothing.

We slide into these arguments unexpectedly. A cat goes sprinting down a stoop before us as we walk along the street: it sparks a conversation about cats and why she doesn't like them, which becomes a conversation about the hissing stray that ran into the house when she was six and lay down in her brother's crib, which becomes a conversation about her nieces and the special cover that her sister bought to stop cats jumping in her daughters' stroller, which becomes a conversation about her sister asking her when we'll have babies of our own. The closer that Alisha and I become—and I don't believe it's possible for me to love her any more than I do now—the guiltier I feel that she's committed herself to someone like me.

But I am trying to get past my insecurities, for both our sakes.

Six months ago, we had the worst fight of our married life. Maybe I was trying to nudge her towards leaving me, not because I wanted her to go, but so I could pre-empt the loss of her on my own terms, control it. The day had started with a pleasant enough breakfast: I made a pan of porridge and, as usual, I teased her for the way that she pronounced it, *pordge*. Afterwards, we sat around my laptop at the kitchen counter, browsing a realtor's images of studio spaces in midtown she'd been mulling over, and we Street Viewed the surroundings to gauge their pluses and minuses. I brewed another pot of coffee and we shared the Saturday papers on the couch. In one of the supplements, there was a profile of a famous sculptor who was digging an enormous hole out in the Arizona desert in the name of art—she was enthused by the spread of landscape photographs accompanying the article: 'Wet-plate collodion,' she said, holding the pages up to catch the daylight. 'Every time I see somebody using it this well it makes me want to throw my camera off the fire escape.' She tried to explain the technicalities to me—a fiddly Victorian process that involved coating a plate in silver nitrate and then exposing it before it dried—but I quickly lost the thread. I said, 'If it appeals to you so much, why don't you try it for yourself?'

'I don't have that sort of time to lose right now. Too much trial and error. It'd take me years to get any good at it.'

'Give yourself a fortnight,' I said. 'You're a fast learner.'

'Ah, Dan, you're such a sycophant, I love you.' She threw the magazine at me, laughing. 'Seriously, it's taken me this long to figure out the stuff I do already, and I still don't know the half of it. And besides, we're talking about handling some pretty nasty chemicals on a daily basis. I couldn't be around them if we ever started trying or, you know, just thinking of my health in general. The ones I'm using now are bad enough.'

'There's that word again,' I said. '*Trying.*'

'Oh, come on. You know that wasn't on my mind until just now.'

'If you say so, Lish.'

'Well, hey, it has to be a small consideration, doesn't it?'

I looked back at her much too coldly. 'I really wouldn't let it stop you at this particular moment, no.'

'Huh.' She sat up, leaned away from me. 'All right.'

I went and put our cups into the dishwasher.

'Honestly, Dan, I wasn't even thinking of it,' she said.

'Good, then.' The rinsing of the porridge pan was suddenly my priority.

And she called to me again over the noise of the taps: 'But, anyway, so what if it *was* on my mind? I'm allowed to think about it, aren't I? Even if you won't discuss it.'

'Right, like you don't talk about it every other day.'

'Dan, come on—you won't even entertain the fucking subject.'

'I've been entertaining it a lot more than I used to.'

'What's *that* supposed to mean?'

'It means you should know better. I can do without you piling on the pressure.'

'Oh man, you're serious. This is actually what you think.'

I shrugged at her. She shook her head at me. We went on in this mode for some time. I grew more juvenile and intent on causing injury with everything I said, until she was shouting back: 'You know what, Dan? I'm getting pretty sick of this. Not everything is all about you and your misery, okay? I'm going.'

'Where?'

'To the studio.'

'What about the park?'

'Forget the park. I'm not spending any more time than I have to with you today.' And she slammed the door on her way out. I didn't see her for the rest of the afternoon. My righteous indignation buoyed me—I felt absolutely sure that I was blameless. There was work I needed to get done, so I busied myself with it. Around five, she rang to tell me she'd be staying the night at the studio. She wasn't trying to punish me, she said, she'd just got 'elbow-deep into a side project' with a friend of hers. 'Just a stupid screen-printing thing I should never have agreed to. Now I really want to get it over with.' I let these words hang without comment.

I couldn't be alone in the apartment any longer so I took my laptop out with me and walked down to St. Mark's Place. There is a café bar called Vick's that has become a regular haunt of mine. By the standards of the East Village, it's low-key and unpretentious, and the food is ordinary. It has a trellised glass frontage like an old shoe shop you might come across in Covent Garden, and I like to go there after office hours sometimes, to sit with my computer and glass of beer while I review my assistants' spreadsheets and rewrite their clinical prose. That night, I had to finish off a draft of an advisory report I'd been compiling—an overview of recent deal activity from aircraft lessors in Asia, if you want the exciting details. I got so absorbed in the minutiae of my data presentation, and so heedless topping up my beer glass from the pitcher, that I didn't even notice how full Vick's had got around me.

A standing crowd of cocktail drinkers had stolen the whole room. They were staring at the far end of the bar, as though in expectation of a speech. I was penned in to the corner of the place. I could hardly get my chair out. Then a trumpet started blaring in the space behind me. A snare drum shuffled, too. A distorted electric guitar. It was jazz, but not the easy kind—the stuff you need to train yourself to appreciate. The crowd hooted and applauded. I had to boost myself up on my tiptoes to see.

Right at the back of the bar, a trio had begun a set. The trumpeter, in a long white smock and shades, was developing a theme of screeches. An improvised racket that drew whoops of admiration all around me. I gathered up my laptop and tried to get the waiter's attention. The trumpet kept on squalling. The waiter was too far away and too distracted. I didn't want to leave the money on the table, so I had to try and sidle through the jazz lovers to the register where I could pay. 'Excuse me, sorry, excuse me, sorry, excuse me.' The brushed thump of the snare began to swell. I was almost at the counter when a guy in a tight denim shirt turned into me with two martini glasses, and I flinched. The drinks careered into the hairdo of the woman next to us. She turned to me, raging, drenched at the neck. I must've apologised, but I don't think she heard me. 'What the fuck, man?' she said, as I went past her. The trumpet would not stop its lunatic bleating. 'Hey, buddy, you owe me two drinks!' called the man. I apologised again. I just wanted to pay and get out of there. When I got to the counter, I planted two bills under a glass and made sure the barman saw it. Then I felt a prodding in the middle of my back. 'Hey, asshole, what the fuck, man? At least say sorry to my girl.' I must've nodded. I might've mumbled something back to him. I tried to leave without a fuss. The snare drum punched and spat at me. The trumpet was choking and shrill. As I pushed for the exit, my laptop was tugged from my grip. I spun round, and saw the man was waving it above his head, a trophy. He looked at me with tightened eyes and dropped it to the floor. I watched a few smalls chunks of plastic break off as it landed. The trumpet kept on biting me. I bounded forwards. The man took a step back. I grasped his denim collar, shoved him. He skidded and fell down.

I went to rescue my computer from under the legs of a table, crawled on my haunches to retrieve it. But before I could get up again, the man stepped in. He swung his knee into my face and I slumped back to the parquet. The sharpness of the pain inside my cheek was so familiar. It reached my brain. I listened to it. It told me I should hurry up and go. I managed to stand, my mouth seeping blood. I wiped it with my wrist. I didn't react—not yet. My father would've broken him without a moment's hesitation, but I just nodded at the man, apologising: 'I'm going. I'm sorry. I'm going.' He dropped his fists, back-pedalling, proud. The crowd was eyeing me. The trumpeter was waiting with his horn held to his chest. The drummer was standing on his stool with his two brushes. 'Okay, let him through, come on, let him through. Get this guy out of here.' A path to the door opened up for me. I staggered out onto the pavement.

I should've gone to hospital, but I trudged for home. The

city felt unusually calm. My pulse was throbbing in my jaw. I reached an intersection, waited for the bleary lights to change and let me cross. A gleaming SUV slowed down in front of me, wanting to turn right. Its passenger peered through the open window, saying: 'Try the ER, pal. You look like shit.' He laughed so brazenly as the car moved off that people waiting near me on the sidewalk joined in, too. The humiliation of it burned in me. I thought of my computer, abandoned to the floor of Vick's, the hours of work I hadn't backed up, all my private photographs and videos and documents.

When I got back to the bar, there were too many people blocking the entrance, and I couldn't see him through the windows. Bodies huddled, swaying to the music, baying for drinks. The blood was sliding down my chin. I decided it was best to wait for him to leave. All I wanted was my laptop. I sat in the doorway of the building adjacent, a dingy nail salon with a pigeon-soiled awning, pink graffiti on the glass. My eye was closing up already. I leaned back in the alcove and watched as people came and went from the bar: my anger festered there. The traffic on First Avenue kept on hustling through the dark. The jazz ensemble was a muffled din beneath the engine noise. It must have been at least an hour and a half I sat there. My lips had almost fused together by the time he emerged.

He came out with his denim shirt rumpled and sweaty, his red-headed girlfriend linked to his arm. They were laughing and shouting to someone inside: I caught the tails of a joke. 'Take it easy, buddy!' he called, stepping backwards. 'See you Tuesday, Freddie!' someone called out at him. 'Hey, I told you, he ain't gonna be there!' his girlfriend called in, giggling. And as they walked off together, rounding the corner of St. Mark's, I saw he had my laptop clutched under his arm. What kind of person beats a man and takes his property as the spoils? What kind of person lets him? It rattled me, incensed me. I ran after them.

They were stumbling down the rule-straight block as if it were crooked, both of them giddy on cocktails, drunk on each other. Her hand was in the back pocket of his chinos. I slowed down, kept my distance, unsure what to do. My face was agony. They passed restaurants and tattoo parlours and the kosher market. I trailed behind them, onto Avenue A, tracked them all the way over the next two cross-streets, heading north, until they dipped under a scaffold on East 12th, where the giant footings of a condo site were swathed in plywood boards and membrane. A dismal line of strip lights in the temporary walkway. Hard to see in from street-level. No one coming up ahead. I checked behind. Not a soul. I upped my pace. They were only a few metres from me. I could see the edge of the computer bobbing in the crook of his left arm, goading me.

'Hey!' I called, rushing at him. 'It's Freddie, right?' And as he turned, bewildered, I reached out and put my hand around his throat so cleanly it immobilised him. I could feel the stubbled curve of it bracing my palm, all its resistance and its give. He dropped the computer and I heard it strike the concrete. I pushed him back against the boards and glowered at him. His girlfriend yelped, pounded my back. This didn't stop me. 'Get off him, asshole! Get the fuck off him! I'm calling the cops!' What stopped me was the quality of the fear deep-rooted in his eyes—he recognised me from the bar, of course; he understood what I was there for, acknowledged what he'd done to me; but something more than that, I think. He must've seen I had the capability to keep on squeezing if I wanted to.

I leaned right into his face. 'I'm taking my fucking computer back,' I said. 'Got it?'

He slow-blinked at me.

'You do *not* want to make this difficult, Freddie. Take my word for it.'

He spluttered.

I squeezed. 'Do we understand each other?'

'Yeah, man. Let him go. He gets it,' said his girlfriend. 'Jesus. What the fuck is wrong with you?' She stooped to gather my laptop. 'Take it, take it. Let him go.' So I did.

My hands were trembling all the way to my apartment. For a while, I stood at the bathroom mirror, washing the blood from my mouth, padding it with cotton balls and antiseptic. I gulped two Ambien to dull the pain. The right side of my face was plum-red and distended, the eye socket bloated shut. I didn't recognise myself. I ditched my bloody clothes in the hamper and walked out to the hallway, where I'd left the laptop sitting by the doormat. Under the kitchen lights, I studied the damage—the casing was badly dinted and the speakers were shattered, but it still booted up. It went about restoring all the windows that were open when its power dropped out. I plugged it in while it purred through its operations and made myself a cup of tea with two capfuls of brandy. When I checked the screen again, the Google Street View image of a loft in midtown had resurfaced in the web browser. I gazed at it for a long moment without thinking anything, but the pain was still needling me. The pills wouldn't grip. I moved the cursor to the search bar, moved it away, moved it back again. I put my fingers to the keyboard. The carriageways were opening in my head. The child lock was on. 'It isn't far.'

'Stay on this road, we'll reach a junction.'

'If there's anything the matter with that boy, I swear to god, Fran, I'll—'

'What? What are you going to do to me? I'm interested to know.'

'I'll make you suffer.'

'Hard to imagine that right now, Kath, I've got to say.'

'Where the fuck are you taking me?'

'You know exactly where we're going.'

'Just promise me he's going to be there. Promise me.'

'I thought my promises weren't worth anything. Have you changed your mind about that?'

'Just tell me he's all right.'

'You'll find out, won't you? It's only up the road.'

'He'll be frightened on his own.'

'Who said he's on his own?'

'You did.'

'Did I? Huh, that's funny.'

'Just please—promise me.'

'Okay. I promise. There. You trust me now?'

'No.'

'Didn't think so. What's the point in talking, anyway? Drive the car.'

'I fucking hate you, Fran.'

'That's hardly a surprise. I've got a shotgun pointed at you.'

'You never used to be this way.'

'Yeah, well, maybe I got tired of the old me.'

'You don't have to do this. Whatever you're planning.'

'Go left at the church, when we get there. You'll recognise it.'

'Is that where he is?'

'You'll see. Oi—leave that window up.'

'I just wanted some air.'

'You're about to get plenty, believe me.'

Y ou will grow up in an age when it is possible to revisit the forsaken spaces of your life at the touch of a screen. I have never been to Audlem, but I have seen it more than any other place on Earth. I can only view it in the daylight. The route I take to find it is the same as theirs: it starts on the M6, the southbound section of the Sandbach Services, leaves the motorway to join the A500, the A531, the B5071, the A529. An ashy covering of clouds hangs static in the sky until I reach the junction in the village square. Then something odd occurs. I click the cross on the road—it's always there in the same place, under the rear bumper of the Morris Minor van that's always turning left, beside the cast iron streetlamp with its jubilee display of Union Flags always flapping northwards on the breeze, next to the Parish Church of St. James the Great where a white-haired man is always lurking on the kerb in baggy slacks, and two cyclists in luminous jackets are forever sheltering at the bus stop as though rain is imminent. And when I click it, by some miracle, the sky goes blue, the sun comes out, the people change. The images are clearly from a different time, the paintwork of the cottage window frames becomes a fraction darker, the shadows expand on the concrete. In this one stretch of Google maps there is a glitch, a lag, a tract of scenery that hasn't been updated in five years: here, it's June 2011, and a short-haired lady strides off with her crumpled umbrella on the drying pavement, the cyclists have disappeared, relieved by an old couple on a bench, their faces pixelated like two criminals on the news—he is always gazing at the rooftops, she is permanently rummaging inside her handbag (for gum, I like to think, or cigarettes). On the corner, by the turn for Vicarage Lane, the vacant shop with the net curtains is for sale; but click a little further along Stafford Street and that same shop has wooden Venetians and a glossy pastel-green facade. Rotate the view, it's August 2016 again and the streets stand empty, the bus shelter has nobody to serve. Where did they go? What became of them?

This is the only Audlem I can bear to know. A scanned-in village where everything that is about to happen never comes to pass.

Head down Vicarage Lane, just like my mother had to do at gunpoint in the dark, and you will see a family is coming up the slope: the parents are wheeling a buggy, carrying their two young daughters in matching green coats. Their faces are blurred out, of course, but they exude a happiness that you can see without zooming in. Who are these people? Don't they know what went on further down this track? I always get the urge to stop and tell them, but they vanish as I approach.

Down I go, as ever, past the gardens with the trampolines, the allotments and the potting sheds, those three white sheets hung up on the line, the gate with its KEEP CLEAR sign, the disused business premises, the van from the telephone company parked up outside, and the man in overalls nattering into his mobile. Here, it's March 2009—all the trees are bare, the ground is damp. In the paddock where they died, there are no gravestones. Just a horsebox and trailer shrouded in tarpaulins. An outhouse. Trampled grass. So still. There's a small blue hatchback waiting on the muddy apron of the road, the same place he made my mother ditch the Volvo—there is no plaque for her there, no bouquet of flowers tucked into the railing slats. But if you rotate the picture you can see a faceless woman driving past the nursing home's brick gateposts in a silver

Volkswagen convertible, a small dog in the passenger seat. They are captives in the frame, going somewhere, going nowhere. I've been staring at them, on and off, for years. They are never getting out of Audlem, but all I have to do is close the window, keep on going.

I've been trying to show Alisha that I'm worth the drain upon her energy, that I can find a lasting happiness with her. The state she found me in that afternoon at the apartment—bloody-mouthed and tranquillised upon the kitchen counter—saddened her more than it frightened her, as though she'd already resigned herself to situations like it when she married me. She propped me up and put my shoes on, held me upright in the elevator, persuaded me into a cab, and went with me to Bellevue Hospital, ignoring all my protests. She listened to me slur an explanation for my injuries to the doctor, then sat with me in the bright halls of Radiology, asking no questions except if I needed any water from the cooler, if I was comfortable, until the doctor called us in again. There was no fracture in my cheekbone, just a lot of bruising to the facial tissue, enough to keep me out the office for a week. I was shaky and headsore and my teeth felt loose, but I was capable of walking home. Coming out the carousel doors, she held my arm and said, 'I don't care how long it takes, Dan, or how many bar fights you get into in the meantime, but we are going to get you off those pills, you understand me? I'm not letting you destroy yourself like this.' And I told her I would stop, but I'm still taking them. She watches as I sink the tablets before bed each night and makes her disapproval clear to me by morning. I'll spare you my excuses and just say: I'm working on it.

She knows that I've been speaking to somebody lately, but

she doesn't know it's you. I've mentioned Dennis Alma and his grief group at the 10th Street Church so often that she must think I'm close to saying grace at mealtimes, and I can tell she's mindful not to interfere in my progress, whatever has inspired it. She has seen me writing in my notebooks and seems to have assumed that it's some therapeutic exercise I've been allocated by a new psychiatrist, which isn't so far from the truth. This— my coming here and talking to you—is not a secret I am keeping from her, it's a privacy I've yet to share. Alisha is sure to understand the distinction. There's nothing I have said to you that she doesn't know already. Once I've finished here and packed the last of the cassettes into the box with all the others, I'll go straight home and tell her all about them. But these tapes belong to you, and whoever you decide to play them to is your decision.

It has been about five months since I began all this. The routine has given me a sense of purpose, a different compass by which to plot the course of my days—I'll miss it. On nights when I'm not tutoring in Queens or somewhere else, I've been going up to meet Alisha in her studio—she's co-letting a place above a paint and hardware store on 9th and 21st, for lack of an alternative, and I've grown used to the subway ride, the short stroll in the dusky light, the cutting rain, and now the snow.

She buzzes me up and I climb the stairs to her workspace full of stand lights, paper screens, and thrift-store furniture, to lie back on her fainting couch with a mechanical pencil and a notepad until she's ready to leave. On Thursday evenings, I sit mutely for an hour with Dennis Alma and his group, then walk down to my storage locker just a few blocks south of the church. This is where I've been recording everything I write for you. I have a cumbersome stereo tape deck and a microphone here, ten packets of unused Maxwell cassettes (not as hard to find as you'd expect), and for the bargain price of

$179.95 a month, I'm guaranteed no scrutiny from the outside world, no interruptions.

It's nothing much. An aluminium-sided room, ten feet square, but it means more than that to me. Perhaps it's just another place to hide. I can come and go whenever I please—there's always someone manning the reception desk—and I've organised the space to serve my needs: a Turkish rug, a folding table, an armchair, and a reading lamp. In the metal cabinet, you'll find nearly three hundred pairs of antique spectacles, individually wrapped in plastic bags and boxed with tissue paper—you might not share my interest in them, or be glad to inherit them, but their accumulation has been my most productive waste of time, a necessary distraction from so many other thoughts. If you look inside the stacks of archive boxes here, you'll see they're filled with videos—official series compilations of *The Artifex* from 1994–97, acquired in charity shops, garage sales, online, copy by copy. And somewhere in among them are the VHS originals I made when I was twelve, still in their shabby cardboard sleeves with my own childish writing on the labels. In this room are many duplicates of *The Artifex Appears*—I make spares to save the magnetism of the library tapes at my apartment—and I play them through cheap headphones from the dollar store, because the sound of Maxine Laidlaw's voice through anything else is not the same. This used to be the place I came to listen when I needed consolation; now it is the place I come to talk. That's a measure of improvement, I suppose.

The diaries my mother kept between the ages of eleven and eighteen are not here—I have them in a safe at home, along with her jewellery and other personal effects. They were found in my grandparents' attic during the clearance of their house in Bradenham: six fat volumes of her day-to-day thoughts, zipped into an old sports backpack with her school folders. What I've got here are the photocopied pages. On 7th January 1983, she wrote this: *Francis doesn't like how much time I spend with my diary & thinks it's something only kids do ha ha ha! It's like having an imaginary friend he says. He thinks I'm always whining that I don't have time for other things but somehow I've got ages to be scribbling in a book. I told him it was stupid to be jealous of a diary & he said it was stupid to love talking to yourself as much as I do & it turned into a silly fight. We haven't really made up yet. I said that I would write less just to shut him up but I don't know.* Her last entry was 11th February of that same year—a perfunctory account of her uneventful Friday at the office and her expectations for the weekend: another camping trip to Cornwall in the rain. There is no mention of late periods or pregnancy in these final pages—she just stops writing. But the arithmetic is simple to perform.

It was reading back through all her diaries that made me think of you. In the week I spent away from work last June, recovering from what I told the partners was an accident on the squash court, I couldn't rest—no matter what Alisha did to keep my mood from darkening, I didn't have the regimen of going to the office and burying myself under the wing of VSK. By Wednesday, I felt directionless and agitated, distant from myself. When Alisha left to pick up groceries that afternoon, I went and took the diaries from the safe. I needed to be closer to the patterns of my mother's voice again—the memories I hold of her are always shifting, but the person in those diaries is changeless.

I had forgotten what her teenage mind was like—all the hypertensive rants about her parents, the rambling contemplations, how often she insists my father is a fling, a station on the path to somewhere better. She's thorny in her diaries, full of attitude, a work in progress. But I never fail to recognise my mother in them. Her consciousness is always there for me. A small reality survives in what she writes. I cannot overstate how much it's worth to have her thoughts preserved like this, available for reference when I need her. And it occurred to me, as I was going through them, that any child of mine could have the same.

I'm doing this so you won't ever have to speculate about the man I was before you met me. All the good and worthless things I know about myself have been laid out for you. I have spoken everything out loud so you can hear the way the truth sounds in my voice. Use these tapes to gauge the weather that might follow. Listen through your headphones in the dark. Understand where you have come from. Maybe there will come a day when I can lie to you as easily as I can pick my teeth—it's likely in my nature, and I can't promise you I'll notice when it happens. These tapes are my insurance against that. Whoever I turn into, however I might disappoint you, whatever transpires from this point on, you'll always have the person I am now. I hope there'll never be another version.

Before I met Alisha, you were not even a mote of possibility inside my head, and now you have become one of the first considerations of my day, my best distraction. When my inbox settles into silence every morning, and I've checked and organised my diary, and skimmed the *Journal* and the *Times*, I have half an hour to myself before I leave for work. This used to be the time I'd trawl the web, excavating any mention of *The Artifex* that I could find, hovering the cursor over video clips and stills, removing links from Wikipedia pages, buying unclaimed VHS originals, doing what I could to stop the show from circulating—anything to make Fran Hardesty extinct. Now I have a better occupation. I sit down in the quiet apartment and imagine you. The morning feels so different with you in it. I don't know when you'll be here. A year or two, or maybe more. But I'm certain what I want.

I want to look at you some day and feel the great electric charge my father never felt for me, the immutable connection to your bones. I want that flush of astonishment my mother had when I spoke phrases she had taught me, all the ways of being that I learned from her. I want to teach you how to drive. I want to know your fascinations and watch you in pursuit. I want Alisha to explain this city to you. I want to show you England. I want to go with you to Audlem, press my heart against the ground and get back up. I want you to be raised outside disaster, without limits, beyond blood.

ACKNOWLEDGEMENTS

Everyone needs a friend like Adam Robinson, who drove me on the slowest roads to Wasdale Head one rainy weekend without asking for an explanation—the existence of this book owes much to him and his knowledge of the Lakes.

Ed Park's insights on the first draft were profound and crucial. Rowan Cope lent my work the same pin-sharp editorial eye and helped me find solutions I hadn't considered. Thanks to Maisie Lawrence, Jo Dickinson, and the whole team at Scribner. Thanks to my ever wise and thoughtful agent Judith Murray, and to Gráinne Fox and Kate Rizzo. Thanks to Caroline and Peter Hesz, Sharon Evans, David Lloyd; and to the much-missed Giles Waterfield for kind words I'll never forget.

My brother Nick inspires me daily, in ways he doesn't even realise—this one's for him—and Katy Haldenby was an enthusiastic early reader. My wife Steph was always there to help me navigate the darkness that descended in the writing of this story, and has supported me with her great heart and mind at every stage. Thank you, most of all, to Isaac—true happiness is the mere thought of you, my son.